William Russell

The Heir-At-Law

And Other Tales

William Russell

The Heir-At-Law
And Other Tales

ISBN/EAN: 9783337248093

Printed in Europe, USA, Canada, Australia, Japan

Cover: Foto ©Andreas Hilbeck / pixelio.de

More available books at **www.hansebooks.com**

THE

HEIR-AT-LAW,

And other Tales.

BY

WATERS,

AUTHOR OF "RECOLLECTIONS OF A DETECTIVE POLICE-OFFICER,"
"A SKELETON IN EVERY HOUSE," ETC., ETC.

LONDON:

WARD, LOCK, & TYLER, WARWICK HOUSE,

PATERNOSTER ROW.

CONTENTS.

THE HEIR-AT-LAW.

CHAPTER I.

THE annals of the British aristocracy have already furnished the historiographer with numerous chapters of family romance; but those archives of an order, wherein a place is esteemed by the many as the highest guerdon that beauty, bravery, genius, can win, must necessarily be inexhaustible in such revelations. Here is one that not long ago fell within my own experience; and, by simply restoring the original names and localities—altered by me for reasons that will be obvious—it would in all essential particulars faithfully reproduce an episode in the domestic history of one of our great county families; not, it strikes me, interesting only from the collision and evolvement of curious and striking incidents, but pointing an instructive moral, which they who run may read—although the catastrophe may not be thought to reach quite to the ideal standard understood by *poetical* justice—an objection to which the romance of real life will, I fear, be always more or less obnoxious.

The bankruptcy, in 1842, of Mr. Ansted, a city merchant, in whose amiable family, domiciled in one of the squares of Tyburnia, I had officiated as governess since I left Lancashire—a lapse of nearly seven years—threw me once more upon the world in search of dependent bread. As I was an orphan, and had no relative that I knew of capable of assisting me to reach a more eligible path of life, there was, of course, nothing before me but to obtain as quickly as possible a like situation to the one of which Mr. Ansted's commercial calamity had deprived me: even that would not, I feared, and with reason, judging from the crowded state of the governess' columns in the *Times*, be of very easy accomplishment. Happily a caprice, that of advertising in my own name, Miss Redburn, instead of the stereotyped " A Lady," dissipated my apprehensions, and in a very unexpected and startling manner.

About three o'clock in the afternoon of the day my advertisement appeared, a fashionable barouche and pair dashed up to the door of the house in Upper Seymour Street, where I had taken temporary lodgings, and a lady alighted, elegantly attired in a slightly mourning carriage-dress, whose important presence was instantly announced by a footman on the knocker, with a vehemence that brought half the first and second floor habitants of the quiet street to their windows.

"Is Miss Redburn at home?" was asked by a female voice, the rich tones whereof struck my ear familiarly. The scared serving-girl replied, I suppose, in dumb show, by pointing to the door of my room; for with hardly a pause between, the same voice said: "Thank you; that will do: I will introduce myself:" and the next moment the carriage-lady was before me—in my arms! The flashing light of her dark brilliant eyes greeted me as joyfully as did her sisterly embrace and glad exclamation: "Dear, dear Gertrude, I am so delighted to have found you! Surely," she added with a gay laugh, and partially yielding to a sort of instinctive effort I made to free myself from her clasping arms— "surely you cannot have forgotten your old friend and pupil, Clara?"

"Clara Selwyn!" I exclaimed, forcibly releasing myself, as a dreadful thought arose involuntarily in my mind—"Clara Selwyn!"

The lady's flushed cheek and haughtily curling lip showed that my ungenerous suspicion was read aright. "Yes," she coldly replied, "Clara Selwyn, when you knew me, Gertrude, but Mrs. Francis Herbert not very long after you left Lancashire, and now for several years a widow."

"Francis Herbert, of Ashe Priory!"

"Just so. Should that so much astonish you?" she added, glancing proudly at the mantel-piece mirror. "You perhaps imagine that the magnificent Mrs. Herbert, the dowager, would have sufficient influence over her son to dissuade him from such a *mésalliance*. It did not prove so," continued my charming visitor with a sweet silvery laugh, and resuming her previous caressing tone and manner; "those are obstacles, dear Gertrude, which light-winged, youthful love easily o'erleaps; and we were privately married within, I think, six months of our first meeting."

" Privately married!"

" Certainly. My husband's stately mother's many excellent qualities, both of head and heart, were strictly subordinate to her all-mastering pride of birth, and to have asked her consent would have been an absurdity. Nay, the after chance discovery of what had taken place almost proved fatal to her life, suffering as she did from disease of the heart. Happily, that peril passed away, and we were *quittes pour la peur*. Still forgiveness was not to be hoped for, and we left England to vegetate in obscurity abroad, till time and the stars should permit us to return and assume our proper position. Exile, poverty, in a comparative sense," added Mrs. Herbert—a dark cloud for a moment veiling her lustrous loveliness—"would have touched me little, but for the loss of my husband barely three years subsequent to our marriage. Since then, I continued to reside in the south of France, with our only child, little Francis, and mamma, till about two months ago, when the sudden death of Edmund Herbert summoned us home to fortune—greatness."

" What a bewildering turn of the wheel! I read a notice of Mr. Edmund Herbert's death in the newspapers. He died of *tetanus,* or locked-jaw, did he not, resulting from a gunshot wound in the hand?"

" Yes; and his mother, to whom he was devotedly attached, did not survive the shock more than a few hours. He was, you are aware, my husband's elder brother, and several years his senior, but had never married. I knew him by reputation only—not, it so chanced, personally—and that he was one of the highest-minded, most generous of men. But enough of this for the present. We shall have plenty of time hereafter for indulgence in gay or gloomy reminiscences. My present business here, Gertrude, is to offer you a home at Ashe Priory, as preceptress to my son—as companion and friend to myself. You will not refuse, I see," she added, affectionately kissing me. "We shall be sisters, as we were in the old time. So extremely fortunate—was it not?—that I to-day glanced over the advertisement part of the newspaper—so rare a thing for me to do."

I expressed my grateful thanks as clearly as the strong emotion which agitated me permitted, and presently said: " Your sister Mary, dear Mrs. Herbert, she who so well deserves happiness, has not, I fear, drawn a prize in the strange lottery of life?"

Beautiful Clara, variable and sensitive as a child, was instantly sad again. "Alas! no; and she, too, is a widow. But Mary and her little boys must, and shall," she added, "spite of mamma's unreasonable objections, take up their abode with us; and therein, Gertrude, I shall also need your aid and sympathy. But of this hereafter. That which we have now to understand thoroughly is, that you breakfast with us to-morrow morning at the Clarendon, Old Bond Street, where we have been staying for the last ten days, and whence we set off, at twelve precisely, for Ashe Priory."

It was so settled; and Mrs. Herbert left me, half doubtful that I had heard aright; and it was far into the night before my brain had ceased to throb and sparkle with the thick-coming images—the rekindled memories of some twenty years—which her unlooked-for presence and strange news had awakened into life. A brief resumé of those thronging reminiscences must necessarily precede the telling of the story sequential to them, in which I was now about, unwittingly, to become an actor as well as auditor.

The Selwyns and ourselves were next-door neighbours, though living half a mile asunder, in a rural parish of Lancashire, the metropolitan village whereof —about a quarter of an hour's smart walk from our sequestered dwellings—was as dull, decorous, old-world a place as could, I imagine, be found in the most agricultural county in Great Britain. Both families had been thus domiciled as far back as my own personal experience extended, but I knew that in his early manhood Mr. Selwyn had attempted to practise as a solicitor in our little market-town, with such lamentable fortune, that he contrived not only to lose the only suit of importance he had ever been intrusted with, but to blunder so outrageously in the conduct of it, as to render himself liable in heavy damages to his own client. These first-fruits of his legal exertions so disgusted Mr. Selwyn with the profession, that he resolved to espouse forthwith Mary Everett, the daughter of a deceased clergyman, and withdraw from ungenial business avocations to the sylvan quietude of Beach Villa, a largish and showy cottage *orné*, standing in its own grounds, of about an acre in extent, with the hope of there gliding through life unvexed by the cares, vanities. and ambitions of the rude, bustling, outer world. As he was possessed of a clear eight hundred a year, and married a gentle, well-principled, true-hearted woman, this expectation, though not destined to be realized, cannot, I think, be said to have been unreasonably based. His wife, unfortunately, died in giving birth to their first child, a girl; and deeply as Mr. Selwyn was thought to feel her loss, his plastic nature so readily again yielded to feminine influence, that the orthodox year of mourning had barely expired when he appeared for the second time at the marriage-altar—his bride on this occasion being Clara Stapleton, an intimate acquaintance of his first wife, though an altogether different person. Clara Stapleton must have been endowed with rare personal charms, for she was still singularly handsome sixteen years later, when I had attained an age capable of appreciating such attractions; but the spirit within matched ill with the unflawed beauty of its mortal covering. Not that Mrs. Selwyn was a bad person in a direct and positive sense: she would not have uttered an absolute falsehood—have committed a manifestly evil deed; but vanity and pretence—the prolific sources of not less real, if unspoken deceit, meanness, and injustice—were her besetting sins. Though greatly bettered in circumstances by marriage, she quickly wearied of the dull monotony of Beach Villa; and as her empire over good, easy Mr. Selwyn was absolute, an absurdly pretentious style of living was attempted, which treble her husband's income would hardly have justified. The result was not only pecuniary embarrassment, but frequent social mortification and discomfiture at the hands of the local aristocracy, sought to be propitiated by a tinsel imitation of their own, after all, not very splendid glories. Two considerable legacies were squandered in bolstering up and prolonging Mrs. Selwyn's ambitious aims; but the end was visibly at hand by the time Clara, Mr.

Selwyn's only child by his second wife, was in her eighteenth year.

Mr. Selwyn had been for some time rapidly breaking—borne down, not by years, he was little more than five-and-forty, but by mind troubles—when the crash came, and put the finishing stroke to his broken fortunes and failing life. An execution which he could not pay out, was sent into Beach Villa, and driven to extremity, he did that which, a few years previously, might have saved him—placed his affairs in the hands of his old friend Mr. Thornley, a thorough man of business, and now, I have heard, one of the largest holders of railway stock in the kingdom. That gentleman readily undertook the ungracious charge; and a thorough investigation ensued, by which it was ascertained that when all just claims were satisfied, not more than one hundred a year, at the utmost, would remain to the Selwyns, exclusive of Beach Villa—upon which there was a heavy mortgage—and its gewgaw furniture. This decisive disclosure frightened Mrs. Selwyn into submission, and she peevishly acquiesced in the discharge of the servants, with the exception of a maid-of-all-work, and the sale of the phaeton, horses, Clara's Arab pony, &c. Poor Mr. Selwyn did not long survive this calamitous downcome. I was at home at the time, having not long previously returned from Liverpool, where I had been studying to qualify myself for the precarious profession which, it had

been for some time foreseen, would, ere many
years—perhaps months—be my only earthly resource; and being a good deal with Mr. Selwyn,
I soon came to know that the carking anxiety which
chiefly weighed upon his mind, was not for his
wife, whose criminal follies, weakly acquiesced in by
himself—that was the sharpest pang—had greatly
lessened, not to say destroyed, the love he once
bore her; nor for his eldest daughter, Mary, was his
mind haunted by sinister forebodings—she would, he
felt, walk erect and unswervingly along the slipperiest
and most perilous life-path she might be required to
tread; but Clara, what, with that dangerous gift of
unmatched loveliness—that impulsive, ambitious disposition, derived from her mother, though, it might
be hoped, attempered to loftier issues—what, in the
dark future, might become of her, left unbucklered
from the sordid world by his, her father's, dastard
lack of firmness? That was the sting of death; and
eagerly did his fainting spirit toil to devise means of
atoning, if but partially, for his grievous fault. A
will was drawn up and executed, by which Mary
Selwyn, who had just passed her majority, was constituted sole trustee of all he might die possessed of,
and absolute guardian of her sister Clara. To the
last, this thought dominated all others. I was present
when the final summons came, and well do I remember that closing scene. His wife had been
almost forcibly removed, at the dying man's request;

her wild remorseful outcries rendering it impossible
that he, feebly struggling in the close grasp of the
Destroyer, should fulfil the purpose nearest his heart
—the earnest commending of Clara to her sister's
watchful care and tenderness; and the impressing
upon Clara that to her sister—not mother—she must
look for counsel and guidance, and in all essential
things yield her true and loving obedience. The
pledges so solemnly demanded were as solemnly
given by the weeping daughters; and a gleam of
placid joy lit up for a moment the darkening eyes
of the dying father, whose quivering lips, whilst his
wasted hands rested upon the bowed heads of his
children, seemed to be invoking a blessing on them.
Presently, the feeble hands slipped aside, the slightly
raised head fell gently back upon the pillow, and the
faint light and smile passed away with a sigh, and
the murmured ejaculation, " Thy will be done!"

Death passing through a household but transiently
darkens and interrupts its daily life. The old cares,
duties, vanities, quickly resume, and, till another
arrow strikes, maintain, their accustomed sway. Mrs.
Selwyn's passionate self-reproaches soon changed to
fretful lamentations over the cruel and quite un-
merited reverse of fortune that had befallen herself
and Clara—Mary, her step-daughter, never having
been included within the circle of her selfish sympa-
thies. Clara's radiant bloom stole gradually back to
her cheeks—ay, and Mary's genial cheerfulness be-

fore long again cast its sunny glow on all around. A very admirable person was Mary Selwyn, of a rare sweetness of temper, and gentleness of disposition, combined with unbending firmness and rectitude of character—qualities which required not the attraction of physical beauty to win for her the love and esteem of all worthy hearts that came within the range of their unobtrusive influence. Not that Mary Selwyn was wanting in feminine comeliness and grace—very far, indeed, from that; but her beauty was of a more subdued, less striking type than that of her sister, and, especially to unfamiliar eyes, seemed eclipsed in Clara's presence. Mary was now the sole stay and hope of the bereaved and impoverished family. Mrs. Selwyn ungrudgingly resigned to her the desperate task of keeping house upon a hundred pounds a year; a judicious economy took the place of careless extravagance, and the future gradually assumed a more hopeful aspect. It was settled, that as soon as Beach Villa could be advantageously let, they would seek a less expensive home, at a distance from the scene of their former comparative splendour; and, in the mean time, Mary, with my assistance, set vigorously to work to perfect Clara's educational accomplishments, which a blind indulgence had permitted to fall in some respects sadly behindhand. She was, however, apt and willing, and, no longer interfered with by Mrs. Selwyn, who seldom, indeed, stirred out of her bedroom, made rapid progress.

Some five or six months had passed thus pleasantly and profitably away, when Mrs. Selwyn's ambitious longings, partially rebuked, but ineradicable, unfortunately revived again in the dazzling light of her daughter's beauty, which, she had finally persuaded herself, could not, if judiciously brought into play, fail to secure Clara, and of course Clara's mother, a far higher position in the world than that mother's cruel folly had despoiled her of. It was quite true that the younger Miss Selwyn's rare personal gifts had begun to excite a sort of agitation in our corner of the county, and that her name was in the mouth of every feather-headed fopling for miles around, suggesting sinister or fortunate auguries, as the envious or benevolently hopeful dispositions of the prophesiers determined. One consequence of all this was numerous impertinent calls at Beach Villa, under pretext of inquiring the terms upon which it could be let, and of viewing the premises, by parties who had not the remotest intention of becoming tenants. As soon, however, as it came to be well understood that such visitors would see nobody but Mary Selwyn, or myself, if I happened to be there, the annoyance abated, to be renewed in some instances under a more decorous and less transparent mask. One gentleman, of about my own age I judged, which was a few months more than that of Mary Selwyn, and, to our unskilled appreciation, of remarkably aristocratic appearance and manners, would not

be denied an intimacy to which he had no legitimate
or conventional claim. Finding that Miss Selwyn's
icy reserve could not be otherwise broken through,
Mr. Calvert, as he called himself, produced, with evident reluctance, blushing the while like a school-girl,
and presented to Mary, a letter written by her father—
there could be no doubt about that—expressing the
warmest thanks for some service or favour which the
writer had received at the hands of the person addressed. Miss Selwyn read it with emotion, but
presently remarked in a partly apologetic tone:
" There is no address, sir, at the foot of this note.
You have the envelope, of course ?"

The gentleman, instead of firing up, as I should
have thought he would at the implied suspicion,
changed colour, and, with something of agitation in
his voice and manner, said, " No, I have not ; it has
been mislaid or lost. But surely Miss Selwyn cannot think so meanly of me as to believe that I would
assume, falsely and basely assume, to have rendered
the trifling service alluded to ; that I—I——"

He stopped for want of words or matter, and Mary,
who had intently observed him, said, " I do *not* believe so, Mr. Calvert. Will you walk in ?"

From this time, Mr. Calvert became a very frequent visitor indeed ; but invariably, as I afterwards
frequently recalled to mind with a pang of regret at
my own want of penetration, at such hours that he
would be sure of meeting with none but the family.

I very much liked this Mr. Calvert withal; his conversation was refined and intellectual; and, witless
dogmatist that I must have been, if what I heard of
him about a year after my removal to London was
correct, I—piquing myself, too, upon accurate per-
ception of character, and especially male character—
pronounced him to be a person of large conscientious-
ness and self-sacrificing amiability! Constancy,
indeed, if we had rightly divined his mission at
Beach Villa, was not of the number of his virtues,
for it was before long very apparent to me that Mary
Selwyn, not her all-conquering sister, was the com-
pelling loadstone that drew him there; and it was
becoming pretty clear, moreover, that his preference
would at no great distance of time be reciprocated,
when an unexpected incident showed me, or seemed
to do so, how little I comprehended Mr. Calvert, or
the impulses by which he was governed. Clara and
her mother had accepted an invitation to pass a week
with the Lumsdens, retired and tolerably wealthy
tradespeople, who had removed not long before the
Selwyns' downfall from our neighbourhood to a place
about ten miles off; and a letter from Clara, ostensibly to announce a prolongation of the visit, startled
her sister and myself, not only by informing us that
Captain Toulmin, son of the Hon. Mrs. Toulmin, a
widow-lady related to the Herberts of Ashe Priory,
was a daily guest at the Lumsdens'; but, by the girl-
ish exultation of tone in which she wrote, evidently

inspired by the belief that she had made a serious and important conquest.

Mary Selwyn was both vexed and angry. "This meeting between Clara and Captain Toulmin," she said, "has, I have no doubt, been concerted between him and the Lumsdens—worthy, well-meaning people enough, but incapable of saying 'No' to the son of an honourable. I will write to-night, and insist upon her immediate return home."

I agreed that it would be proper to do so, and was leaving the room, when Mary said with a kind of anxious bashfulness, a bright blush the while mantling her sweet face with scarlet: "Mr. Calvert, Gertrude, will probably look in for a few minutes this evening. He, I have no doubt, knows this reputedly gay and fashionable captain; and if you, when I am not present, were in an off-hand, indifferent manner to sound him relative to the said gentleman's character. I should, or I err greatly, be furnished with reasons for insisting upon Clara's instant return, which even Mrs. Selwyn could not gainsay."

I undertook to do so; and very blunderingly did I redeem my promise. Mr. Calvert, with his quick, eager, confounding interrogatories, drew from me, before I well knew what I was saying, the exact motives of my awkward questioning; and the effect which that knowledge produced upon him was extra-ordinary. The flush and animation of his counte-ance, which, in my wisdom, I had attributed to his expectation of presently seeing Miss Selwyn enter the room, became, as I spoke, pallid and stern—with jealous anger, I concluded, what else could it be? and his tone was high and wrathful as he replied: " Inform Miss Selwyn that I *do* know Captain Toulmin, and so well, that I advise, that I entreat, beseech her, not to lose an hour in removing her sister from the contamination of his society. She must be firm, too, as well as peremptory, for Toulmin is not a man to be easily turned aside from any purpose, however infamous, he may have formed. He will follow Clara Selwyn here, of that be assured ; and nought but evil *can* ensue if he be permitted, under any pretence, to thrust his presence upon this family."

Surprise at this fiercely-uttered outburst held me dumb, and three or four minutes' silence, meditative on Mr. Calvert's part, followed ; then starting suddenly from his chair and seizing his hat, he said : " Make my excuses to Miss Selwyn, if you please, for thus hurrying away ; but it just occurs to me that an important business-matter, which had slipped my memory, must be attended to at once ; good-evening, Miss Redburn."

He was gone ; and before he could have reached the else unused stable, where his horse was usually haltered during his visits, Mary came in, to whom I of course related what had just passed. She was greatly surprised—shocked is the more accurate word —and it was plain that a pang of wounded pride mingled with the painful solicitude excited by Mr. Calvert's words and manner as reported by me; for Mary Selwyn, good and amiable as she might be, was still a woman withal. She had turned from me, and was looking out of the window: "He must, indeed, be greatly agitated," she said, with a tremor in her tone almost successfully repressed. "Look, Gertrude!" I did look, and saw the usually sedate, mild Mr. Calvert galloping fiercely off, as if life depended upon his speed. "He does love her, then," murmured poor Mary, as horse and horseman disappeared at an angle of the road. "Well, he could hardly help doing so." A minute or two afterwards she kissed and left me, her fine eyes bright with excitement and wet with tears.

CHAPTER II.

Mary Selwyn rose early on the following morning, and when I joined her at breakfast, she had, in appearance at least, quite recovered her usual cheerfulness and equanimity. She had determined, instead of writing, to go personally, and insist upon Clara's immediate return home. Another consternation awaited us: a note arrived from Mr. Calvert, containing, besides the ordinary compliments, &c., a brief intimation that important affairs obliged him to leave that part of the country, and that some

months would probably elapse before he could promise himself the pleasure of again calling at Beach
Villa. "Very extraordinary conduct this," I exclaimed; "upon my word, the man is a perfect
riddle!"

"True," was the low-voiced reply; "and one
which those who have duties to perform should
not waste time in endeavouring to solve. Ah! here
comes the fly Susan has ordered. Good-bye, Gertrude, till the evening. We shall not be late home,
I hope."

It was, however, past ten o'clock before the fly
returned, bringing the two Misses and Mrs. Selwyn,
the last still swelling and panting with the but partially abated storm of rage which Mary's determined
insistance upon her sister's return with her to Beach
Villa had thrown her into. Clara, who, one could
see, had been profusely weeping, retired to bed at
once; but Mrs. Selwyn, whose excitement precluded
rest or a wish for it, remained up to vent her indignation—first upon Mary, and, when she had withdrawn, upon hapless me, who could not well refuse
to listen. I gathered from the irate lady's objurga-
tions, that there had been a violent scene at the
Lumsdens'; that Mary Selwyn's firmness prevailed
with difficulty, and not till Clara herself—upon being
reminded, I had no doubt, of her father's dying
injunctions, ever a potent spell with her—had
decided for her prim half-sister against her own

mother. It seemed, moreover, that *two* gentlemen had been dangling after Clara—Captain Toulmin, the young lady's favourite it was intimated, and his friend, Mr. Francis Herbert, the second son of the dowager Mrs. Herbert, of Ashe Priory, the towers whereof were, on a bright clear day, dimly visible from the garret-windows of Beach Villa, who Mrs. Selwyn was evidently mad enough to hope might be hymeneally caught in the meshes of her own and her daughter's ambition. This struck me as so utterly preposterous, the Herberts ranking amongst the highest magnates of that division of the county, that I could hardly forbear laughing in the silly woman's face. Reflecting, however, that maternal vanity has ever been a chartered dreamer, I main- tained, though with difficulty, a serious expression of face; and Mrs. Selwyn, having at last exhausted for a time the phials of her wordy wrath, muttered a sour good-night, and went to bed.

The next day but one, Beach Villa was let upon terms which had been several times previously re- fused; and within twenty-four hours of the comple- tion of the bargain, the Selwyn family were on the road to Preston, near which a habitation more suit- able to their means had been taken for them by Mr. Thornley. Personal intercourse with my young friends was thus necessarily terminated; and that by letter, chiefly from the swift coming on of trouble in my own home, soon became infrequent, and before

I left Lancashire had entirely ceased. My father, a lieutenant in the royal navy, who had served with Nelson, was released at last by the welcome hand of death from sufferings he had bravely borne for several years : and in about two months only my mother sickened of the malady which was soon to reunite both parents in their long home. In the presence of these griefs, all minor regrets were of course rebuked and hushed ; the Selwyns and their self-created difficulties were for the time forgotten ; and I nerved myself to pursue with hope and courage the strange and solitary path of life before me, and over which thick darkness had so early fallen.

It was some time before I succeeded in obtaining the engagement with Mrs. Ansted ; and how that terminated, together with the sudden apparition of Clara Selwyn, bewilderingly transformed into Mrs. Francis Herbert, of Ashe Priory, the reader has already been informed. The only tidings of the Selwyns which reached me after leaving Lancashire, was a hurried answer to a question addressed by me to Mr. Thornley, whom I met at the Euston Station, just as the train in which he had taken his seat was about to start. I had inquired after Mary Selwyn, and his reply was to the effect, that she had long since thrown herself away upon a mean adventurer of the name of Calvert, and was, he understood, living in obscurity somewhere in

Wales, with her husband and one or two children. He had not time to add, that his information was solely derived, as I afterwards knew, from Mrs. Selwyn, or I should have more correctly estimated the probable truth of the imputation upon Mr. Calvert.

After this recapitulation of bygone events, it will not, I hope, appear surprising that I was bewildered by the unexpectedly announced and marvellous change in Clara's fortune, drawing after it a minor but still very appreciable improvement in my own. And, for the life of me, I could not at all realize that change. It seemed to be an impossible, dream-like extravagance—a *coup de théâtre*, only to be met with in a play or a novel, and I was half tempted to doubt, whilst proceeding the next morning in a cab to the Clarendon, whether I should really find the Selwyns in that aristocratic hotel. So far, however, there was no illusion ; Mrs. Selwyn, who was looking exceedingly well, received me with prodigious con-descension, and *Redburn'd* me over again and again with untiring self-complacency. With Clara, I was still "dear Gertrude," as in the old time ; and her son, a nice little boy of about five years of age, had, I found, been tutored to address me as his mother did.

Precisely at twelve o'clock, we set out in a travelling-carriage, with four post-horses, for Ashe Priory—Mrs. Selwyn being of opinion that journeying by rail was essentially vulgar and plebeian—and in due time were safely deposited at our destination. Arrived at that splendid abode, the feeling of unreality—a sense of the precarious tenure by which the lordly pile and its adjuncts *must*, I felt, be held by the present apparent mistress, returned upon my mind with aggravated force; and if I rightly read Clara's brightly flushing face, and nervous, unquiet looks, the same thought was beating at her heart, as, encompassed in each other's arms, we, with a shrinkingness, a timidity impossible to shake off, ventured through the stately and solitary apartments. Clara Selwyn —thus ran my thoughts whilst making a hurried dinner-toilet – Clara Selwyn the indisputable mistress of all this splendour—impossible! The same law-legerdemain which has installed her here in right of her son, will, I fear, by some counter-trick, dissipate the glittering dream! In right of her son! Ay, that must be the substance which casts these ominous shadows! Clara's grandeur, at the best, can be commensurate only with the life of that frail boy; and not grandeur only, but bare competence; for now, when calling to mind the fragments of conversation between Clara and Mrs. Selwyn during our journey, I remembered they talked of a legal opinion having been given that Clara's husband, Francis Herbert, having died before his elder brother, when he was consequently not possessed—seised, I recollect, the term was—of the property, she therefore, as his widow, was not entitled to her thirds of the personals. They spoke, too, of a sealed packet of papers found in the elder brother Edmund Herbert's escritoire, directed to an intimate friend of his, a colonial bishop, and of course duly forwarded, which, it is thought, may possibly contain a will disposing of the large personals, the landed property being strictly entailed on the heirs-male ; and the alarming conclusion is, that the death of her son, the child heir-at-law, would at once hurl Clara from her present brilliant position into the abyss — by contrast made more terrible — of poverty and dependence! This boding train of thought pursued me as I sat at dinner—a cumbrously comfortless one, by the bye, except to Mrs. Selwyn, who really seemed to feel that dining with a tall lacquey posted behind her chair was her natural though shamefully delayed destiny ; and I intently scanned the *physique* of the pale boy, who his mamma insisted should dine with us, in fruitless quest of decisive indications pointing to a brief or a prolonged life.

These panic terrors had, to a great degree, subsided by noon on the morrow : the air was bright, clear, and invigorating to both mind and body : rest had restored the child's ruddy colour, and it was, after all, I reasoned in my improved mood of thought, likelier, or at all events quite as likely, that he would live to be the father of a family, as perish prematurely in his nonage. And the affair altogether, after

a time, no longer struck me as being so monstrously absurd, so utterly incredible. The servitors, old as well as young, all acquiesced, undoubtingly, in the rule of the new dynasty; the numerous cards left by the notabilities for miles around were, to my silly thinking, so many attestations of the belief of those persons in the stability of the existing state of things; and I gradually ceased to torment myself by too curiously prying, or striving to do so, into the fateful and impervious future.

Clara, notwithstanding Mrs. Selwyn's vehement dissuasion, did not delay writing to her sister Mary (Mrs. Calvert), urging her, in the kindliest terms, to come and take up her abode with her two sons at Ashe Priory. Mary's answer—dated from the neighbourhood of Douglas, Isle of Man, where she had chiefly resided since her marriage—was a refusal of the invitation, at all events for the present. She did not propose leaving home till the arrival of a gentleman, then abroad, to whom the settlement of her deceased husband's affairs had been intrusted. Clara, the letter stated, had been misinformed with respect to her (Mary's) pecuniary resources, which had always sufficed, not for the necessaries only, but for the elegancies of life, and would do so amply in the future. One brief phrase, alluding to the writer's bereavement, was conclusive with me, spite of Mr. Thornley's second-hand story, afterwards very positively re-indorsed by Mrs. Selwyn, that Mr. Calvert had been in every respect worthy of the strong love which dictated it. More immediately addressing Clara in the old tone of affectionate warning, Mary adjured her with almost pathetic earnestness, not, spite of the present cloudless sunshine of good fortune, to rest her future happiness and peace upon worldly elevation and grandeur. This was repeated again and again in varying terms, but always with a fervency which showed they were not mere cant · words of course, but grave, and, in the writer's judgment, much-needed counsels. The menacing chance, then, that Clara's son might die during legal infancy, had painfully impressed her sister's mind as well as mine! —not prophetically, I could only hope and pray.

Although Mrs. Calvert declined an asylum at Ashe Priory, another lady, the Hon. Mrs. Toulmin, whom her son, Captain Toulmin, had by his reckless follies, it appeared, literally beggared, gladly accepted it, when pressed upon her with much delicacy and generous feeling by Clara. A remarkable compound of pride and kindliness, buckram and benevolence, was that tall, pale, dignified, and very courteous personage. She could not but feel, and that acutely too, that Captain Toulmin, the next male heir to the domains of her ancestors, as well as of the Herberts, had been barred from the succession by the madcap marriage of his cousin, Francis Herbert, with a beautiful Nobody; yet did she soon come to love warmly the child of that marriage, who alone stood between her own son and a splendid heritage; and was as proud of the charming mistress of Ashe Priory as if Clara, instead of being a mere *parvenue*, could have boasted of a pedigree as long and unexceptionable as that of the last winner of the Derby. One curious trait in the good lady's character afforded us—that is, Clara and myself—much quiet amusement. Most persons, I have heard, derive pleasure, like honest Dogberry, from being able to boast of their losses; but this, I suppose natural propensity, was, with the Hon. Mrs. Toulmin, exaggerated to monomania. Over and over again, we used to watch her making elaborate and corrected estimates of the money-value of the family plate, jewels, furniture, books, horses, carriages—of every valuable, in brief, whereof she or her son—the same thing—had been despoiled by the law of succession; her self-importance evidently increasing, *pro ratâ*, with the vastness of the sums thus laboriously ascertained; and when, as sometimes happened, a property was spoken of in her presence—a farm for instance—of which she had not before heard, she would eagerly inquire its gross value, note it instantly with a pencil upon her ivory tablets, adding it to the previous total, and then mentally glorify herself upon the additional wealth she was thus proved *to have lost!* In sooth, my own opinion is, that all the Herberts were more or less of eccentric intellect. In the dowager Mrs. Herbert before spoken of, the erratic mental predisposition manifested itself in a pride of lineage, of which I could give many ludicrous anecdotes, approaching to insanity in its fantastical extravagance; in Francis Herbert, on the contrary, it displayed itself in contemptuous disregard of the marital code governing his order; and in the Hon. Mrs. Toulmin, not only as just related, but in other modes which it is needless further to allude to Before this narrative is concluded, the reader will perhaps discover additional proof of the soundness of my theory.

The presence of the Hon. Mrs. Toulmin at Ashe Priory naturally drew after it that of Captain Toulmin; and it did not fail to occur to me, that Clara might have had some notion of the kind when she pressed the invitation upon that lady. However that might have been, September was no sooner at hand, than Captain Toulmin rented a sporting-box in the neighbourhood, and thenceforth was a daily guest at the Priory. A gay, handsome, specious man of the world, of about, I should say, five-and-thirty, was Captain Toulmin, a gentleman of polished address withal, and completely master of the little arts of society, which, being constantly in requisition, are so effective in making a company reputation, and concealing essential defects of education and character. Fully determined, too, was he to render himself exceedingly agreeable to Mrs. Francis Herbert, and to marry her, *if* her little boy's health should *not*—as it had already evinced some indecisive symptoms of doing—fatally decline. There was another frequent guest at the Priory, the Rev. Charles Atherley, rector of the parish, though only eight-and-twenty, possessor of a handsome income, and a very different man from Captain Toulmin; the fate of his timid matrimonial aspirations also depended, I could not help believing, upon that of Clara's son. "Poor boy!" I silently soliloquized one afternoon, as, partially hidden by a sun-screen, I watched the demeanour of the two gentlemen, who had been affecting to read, as an excuse for non-intercourse, both being implacably jealous of each other—" poor boy! you little know with what intensity of interest they are contemplating the sudden pallor that has overspread your pretty face —the languid listlessness with which you have just laid aside your play-toys, and stretched yourself upon that couch. You did not see, and seeing, would not have comprehended, the exultant flash, as lurid as fire from the bottomless pit, which broke from the dark eyes of the captain; no more than you would the rector's involuntary glance—*not* of grief—quickly followed by the pang of self-reproach, which has sent him hurriedly across the room to you with those oranges and jujubes, and causes him to speak with such gentle tenderness, that you look up lovingly in his face, and take his hand as if it were your mamma's or mine." The good rector has since then often declared that my surmise wronged him; but I am not for that the less convinced that I was right.

The truth was, he was over head and ears in love
with Clara, and could not shut out from his mind,
try as he might, an instinctive conviction, that were
Mrs. Herbert no longer the lady of Ashe Priory,
and mother of the heir to the Herbert estates, Captain Toulmin would at once cease to be his rival;
and moreover, that possibly the rectory, and something approaching to two thousand a year, might not,
in that case, be thought beneath her acceptance.

All this, I say, was as plain to me, a looker-on at
the play of cross and selfish purposes in progress—
lookers-on proverbially knowing more of the game
than the actual players—as if the Rev. Charles
Atherley, A.M., and Captain Toulmin had told me so
in as many words; but Clara's inclinings I could not
so positively determine. I saw that the handsome
roué was her shadow, whether she remained at home,
or walked or rode out, and that she was flattered,
pleased with his obsequious courtesies, but this was
all; and she invariably, moreover, laughed off every
attempt I made to treat the matter seriously. Then
Mrs. Selwyn was indefatigable in his praises, which
I could very well understand and excuse; forasmuch
that, Captain Toulmin being the next heir to the
entailed estates after little Francis, a marriage with
him would insure Clara's future, and of course her
own, in any eventuality. The Hon. Mrs. Toulmin
also greatly favoured her son's *apparent* intentions;
and after much cogitation, and considerably in-

fluenced by the recollection of what I heard Mr.
Calvert say of Captain Toulmin, I determined upon
writing to Mary, and informing her of my conjectures,
doubts, and fears, not forgetting to add an injunction
to keep my name out of any controversy that might
arise upon the subject. My letter was quickly responded to, and in person; Mary Selwyn--Mrs.
Calvert, I should say—making her appearance at the
Priory as soon as a letter by return of post would
have reached me. Surprised, delighted, I need
hardly say, Clara and I were to see her ; and looking
so wonderfully well, too, spite of the tint of recent
sorrow which shaded and softened the fine glow of
health, and a certain matronly, yet youthful grace
and air which seemed, so to speak, to radiate from
her. I had no idea she would ever have been so
handsome, and the same thought was, I saw, sparkling
in her sister's eyes. Mrs. Selwyn's greeting was of
the coldest, grimmest; and her discontent was
greatly increased the following day when Mary
directly questioned her sister concerning Captain
Toulmin ; and upon receiving what she deemed
unsatisfactory replies, peremptorily insisted, as if
Clara was still a child, and she her absolute guardian,
that the intimacy should be forthwith and unmistakably broken off. This *brusque* mode of proceeding
was certainly not in accordance with the dictates of
Mary's usual calm good sense. Clara, as might have
been anticipated, accustomed as she had of late been

to such obsequious deference, would not tolerate such rude schooling, even from her sister; and Mrs. Selwyn fired up with ungovernable fury. Mary soon recovered her rarely lost command of temper, listened for some time with unruffled composure to the dual storm she had rashly evoked, and at last said in her quietest manner, in reply to a rude taunt of Mrs. Selwyn's, relative to her own comparatively beggarly match with *that* Calvert, and rising as she spoke to leave the room—" I do not reply to you as you deserve, because my father's wife and Clara's mother will always be at least passively respected by me, even when, as now, she grossly fails in respect to herself. Come with me, Gertrude; I wish to speak with you."

We passed out of the house, and for some time walked silently about the lawn and shrubberies, Mary, as I could feel by the trembling of her arm, for I did not like to speak or peer into her face, being very much agitated—I supposed in consequence of Mrs. Selwyn's coarse and unfeeling allusion to her husband. After a while her emotion passed away, and she had recommenced questioning me on her sister's intimacy with Captain Toulmin, when that gentleman came galloping up the avenue, gallantly waving his hand as he neared the house towards the window of the apartment where we had left Clara and her mother. "Go, Gertrude, go at once and inform Captain Toulmin—privately will be best—that I must speak to him immediately in the library; you, of course, returning with him. This audacious insolence shall be endured no longer."

I was a good deal startled by the energy of manner she displayed, as well as by her words, but nevertheless hastened promptly to perform her bidding. I awaited the captain's return from the stables in the hall, delivered my message *sotto voce*, at which he seemed a good deal surprised, but of course bowed graceful acquiescence, and followed me to the library. Mary was standing at one of the windows, and as the door opened, turned and confronted the nonchalant man of fashion with a commanding sternness of aspect that not only confused and astounded me, but appeared to disconcert greatly the gallant captain himself.

" Mary — that is, Mrs. Calvert," I stammered — " Clara's, I mean Mrs. Herbert's, sister, Captain Toulmin."

Captain Toulmin bowed fiercely, and ejaculated " Ha !"

" I have sent for you, Captain Toulmin," said Mary, with an air befitting an empress, " to request that you will immediately discontinue the offensive attentions which this lady, Miss Redburn, informs me——"

" Good heavens, Mary !" I burst out, interrupting her ; and there I stopped, literally for want of words or breath, perhaps both. Talk of spontaneous combustion—I was red-hot from head to foot in an instant!

"That you will immediately," resumed Mary, with inexorable persistence, " discontinue the offensive attentions which this lady, Miss Redburn, informs me you have presumed to obtrude upon my sister, Mrs. Herbert."

The man's frame seemed to dilate with passion, and his fierce eyes glared at Mrs. Calvert as might those of a wild animal at bay, and about to spring upon the hunter. For a moment only could he confront her steady gaze, and he presently blurted out, " Why—who—what is all this?"

" The request I have made," continued Mary, " is, in fact, a command which Captain Toulmin will not dare to disobey ; and for this reason, that I happen to know where his wife, his cruelly-abandoned wife, Lydia Burdon before marriage, is now residing."

A dreadful imprecation, with which 1 will not stain the paper, burst from the detected culprit's lips ; but he was thoroughly cowed, as well as all but maddened ; whilst Mary, in her calm nobleness of contempt, looked positively beautiful—Juno-like.

" Upon condition, Captain Toulmin, that you at once cease those insulting attentions, that your visits here are very brief, not oftener than once in each week, and that your deportment is that of a person whose presence is barely tolerated from respect to your mother, Mrs. Toulmin, which is the exact truth, I will not, for the present at least, disclose your disgraceful secret to my sister ; my only motive for this forbearance being, that were I to do so, Mrs. Toulmin would be, there can be no doubt, immediately deprived of the only home her son's vices have left her. Now, Gertrude, let us begone," she added, after a slight pause, the captain's convulsing rage not permitting him articulate speech. "This gentleman, I have no doubt, perfectly comprehends his position, and the line of conduct it behoves him to pursue."

We then quitted the library, I in a perfect maze of wonder and excitement, not untinged with passing anger.

"Let us return to the shrubbery," said Mary; "we can converse more freely there. You are surprised, and a little vexed, dear Gertrude," she went on to say as we left the house, "that I should have mentioned you in connection with this unpleasant affair; but you will forgive me, I am sure, after hearing the reasons which induced me to do so. In the first place, it could do you no possible harm."

"I am not quite sure of that. Captain Toulmin has numerous and influential friends; and should it happen that——"

Listen, love," interrupted Mary, "till I have finished, and then object as much as you please. It is necessary, for several reasons, that appearances should, for the present, be saved with regard to Captain Toulmin; and, above all, that Clara's name shall not in any way be mixed up with that of a

married man in the greedy, indiscriminating public
ear. I have now a slight hold of him through his
mother, which, were Clara supposed to be in my
confidence, would of course be at an end. I fear,
besides, that his showy exterior and plausible manners may have in some degree captivated my sister's
fancy; and nothing is more certain to dissipate that
preference, if it exists, than the substitution, on his
part, of an apparently causeless rudeness and neglect
for the honeyed courtesies with which he has of late
assailed her; because, thereby wounding her vanity,
dear Clara's weak point, as you and I may confess to
each other. Poor child!" added Mary, in a low,
musing tone, " she shall not, if I can help it, have
her fall from the giddy state which so delights her,
embittered by the violent disruption of even an
imaginary contract of affection."

" You believe, then, that the life of little Francis
is tainted mortally ?"

Mary looked sharply in my face, hers at the same
time faintly colouring, and said : " To be sure—yes ;
and that is also your opinion, is it not ?"

I confessed it was, and Mary proceeded with her
reasons.

" I heartily wish Clara had never been placed in
her present position. She arrived here a fortnight,
as it chanced to fall out, before I had even heard of
the dreadful accident—the sudden death, I mean—
of—of the elder brother, Edmund Herbert——"

"You are trembling like a leaf, Mary, in this sharp wind : let us return to the house."

"No, no; I have a few more words to say. Do you know," she resumed, quite briskly, " that I very much like the Rev. Charles Atherley, who spent last evening with us; chiefly, I dare say, that he is so evidently devoted to Clara? That, now, is a connection which I would do all a sister might to foster and promote. Engaged to so worthy, so agreeable a person, a handsome independence assured to her, the fall of the present house of cards would not be felt so keenly by her as otherwise I fear it will be."

"You are not unworldly, Mary," I said, with an involuntary smile, " at least for others."

"Nay, nay, Gertrude; do not say that. The chances are, you know, that a will has been made, and that Clara will have a fair share of the Herbert personal property; so that, expectations included, there is no such great disparity of fortune between her and the rector. And now, Gertrude," concluded Mary, " that we perfectly understand each other, let us in and for the future endeavour, by every means within our reach, to promote dear Clara's *permanent* happiness and welfare."

CHAPTER III.

CAPTAIN TOULMIN had, we found, already left the Priory, after hurriedly excusing himself to his mother and Mrs. Herbert, by the pretext of urgent and suddenly-remembered business affairs. He did not re-appear till three clear days had elapsed, and then looking like a man recently fallen from the clouds, and hardly yet certain whether he had alighted upon his head or his feet. His bearing towards Clara was awkwardly but strictly in accordance with the prescribed pattern, a change which terribly mystified Mrs. Selwyn, and for a time evidently disconcerted and annoyed Clara. Pride, however, as her sister anticipated, soon came to her relief, and before the discomfited captain's uncomfortable visit terminated, her manner was as cold and haughty as his was affectedly indifferent and neglectful : there was no longer, thank heaven, any fear that her affections had been seriously entangled. The man was possessed of astonishing self-command ; but, for all that, an attentive observer could easily see frequent flashes of the volcanic rage within break through the exterior mask, prophetic of vengeance upon Mrs. Calvert and her relatives, should fate ever place the means of inflicting it within his power. And that passionately longed-for opportunity would, it daily became more clearly apparent, be erelong afforded him. Little Francis drooped rapidly: he was not precisely ill; that is, no cognizable, definite malady had as yet attacked him, but he suffered under an increasing *malaise,* a dejection of spirit which would almost certainly render him an easy prey to any active disease

by which he might be assailed. This was more evidently than ever Mrs. Calvert's decided conviction,
and greatly contributed, of course, to the pleasure
she felt, and she could hardly help openly expressing,
at observing the fresh life and vigour that marked
the hymeneal aspirations of the reverend rector since
the, to him and others, unaccountable withdrawal
of Captain Toulmin's formidable pretensions. Very
natural in an attached sister was that pleasurable
feeling. A union with the Rev. Charles Atherley
would place Clara high out of adverse fortune's
reach; and that great point secured, no other evil
of any magnitude was to be apprehended. Mary
herself, it was understood, enjoyed a quite sufficient
income, though to what amount was not known, she
being the very reverse of communicative upon the
subject; and Mrs. Selwyn would be fairly enough
provided for by the Selwyn one-hundred-a-year patri-
mony, and the rent of Beach Villa. The future of
myself alone seemed entirely bleak and cheerless;
but even for me Mary had words of encouragement
and hope; and it was in a manner tacitly agreed between us, that if our fears were realized, I should
abide with her till, at all events, a more eligible
home presented itself for my acceptance. The dura-
tion of Mrs. Calvert's stay at the Priory, I should
mention, was governed by two motives: in the first
place, her own children being, as she told me, in
perfect health, and under the care of trustworthy

persons, she was desirous of remaining till a change for the worse or better took place in her sister's son ; secondly, the colonial bishop I have spoken of was shortly expected to arrive in England, and would, of course, pay a visit to Ashe Priory, when the important question relative to the personalty would be set at rest.

The dreaded blow was not long delayed, and our low-whispered apprehensions were bruited through the stately mansion by Dr. Mitchell's announcement, that Francis Herbert was attacked by scarlatina, a disease just then extremely prevalent, and very generally fatal. The rigidly demure, but withal demoniac aspect of Captain Toulmin—now again a constant and defiant visitor at the Priory—presented an unmistakable daily bulletin of the mortal progress of the disease, till the fifth day, when, mocking us with idle hopes, it appeared to be almost miraculously arrested. The fever had certainly abated, there was considerable moisture on the skin, and the pretty patient had enjoyed a brief, but seemingly refreshing, sleep. An incident arose out of this pause between life and death from which I drew, perhaps unjustly. a terrible inference, whether fairly justified by the facts the reader will decide for himself. I was near at hand in one of the corridors, though not visible to the speakers, when I heard Captain Toulmin ask Dr. Mitchell, who was just leaving the house, whether it was true that the little boy was, as reported, so much

better. The physician replied that the child certainly
was very much better, but whether the improvement
would continue or not, he could not say. Dr. Mitchell then passed on; Captain Toulmin entered the
blue drawing-room, as it was called, and I, still unobserved by him, went into the sick-chamber, where
it was my turn to watch, and sent Mrs. Calvert, who
was nearly worn out with fatigue and anxiety, to bed.
It was the close of a dull December day, and when I
sat down by the bedside, no candle, lest it should
disturb the child, who was uneasily slumbering,
having been lighted, it was quite dark, save for a
faint starlight which shone coldly in through the
casement. There was no one, I knew, except Captain Toulmin in the blue drawing-room, the door of
which I heard once, twice, thrice gently opened, and
footsteps, light, stealthy footsteps, approach the sick-
chamber, pause irresolutely, as it were, and go back
again. Once more the steps approached, and this
time came so near that I distinctly saw—the door
being partially open for the admission of air—the
shadow of a man upon the wall just within, and
in the attitude of listening. Two or three slight
knuckle-taps on the door followed, to which I, astonished, anxious, but not in the least alarmed, did
not reply. The next instant Captain Toulmin entered the chamber, walked lightly and swiftly towards
the bed, on the opposite side to where I sat, and
drew back the curtain. "Captain Toulmin," I ex-

claimed, not loudly, suddenly standing up and confronting him, "*you* here!" I could not see his face distinctly, and the start of terror or surprise, which he could not repress, I would gladly not have seen. His agitation, from whatever cause arising, was not easily mastered, and his voice shook uncontrollably as he, not immediately, replied, "Oh, it's you, Miss Redburn—how is the—the child?"

"Better, sir, considerably better, as I heard Dr. Mitchell tell you not many minutes since."

"True, true—I—I know; but it struck me that the nurse, or—or whoever might be here, could give me more positive, more decisive information before I left the Priory for the night. Good evening, Miss Redburn."

This was all that passed, and it scared me terribly —not at the moment, curiously enough, but upon after reflection. If he *did* intend—undeterminedly, as I think, at the worst—intend evil to the child, and had not been baulked, he would have needlessly stained his soul with murder, for before the next day dawned. the disease had accomplished its mission, and the child heir-at-law was no more! I said nothing of the strange appearance of Captain Toulmin in the sick-room; and it was not, I think, till last year that I mentioned it, and then in a manner unintentionally, to Mary. It is a circumstance that my mind, even now, does not love to dwell upon.

Various were the emotions excited by that premature boy-death! Captain Toulmin — and, knowing the man, one can hardly feel surprised at it—had not the decency to affect concealment of his rampant joy, whilst the struggle in his lady-mother's breast between the promptings of sympathetic kindliness of disposition and motherly exultation, was very palpable. Mrs. Selwyn entered forthwith upon her accustomed course of hysterics; Mary, sad, grieving, but calm, entirely devoted herself to soothe the bitter anguish of the bereaved young mother; and as for the Rev. Charles Atherley, it was plain as truth that he was mentally accusing himself of detestable depravity and hardness of heart because that pulsating organ *would* throb with a quicker, wilder beat, and illumine with a brighter glow the tell-tale tablet of his face.

Well, a few flutters only of the wings of Time sufficed to subdue, modify, and harden all those varying emotions and passions. Captain Toulmin, calmed considerably down from the fierce ecstasy of triumph with which he clutched the splendid prize that not very long since appeared to be hopelessly beyond his reach, had taken quiet possession of the Priory, already projected numerous modernizing alterations therein, and had furthermore lent a favourable ear, it was said, to a deputation of numerous free and independent electors. These gentlemen had suddenly discovered, that of all the esquires in that division of the county, there was no one so admirably qualified to fill the legislative seat, soon to be vacated by the retirement of its present occupant from the fatigues and responsibilities of public life, as Captain Augustus Toulmin, of Ashe Priory. It was still but ten days subsequent to the funeral, when Mrs. Selwyn, Mrs. Herbert, Mrs. Calvert, Captain and the Hon. Mrs. Toulmin, the Rev. Charles Atherley, and myself were all assembled in the library, awaiting, with at least outward composure, the expected arrival of his lordship, the colonial bishop, from whom a letter had been received, addressed to " Mrs. Herbert, Ashe Priory, Lancashire," announcing his lordship's intention of calling on her that day about twelve o'clock, on his way to North Wales—a communication which, brief as it was, suggested the probability, aware as his lordship must have been of her son's death, that he was in possession, or cognizant, of a will distributive of the personals, in which Clara was interested. The desirableness of awaiting the bishop's arrival in order to the decisive clearing up of that essential point, was the reason, I understood, that we had not yet taken our departure from a residence where even its late mistress was already looked upon as little better than an unauthorized, unwelcome intruder. Clara, poor, timid, nervous Clara, would have yielded entire possession of everything without a struggle or a word of protest; but her sister—who really seemed made for occasions of difficulty, with such admirable firmness and decision did she act when there was a right to be vindicated, or insolence to be repressed—would not hear of her leaving Ashe Priory till after the bishop's visit; and Captain Toulmin, with a very ill grace, acquiesced, probably because he could not legally do otherwise.

It was, however, not near twelve o'clock when we thus met, our being gathered together so early having been arranged—except as regarded the rector, who, as usual, was self-invited—by dear, fidgety, well-intentioned Mrs. Toulmin. The worthy lady's never quite accurately poised mind had been sadly thrown off its equivocal balance by the domestic revolution that had just taken place, and a vague notion been set floating in her brain, that the lover intimacy formerly subsisting between her son, Captain Toulmin, and "sweet Mrs. Herbert," which had been so suddenly and mysteriously broken off, might be renewed by the genial influence of a sort of family-council, and possibly—so altogether flighty had she lately become —that the right reverend gentleman about to appear on the scene might conclude the affair connubially off-hand without further ado or delay, and thereby reconcile the conflicting emotions by which she was agitated. The aspect of the "council" would have sufficed to convince any one less hopelessly obtuse than the Hon. Mrs. Toulmin, of the desperate character of her enterprise. Her admirable son was lolling, sublimely insolent, upon a luxurious leather-chair near the fire, and fondling Ponto, a huge Newfound-

land dog, one of the numerous quadrupedal additions
he had already made to the establishment at Ashe
Priory; his elaborately got-up sardonic smile and
sneer saying, as plainly as he could make them say:
"You, Ponto, my fine fellow, are the only creature in
this room I care a button for, or that has any right
to be here." Clara, as pale as a lily, frightened-look-
ing—tears in her eyes, that a jarring whisper would
cause to overflow—was standing at the further end of
the apartment, as far away from Captain Toulmin as
she well could be, with one hand clasped tightly
round her sister's waist, looking or pretending to look
over huge portfolios of prints and drawings she had
seen twenty times before, which the delighted rector
was lugging from the library-cases, and displaying
before her with a zealous assiduity, infinitely rewarded
by the occasional faint smile and blush of thanks
which it called forth. For myself, seated near the
fire opposite Captain Toulmin, I was soon thoroughly
absorbed in painful retrospection, especially of the
former scene I had witnessed in that library between
Mary and Captain Toulmin, and the different posi-
tions in which they stood to each other then and
now—a train of ill-boding reverie, from which I was
suddenly roused by loud, sharp, pellet-like sentences
emitted by the Hon. Mrs. Toulmin, the precise tenor
of which I did not catch, in answer to some observation of her son's, as was evident by his rude rejoinder:
" Really, madam, you are too absurd in persisting

that a pastime which may have amused an idle hour
or two, indicated a serious purpose. *N'est-ce pas*,
friend Ponto ?"

This was said in a sneering, taunting tone, clearly
intended to be heard and understood by the group at
the further end of the library. That it was quite
perfectly heard and understood, Clara's agitation and
varying colour—the Rev. Mr. Atherley's fierce, I had
almost written fighting look, directed full at the insolent speaker—and Mary's angry, yet, if the phrase
may be permitted, *pleased* disdain, abundantly testified.
Captain Toulmin no more comprehended that puz-
zling expression of Mary's countenance than I did,
though it greatly irritated him, or even *he* would not
have replied to it by saying: " As to your proposal
of last evening, my lady-mother, that I should allow
the fair widow of my cousin, Francis Herbert, a
pension, or something of that sort, I do not, as at
present advised, see any necessity for doing so; her
portion of the hereditary Selwyn property being
doubtless amply sufficient for the needs of an unencumbered young lady."

I do not believe that this brutality was levelled at,
or deliberately meant to annoy Clara; it was a sudden
savage retort upon Mary for the bitter humiliation to
which she had subjected him in that very room, and
which the queenly look she had now, as then, assumed, must have vividly recalled to his mind, as
it did to mine. " Mary," I for the hundredth time

mentally exclaimed, " is wonderfully changed. Her husband, I remember, was a person of distinguished air and carriage; it must have been through long companionship with him that she has learned that lofty bearing."

The Hon. Mrs. Toulmin said something I did not hear, to which Mary replied : " Pray do not apologize, my dear madam: your son's words, I have no doubt, quite faithfully reflect his peculiarly constituted mind. I have only to remark, though it is scarcely worth while to do so, that under no possible circumstances will Mrs. Francis Herbert condescend to hold the slightest avoidable intercourse with Captain Toulmin. As to pensions, it is quite possible he may yet be the suppliant to her for such favours, instead of the bestower of them."

" Come, come," interposed the Hon. Mrs. Toulmin, who alone of us all did not appear to heed the implied menace contained in the last sentence ; " that is a little too harsh : you should not forget——"

" I forget nothing, my dear madam," interrupted Mary ; " and I must beg that the subject be let drop. These painful, but, I have no doubt, fleeting trials," she added, addressing the excited rector, and seating herself on a couch beside her sister, so as to screen her from observation, " will, I trust, be sanctified to her, and—— Ha ! here, at last, I hope, is the bishop's carriage."

It was the bishop's carriage ; and in a very few

minutes the right reverend gentleman entered the library, and saluted the two sisters with an almost undignified briskness of cordiality. To Clara he addressed a few words of pious condolence; congratulated Mary upon her health and cheerful looks; inquired for her sons; appeared surprised they were not at the Priory; then made a comprehensive bow, and seated himself: his stay could not, his lordship added, be longer on this occasion than a quarter of an hour at the most, he having to attend a church missionary-meeting twelve miles off at three o'clock precisely; but on his return he would, if permitted, make a longer stay. This being the case, instead of adjourning to partake of the luncheon prepared in the dining-room, some sherry and biscuits were brought into the library at his request.

"Your lordship being so pressed for time," presently observed Captain Toulmin, "will hardly be able to do more than acquaint us with the general purport of the important papers forwarded to your address immediately after the decease of Mr. Edmund Herbert."

"This gentleman is——?" queried the bishop, averting his gold hand-spectacles from the speaker's face towards that of Mrs. Calvert.

"Captain Toulmin," replied Mary quickly, "this lady's, the Hon. Mrs. Toulmin, son."

"I remember—I remember: a distant relative of the family's. Well, sir, I *did* receive some important papers, as you mention; that is to say, they would be important were any one insane enough to dispute that a Herbert could have contracted a valid marriage with an estimable lady, though not of his own rank in life."

" No one wants to dispute that, your lordship must be quite aware," said Captain Toulmin.

" Exactly so," replied the bishop; "in which case the papers are *not* very important."

" There was no will, then, amongst them, I conclude?"

" There was not," said the bishop, " which I regret —which I regret," repeated his lordship, who had paused for a moment, startled by the demoniac glance of triumph that Captain Toulmin darted at Mary; " as it would be more satisfactory to all parties if his wishes could be known with precise accuracy. This lady, Mrs. Francis Herbert, he intended, as I know from one of his letters, to provide handsomely for. But, after all," added the bishop, " the absence of a will can be of little consequence, under the actual circumstances. Edmund Herbert knew, as I know, that his intentions will be substantially fulfilled, as certainly as if engrossed and sealed upon parchment."

" Permit me to differ from your lordship upon that point said Captain Toulmin with a sneering laugh " I have already declared that I feel bound by no obligation, moral or legal, to provide for Mrs. Francis Herbert."

"*You* have already declared!" said the bishop, looking bewilderedly towards Mrs. Calvert. "Really, I don't understand! What does the gentleman, Captain Toulmin, mean?"

The bright smile curling Mary's lip, and dancing in her eyes, sent a wild electric thought, hope, through me; and so fiercely did my heart beat with the bare imagination flashing in my brain, that I caught at the back of a chair for support. But no—no, that were too good—too glorious to be true; and yet ——

"Not understand me!" Captain Toulmin was saying the while, though, why I know not, his voice sounded as if speaking at a great distance off. "I do not, for all that, speak in parables. The late heir-at-law to the Herbert property, Mrs. Francis Herbert's son, being dead, I am of course the present heir-at-law: that is plain English, I believe."

"The late heir-at-law, Mrs. Francis Herbert's son, being dead," echoed the bishop, still with his eyes intently fixed upon Mrs. Calvert, "he is of course the present heir-at-law!"

"Your lordship must understand," said Mary, "that I have disclosed nothing: I had powerful reasons for not doing so till you were present."

"Oh, now I comprehend," exclaimed the bishop, rising from his chair, a motion which, from sympathy I suppose, lifted everybody else at the same moment to their feet. "It is not known, then, to you, ladies, and to you, gentlemen, that this lady, who, for perfectly justifiable reasons, has for a time borne the name of Calvert, is in reality the widow of Mr. Edmund Herbert, to whom she was espoused by myself in the church of the parish of which I was then rector, in his own proper name; and that, consequently, her eldest son, *not* Captain Toulmin, is the heir-at-law to the Herbert estates, real and personal."

A silence like that which follows crashing thunder—a silence that could be felt in the audibly-beating pulse—followed the bishop's announcement. What others felt, or how they looked, I know not; I remember only that my own almost suffocating emotions at last finding vent, I threw myself, in a paroxysm of sobs and tears, into Clara's arms, almost strangling her in an excess of delight very little short for a time of delirium. When I partially recovered, I saw that the terrible counter-stroke had prostrated Captain Toulmin, who was lying, pale and senseless, upon a couch—his mother, to whom Mary was speaking kindly, standing over him, chafing his temples, and wildly sobbing. Then the scene closed in again, so far as I was concerned, for I fainted, and was carried insensible to bed. In truth I had been weak and ill for some days past, and was therefore not so well able as usual to bear up against such a sudden revulsion of feeling.

I think I only need add, by way of postscriptum, that the Hon. Mrs. Toulmin is still a permanent guest at Ashe Priory; that Captain Toulmin, who was treated much better than he deserved, is an officer in the service of Austria; that Mary is, if possible, a more admirable person than ever; that her two sons are fine young men, who will, I doubt not, some of these days, do honour to the ancient, but, there can be little doubt, in some degree, till the introduction of fresh blood, partially decaying stock of the Herberts; that Clara is the happy and honoured wife of the rector—again a mother, and quite as much mistress of Ashe Priory as ever she was; that Mrs. Selwyn has been of necessity relegated, upon a sufficient income, to Beach Villa; and, finally, that I have been for a long time settled in London, and that my name, when I left Ashe Priory, ceased to be Redburn.

THE MAGIC MIRROR.

"Dear, ingenuous girl!" exclaimed Henry Rivers with rapturous enthusiasm as he kissed for at least the twentieth time a perfumed note which he had received about half an hour previously: "what a tenderness and grace; what a contempt, or rather forgetfulness, of mere extrinsic advantages, breathes through the charming delicacy and reserve of these dear lines! And I, mistrusting infidel that I was, to delay the offer of my hand till the *Gazette* officially announced my colonial appointment, lest, forsooth, Ellen Danvers should, on account of the want, on my part, of a sufficiently handsome income, decline the proposal she has so frankly, so gracefully accepted! I would wager my existence that when she perused my letter, the fact of eight hundred pounds per annum having been added to my previously very modest revenue did not so much as glance across her mind, far less influence in the slightest manner her acceptance of my suit. Beautiful Ellen! what would I give to have been present when the modest gratitude, the amiable confidence which dictated her written reply, rose in gentle murmurs to her lips, and flashed with radiant eloquence from the clear depths of her dark blue eyes!

Mr. Henry Rivers, who was seated at his solitary dessert, here paused in his passionate soliloquy to help himself to a glass of wine and some grapes. I had better improve the interval which elapsed ere he resumed his rhapsodies to jot down a few particulars relative to his parentage, education, and present position in the world.

Henry Rivers, then, was the third son of a highly-respectable country solicitor, who, fancying he discerned in him the material of which chancellors and chief-justices are fashioned, sent him at the proper age to "eat his terms" in Lincoln's Inn. This stage of the journey towards the woolsack Mr. Henry Rivers performed in a very efficient manner indeed, and he was in due time called to the bar by the benchers of that distinguished and venerable inn of court. Whether, however, his respectable parent had, with excusable partiality, overrated his forensic aptitude, or whether the attorneys of the Queen's Bench had entered into a conspiracy to ignore the young gentleman's abilities, certain it is that exceedingly few briefs found their way into his hands. About five years after he had assumed the wig and gown, Mr. Rivers, senior, departed this life, bequeathing his excellent business to his two eldest sons, and two hundred pounds per annum in ground-rents to his favourite Henry. The still youthful barrister, amidst his grief for the loss of so indulgent a father, felt wonderfully consoled by the reflection that the means of a future decent maintenance did not depend upon the exertions of his own brain, in which organ, his modesty had for some time whispered, *too* great reliance ought not in prudence to be placed. Not that Henry Rivers was deficient in average ability, or unpossessed of talent of a certain kind, only it did not happen to be of the kind suited to the profession chosen for him. His imagination especially was a very brilliant one, and could at a moment's notice

> " Clothe the palpable and the familiar
> With golden exhalations of the dawn ; "

a faculty which, in an argument upon a demurrer, would, it may be easily conceived, prove rather in the way than otherwise. Still further to excite his already overheated fancy, and withdraw his mind from the delightful study of " Coke upon Littleton," he had managed to fall desperately in love with a young lady of great beauty and accomplishments, the second daughter of Mr. Cuthbert Danvers, and a very amiable, well-principled person, but possessed withal of no dowry save her beauty and her virtues. He had been long mentally debating whether—— But I must follow him in his quickly-resumed flights of fancy.

" Love and friendship ! friendship and love !— divinely-varied essence which, sprinkled upon the common-places of existence, converts the parched and dusty earth into an elysium, fragrant with bright flowers, and rich in glorious fruits, from which flows nectar for the gods—— "

He was interrupted by a slight tap at the door; and in as ordinary a tone as he could at the moment command, he bade his visitor " Walk in."

" Dear Aunt Barbara, is it you? I am delighted to see you. It is, I think, but three days since you were here, but an age has been crowded into that brief point of time."

" Whom were you addressing so loudly when I knocked? I was afraid you had company."

" I was soliloquizing, dear aunt: indulging in irrepressible utterance at the happiness, the joy, the bliss, with which this charming note has inspired me! Read it, and imagine my transport at its reception."

" A very lady-like, proper reply," said Aunt Barbara, after a slow and minute perusal of it. " Ellen Danvers is a sensible, superior person; her family, too, are worthy people."

" Sensible—superior! How wretchedly cold and formal your expressions sound! The mild radiance of maidenly regard which shines through every line you have been reading might, one would think, have kindled a warmer —— "

"Nonsense, Henry!" interrupted Mrs. Barbara Rivers. " Do you take me for a school-girl, or has your good fortune utterly crazed your brain? Pour me out a glass of wine: I have walked all the way from Aldermoor to congratulate you on your appointment. There can now be no mistake about *that*."

"Certainly not. Perhaps you would like to read Sir Edward Aytoun's letter announcing his success in procuring it for me. Here it is."

"Very kind indeed; but he might have been less profuse of his foolish compliments. A real service such as he has rendered you requires no such silly tinsel to enhance its value."

"Foolish compliments!" exclaimed Henry Rivers with some asperity: "I believe Sir Edward is perfectly sincere in every expression he has used. You need not, Aunt Barbara, elevate your eyebrows in that manner. I do not of course mean that I *deserve* the high compliments he is pleased to pay to what he calls my great ability and superior fitness for the office—in which encomium, by the way, it appears the minister fully concurs—but I am quite sure Sir Edward *thinks* precisely as he writes. He and I, you know, were college friends."

"You silly boy! Yet it is perhaps better you should believe so: we gain nothing by prying too curiously beneath the surface of the world's conventionalisms:—

'Glissez, mortels; n'appuyez pas,'

is a maxim of sound worldly wisdom; but let us change the subject. I am very glad you took my advice not to make Ellen Danvers an offer till your appointment was gazetted."

" I doubt," rejoined Henry Rivers with increasing ill-humour, " that either Ellen or her father bestowed a thought on the subject, or were in the slightest degree influenced in their decision by my increase of fortune."

A merry laugh broke from Aunt Barbara's lips, but she made no answer in words.

" Still as ever, I see, a disbeliever in the ethereality of either love or friendship. According to you, aunt, the purest emotions, the highest actions, have all necessarily an alloy of earth about them."

" Perhaps so ; but I am not so foolish as to wish to cloud the mirror in which the speech and actions of mankind love to glass themselves, by needlessly raking amidst the selfish sediment which, I fear, lies at the bottom of almost all human motive."

" There, aunt, I differ entirely with you. I would have all polite shams, all make-believes, banished the world, and replaced by a constant and frank sincerity."

" And so disenchant the world of its romance, its poetry, its innocent and agreeable illusions ! Insist that people should be perpetually annoying and in-sulting each other by irritating, useless sincerities ! Society, my dear boy, under such a *régime* would not be endurable. Much of the present, as well as the future, is wisely hidden from us."

A long and wearisome discussion ensued upon this knotty point, during which both speakers occasionally manifested very natural symptoms of drowsiness. Henry Rivers persisted in stoutly maintaining that affection, friendship, contaminated with the slightest admixture of worldliness, was not worth acceptance. But he was at length disgusted with his aunt's obstinacy, and his eyes, in spite of himself, began to close. Still he struggled manfully against the unpolite feeling, sipped a little more wine, and even fancied for a moment, from his aunt's silence, that she was giving in. But suddenly the placidity of his respected relation was broken as if by a squall, and she displayed a warmth and vehemence quite foreign to her usual placid manner. Her very features appeared to dilate and charge with passion as she pursued her energetic argumentation.

At length, after concluding a long and fierce invective, in which doubts of the angelic disinterestedness of Ellen Danvers and Sir Edward Aytoun were strangely mixed up and confused, she pointed with a significant gesture to a small oval hand-glass which happened to be lying on a side-table—" You remember on what occasion I presented you with that toilet-glass ?"

" Certainly I do."

" I have never yet informed you of its strange qualities, though I have been frequently on the point of doing so. It is a *magic* mirror, and will confer on you, as it has conferred on me, the wretched privilege of seeing and hearing all things that concern yourself without deception or disguise."

"Is it possible? But you must be jesting!"

"I was never more serious. The proof is easy. Breathe thrice upon it, and the scene your wish suggests will instantly be pictured there. You will also hear every syllable that passes between the persons summoned before you."

Henry Rivers seized the glass with a confused feeling of delight and vexation. Was his aunt mocking him, or did he really possess a talisman which would enable him to look beneath the outward shows and shams of the world, and bask in the sunlight of truth, undimmed, undistorted, by the false media through which it reaches unprivileged eyes and ears? Surely the age of magic, of mysticism of all kinds, was past; and yet—— There could be at all events no harm in making the trial.

He breathed thrice upon the mirror, and expressed a wish that the interview between his friend Sir Edward Aytoun and the colonial minister should pass before him.

Magical indeed! The glass in an instant displayed a large, handsome apartment, the business cabinet apparently of a great personage. Subordinate officials, secretaries, glided in and out with deferential manner, and in observant silence, except when addressed, and then only answering with 'bated breath and whispering humbleness.

" Sir Edward Aytoun has been waiting some time, my lord," said a gentleman, who had just entered, in a low voice. " He is becoming impatient."

An expression of extreme annoyance passed over the great man's features as he muttered, " That is the most persistent personage that ever besieged and worried a government for favours. He is, however, too important an animal to be slighted. Ask Sir Edward to walk up," he added in a louder tone.

Sir Edward Aytoun entered, and it was marvellous how rapid a change the noble lord's features underwent.

" My dear Sir Edward, I am so glad to see you! I have been longing to talk over your last night's speech. It was—you know I am not in the habit of flattering—a first-rate thing. Palmerston was delighted with it. He had intended, I know, to speak himself, but felt, when you had concluded, that nothing more was to be said."

Sir Edward bowed, and looked pleased. He did not, however, reply, but silently kept his seat in an expectant attitude and manner which no secretary of state could possibly misunderstand. Comparatively young as he was in years, the baronet was already far too old in public life to be amused or diverted from his purpose by empty compliments.

"I suppose, Sir Edward," said the minister, after an embarrassed pause, "you have called respecting the appointment you have solicited for—for——"

"Mr. Henry Rivers," suggested the baronet.

"Yes, Rivers. Are you *very* desirous of obtaining it for him? because I had partly promised it to——"

"I *am* desirous," interrupted Sir Edward, tartly, "that your lordship should oblige me in this matter. It is, I think, a favour to which my unvarying support of the administration fully entitles me."

"Excellent man! true-hearted friend!" ejaculated Henry Rivers, averting for an instant—as, gazing upon the ceiling, he appeared to contemplate the altitude of Sir Edward's merits—his eyes from the mirror, "this is indeed friendship in its true essence. Here, too, there is no disguise, no false colouring." He looked triumphantly at his aunt; but observing, to his great surprise, that that lady's countenance still retained the cold, cynical expression it had lately assumed, turned again to the magic glass.

He must have missed a sentence or two, for the noble lord was saying, "Quite an undistinguished man, I understand, though called to the bar five or six years ago; has never, I believe, held a brief; did I not so understand you, Mr. Quill?"

"Four only in five years, my lord. The last he held was in a pauper-removal case, when his law was corrected by an alderman, before whom the matter was argued."

"Confound the fellow!" muttered Mr. Henry Rivers, colouring at the same time to the very tips of his ears: "how came he to know that, I wonder?"

"This colonial office," interposed Sir Edward, "requires, I believe, no remarkable ability in the person filling it. If it did, believe me I should hesitate greatly in asking it for Henry Rivers. He is a young man of, I have no doubt, good principle; but as to great quickness of intellect, that is quite out of the question."

The holder of the magic glass turned his face stealthily towards his aunt, but snatched it swiftly back as his eye encountered the mocking, triumphant smile which curled her lip.

"If you press it," rejoined the minister, "we must oblige you; but really, since the person to be benefited is so mere a nobody——"

"Your lordship mistakes the matter," interrupted the baronet: "I care very little about Henry Rivers, though I believe him to be a worthy fellow enough; but the fact is, his brothers, the attorneys, are busy, influential men in the county: *you* know how closely parties are divided there; and I really cannot *afford* to lose their support, as I unquestionably should if this appointment were not conferred upon their somewhat feather-headed brother!"

"Enough—enough! he must have the appointment. Send him a civil message from me, and say

I will appoint an interview with him before he leaves the country."

" I will; accompanied by my very best congratulatory compliments. *Cela va sans dire.*"

Henry Rivers laid down the magic mirror. This, then, was his *friend;* the man for whose sincerity of soul he would have pledged his life! Never would he place faith in mortal man again—never! A few minutes' reflection, and a glance at the *Gazette,* which was lying on the table, suggested other thoughts. " Sir Edward has certainly rendered me an essential service; and what he said was perhaps, after all, not entirely incorrect: and yet I can no longer look upon or feel towards him as I did. Confound the mirror!" he exclaimed with sudden passion, and as if about to dash it on the ground. " Aunt Barbara was right—with regard at least to *male* friendships," he added, restraining himself, and speaking more calmly. " But the love of a maiden for her betrothed —the gentle guilelessness of a virgin heart palpitating with the pure and sweet emotions of a first affection; these feelings caught from heaven, unstained of earth, cannot be too nearly contemplated— too minutely analyzed!" Once more his breath thrice dimmed the magic glass: then,

> " Like the murmur of a dream,
> He breathed *her* name,"

accompanied by a wish to witness all that passed

from the receipt of his marriage-offer till the answer was despatched.

The wizard depths of the mirror instantly disclosed a handsomely-furnished sitting-room, opening with French windows upon a shrubbery and flower-garden, through which presently entered beautiful Ellen Danvers, attired in an elegant white morning-dress, and with a bouquet of brilliant flowers in her hand. A servant approached, presented a letter—*the* letter—and retired. Ellen Danvers placed the flowers upon a marble stand, and glancing curiously at the seal, whilst a charming blush mantled her fine features, with some precipitation removed the envelope.

The blush deepened as she read, till its hue mocked that of the freshly-gathered roses by her side; a bright smile parted her sweet lips, and a soft, low sigh, as she seated herself in pensive mood and attitude, escaped her gentle bosom.

" Thrice-blessed mirror! "

She was roused from her reverie by the entrance of her sister Marian, a gay, light-hearted damsel, about two years younger than herself.

" Ellen, papa wishes to see you in the library. He looks as grave as a bishop. Mamma seems equally solemn, and you—— Why, Ellen, your eyes are filled with tears! What, for mercy's sake, can it all mean ? "

" Read this, Marian," said Ellen, proffering the letter, and passing at the same time an arm round her sister's waist. "Papa has doubtless received a companion epistle."

Marian read, and when she had finished, exclaimed, with a kind of regretful archness—"A proposal of marriage from Mr. Rivers, as I'm alive! No wonder everybody seems struck of a heap! But I forbid the banns!"

"Do you, Marian; and for what reason?"

"Reason, Ellen! as if reason had so much to do with these affairs! In the first place, then, you would have to leave us: in the next, he is nothing like so handsome as Frank Mildmay. Ah, that blush, Ellen! Need I further explain why these banns must be forbidden?"

"Mr. Mildmay, Marian, is out of the question. Papa has, you know, forbidden his addresses, and I entirely acquiesce in his decision."

"I wish Caroline and Fanny were at home. It's my impression," added Marian pettishly, "that Mr. Rivers is humpbacked!"

"Nonsense, you silly madcap! A little round-shouldered, perhaps."

"The devilish glass!"

A servant entered, iterated Mr. Danvers' desire for Ellen's presence in the library, and the sisters left the room.

A moment, and the library was disclosed, with Mr. and Mrs. Danvers, Ellen and Marian, seated in council.

"Well, Ellen," said her father, "what answer shall we make to this ardent, eloquent lover of yours?"

The blushing girl did not raise her head, nor immediately reply. At last she said, "Do you not think, papa, I am too young as yet for so very serious an engagement?"

"You are one-and-twenty years of age, and your mother was, I think, a twelvemonth younger than that when we were married. Is that your only objection to the proposal of Mr. Rivers?"

"But, papa, I have seen so little of him, that I—— Really you must decide for me."

"You do not *dis*like him, Ellen?" inquired Mrs. Danvers.

"No, mamma; certainly not. I esteem him, and, as an acquaintance, rather like him : nothing more."

"Accursed mirror!"

"It is, I think, a very eligible match," said Mr. Danvers, "for a girl without a fortune ; and I do not think it at all essential to married happiness that the lady should be at first what is called in love with the gentleman. You will make a good and affectionate wife—of that, Ellen, I am quite sure. By the appointment conferred upon him, and which is, you know, gazetted, Mr. Rivers' income is now at least a thousand a year ; and that, where you are going——"

"Papa!"

"Well, where at all events *he* is going, will maintain a very handsome establishment. Then his character is unexceptionable, and his temper one of the easiest in the world. Altogether, Ellen, I think you have drawn a fair prize in the matrimonial lottery."

"The climate is very healthy, I believe?" said Mrs. Danvers.

"Entirely so; and society there is of a somewhat high cast for a colony."

"I suppose," said Ellen Danvers, blushing still more deeply than before, "from Mr. Rivers' official position, his—his wife will take precedence after the lady of the lieutenant-governor?"

"Certainly, Ellen—no doubt about it," replied Mr. Danvers with a quiet smile. "Now run away and write your answer; mine will be ready in two or three mintues."

The young ladies tripped off to another apartment, followed by their mother; and a change of scene immediately exhibited Ellen seated at a writing-desk, and endeavouring, whilst Marian peeped over her shoulder, to indite a fitting acceptance of Mr. Rivers' passionate proposal. But the task seemed an endless one. Sheet after sheet of note-paper was wasted in vain attempts; but ultimately she placed a rough draft for approval in her mother's hands.

"Far too stiff, too cold, too formal, Ellen. This will never do."

"Then pray, mamma, write it yourself, and I will copy it."

Mrs. Danvers complied; and the missive which had so charmed Mr. Rivers was, after some emendations by Marian, fairly copied and subscribed by Ellen Danvers.

"Heigho!" sighed the affianced bride as the three left the apartment. "No doubt you and papa know best; but I *do* wish I could reciprocate a little more warmly the poor gentleman's vehement passion for insensible, and, I fear, not over-grateful me."

"You will be a happy wife, Ellen," replied Mrs. Danvers, "and Rivers will be a fortunate husband." The door closed, and the glass was a blank.

"Infernal mirror!" exclaimed Henry Rivers, whose fierce emotions during the scenes unrolled before him I have but interjectionally attempted to describe— "infernal mirror! you have robbed love, life, of all its charm! Frank Mildmay, too! I have seen him there! Madman, idiot that I was to avail myself of such devilish agency!" and again seizing the mirror, he dashed it furiously beneath the fire-grate.

The crash of the glass was echoed by the voice of Aunt Barbara, exclaiming at its shrillest pitch, as she shook her nephew roughly by the arm, "Good heavens, Henry, what do you mean by smashing decanters in that frantic way?"

"Decanters, Aunt Barbara!" stammered Henry Rivers, starting to his feet, and thoroughly bewildered; "wasn't it the mirror?"

"The mirror! Henry, Henry, you have been

taking too much wine. I left the room only about half an hour ago, and on my return, behold you are pitching decanters into the fire!"

"It was a dream, then, thank God! Aunt Barbara, you were quite right; and now, if you please. let us have tea."

About eight years after these events, **Mr. Henry Rivers** was seated on a pleasant summer evening beneath a verandah of trellis-work, festooned and canopied with gorgeous flowers, watching with calm delight the gambols of his three charming children. Near him sat his still beautiful wife, turning over a file of English newspapers that had just arrived. Presently an exclamation of surprise escaped her.

"What is the matter, Ellen?" inquired Mr. Rivers.

"Nothing affecting us, Harry, though it startled me somewhat; Frank Mildmay——" It was now the husband's turn to start. "Why, you did not, I think, know him?"

"No matter; what *of* Frank Mildmay?"

"He has broken his neck in a steeple-chase. Do you know, Harry," she added, after a few moments' pause, and with one of the sweetest, happiest smiles that ever lighted up woman's face, "that I once quite liked Frank Mildmay? and I do believe that, had it not been for dear, good, sensible papa, I should have accepted him rather than you. What a providential escape for both of us! Was it not, Harry?"

" Providential, indeed," replied the husband, fondly pressing his wife's proffered hand. Presently afterwards he added in a musing tone, but unheeded by Mrs. Rivers, who was again busy with the newspapers, " A remarkably clever woman is Aunt Barbara. I should like to hear her opinion upon ' the philosophy of dreams '—

' Glissez, mortels ; n'appuyez pas.'

Sounder philosophy than that never fell from human lips."

MR. ROBERT SIMPSON'S COURTSHIP

About three years have elapsed since Mr. Robert Simpson succeeded, at the demise of Mr. Isaac Simpson, ironmonger by trade, fishmonger by Livery, and common-councilman of the City of London by election, to the prosperous business and municipal honours established and acquired by his respectable, painstaking parent. Some natural tears he shed; but, the exigencies of business and the duties of his corporate office—replacing, as he immediately did, his father in the representation of the important ward in which his shop was situated—not permitting a protracted indulgence in the selfish luxury of woe, he fortunately recovered his equanimity in a much less space of time than persons acquainted with the extreme tenderness of his disposition had thought possible. Mr. Robert Simpson, albeit arrived at the mature age of thirty-five, was still a bachelor; and not only unappropriated, but, as ward-rumour reported, unpromised; at perfect liberty, in fact, to bestow himself, his very desirable stock-in-trade, business premises, and three freehold houses in the Poultry, upon any fair lady fortunate enough to engage his affection, and able to return it. Indeed, to this circumstance, it was whispered at the time of his election, he owed his unopposed return to the municipal niche so long and worthily occupied by his departed father; Mr. Crowley, the highly-respectable spectacle-maker, having suddenly withdrawn from the contest on the very day of nomination; thereto induced, hinted gossips of the City, by the fact that Miss Crowley, who chanced to meet Mr. Robert Simpson on the previous evening at the house of a mutual acquaintance, had been by him most courteously and gallantly escorted home. The matrimonial inference drawn from so slight a premise as a few minutes' walk along unromantic Cheapside, by gas, not moonlight, proved, as might be expected, an altogether erroneous one. The Fates had other views regarding the prosperous ironmonger; and as those " sisters three," like most ladies, generally contrive to have their own way, Mr. Simpson was ultimately quite otherwise disposed of; and Miss Crowley, for aught I know to the contrary, remains Miss Crowley to this day.

Not that Mr. Simpson was by any means insensible to female fascination: he was, unfortunately for his own peace of mind, somewhat too susceptible; an ardent admirer of beauty in all its hues and varieties, from the fair and delicate grace and beauty of the maidens of the pale north, to the richer glow and warmer tints of orient loveliness. The strict surveillance of his honoured father, joined to a constitutional timidity he was quite unable to overcome, had, however, sufficed during that gentleman's lifetime to prevent rash impulse from eventuating in rash deed. He was also, I must mention, extremely fastidious in his notions of feminine delicacy and reserve; and his especial antipathies were red hair, or any hue approaching to red, and obliquity of vision of the slightest kind. Such was Mr. Robert Simpson, who, about two o'clock on the afternoon of March the 1st, 1847, stepped, richly and scrupulously attired, into a brougham, specially retained to convey him to dine at his friend Mr. John Puckford's modest, but comfortable establishment at Mile End, where he was by express arrangement to meet his expected, expectant bride. Before, however, relating what there befell him, it will be necessary to put the reader in possession of certain important incidents which had occurred during the three previous days.

On the evening of the preceding Tuesday, Mr. Simpson finding himself at the east end of the town, and moreover strongly disposed for a cup of tea and a quiet gossip, resolved to " drop in " upon his new acquaintance, Mr. John Puckford, hoping to find him and his wife alone. In this, however, he was doomed to disappointment; for he had scarcely withdrawn his hand from the knocker, when he was startled—

Mr. Simpson was, as I have before hinted, a singularly bashful person in the presence of the fairer and better half of creation—by the sound of female voices issuing, in exuberant merriment, from the front parlour. There was company, it was evident; and Mr. Simpson's first impulse was to fly; as the thought crossed his mind, the door opened, and Mr. Puckford, who chanced to be in the passage, espying him, he was fain to make a virtue of necessity, and was speedily in the midst of the merry party whose gaiety had so alarmed him. That the introduction was managed in the usual way, I have no doubt; but the names, however distinctly uttered, seem to have made no impression upon the confused brain of the bashful visitor; so that, when, after the lapse of a few minutes, he began to recover his composure, he found himself in the presence of three ladies and one gentleman, of whose names, as well as persons, he was profoundly ignorant. The ladies were two of Mrs. Puckford's married sisters, and Miss Fortescue, a young lady of reduced fortunes, at present occupied as teacher in a neighbouring seminary. The gentleman was Mr. Alfred Gray, a bachelor like Mr. Simpson, but nothing like so old, and scarcely so bashful. Mrs. Frazer, the eldest of the two sisters, a charming lady-like person, of, you would say, judging from appearances, about twenty-three or twenty-four years of age, seemed—after some oscillation between her and Mrs. Holland, whose fuller proportions, dark

hair, and brunette complexion, contrasted not un-
favourably with the lighter figure, and fair hair and
features of her sister—to engross Mr. Simpson's
whole attention, and to arouse after a while all his
conversational energies, which, by the way, were by
no means contemptible. Mr. Simpson's time was
come: ere a couple of hours had fled, the hapless
ironmonger was hurt past all surgery; had fallen
desperately in love with a married lady, and the
mother of three or four children! On the only single
female present, Miss Fortescue, Mr. Simpson had
bestowed but one glance on entering the apartment;
that had been quite sufficient to check any desire for
a more intimate perusal of her features. The lady
combined his two antipathies : her hair was decidedly
red, and a strong *cast*, to use a mild term, detracted
from the uncommon brilliancy of her mind-glancing
eyes. She took very slight part in the conversation ;
and that little, so absorbed was Mr. Simpson, was by
him utterly unheeded. She wore, like her friend
Mrs. Frazer, a plaid dress, and the baptismal name
of both was Mary.

The ladies departed early, and Mr. Simpson and
Mr. Gray followed their example a few minutes afterwards.

" Mr. Gray," said the former gentleman, as he took
leave of his companion at the end of the street,
" what is that charming person's name? I have
quite forgotten it."

F

"Which charming person?" inquired Mr. Alfred Gray, with a quiet smile.

This Mr. Simpson thought a very absurd question; he, however, replied—"The lady in the plaid dress: Mary, Mrs. Puckford called her."

"The lady in a plaid dress, whom Mrs. Puckford called Mary, is a Miss Fortescue: she is a teacher of music and drawing," rejoined Mr. Gray, with demure accent.   It was too dark for Mr. Simpson to see his eyes.

"Thank you, sir: good night," rejoined the en-amoured municipal dignitary.

Mr. Simpson was soon at home, and before an hour had elapsed, had carefully penned, and posted with his own hands, a letter to his friend Puckford. He then retired to bed, and dreamt dreams.

"Sarah." said Mr. Puckford the next morning to his wife, after reading a letter, just delivered, with a perplexed expression of countenance, "did Mr. Simpson seem to you particularly struck with Mary Fortescue yesterday evening?"

"With Mary Fortescue? Surely not. Why do you ask?"

"Only that here is a letter from Simpson, professing violent love for her, and stating his determination, should you and I be able to assure him, which he scarcely dares venture to hope, that she is disengaged, to immediately solicit her hand in marriage!"

"Gracious!—Is it possible?"

"Read the letter yourself. Her beauty, he observes, is, he is quite sure, her least recommendation. Comical, isn't it?"

"Well, it *is* odd; but she is, you know, a most amiable creature, and will make, I am sure, an admirable wife."

"And he, too, that so especially detests red hair, or the slightest twist in the organs of vision——"

"Mary Fortescue's hair," interrupted the wife, "can scarcely be called red: a very deep gold colour I should say——"

"Very deep indeed—remarkably so," interjected Mr. Puckford.

"And as to the slight cast in her eyes, *that* no one observes after a few days' acquaintance with her."

"I suppose we may with a safe conscience assure him that she is not engaged?"

"Of course we may. It is a wonderful match for her, and we ought to do all we can to forward it. Friday next, the 1st of March, is Alfred's birthday; suppose you ask him to dine with us on that day to meet her? We need have only the same party he met yesterday evening."

This was finally agreed upon; and accordingly, as soon as he had finished his business in the City, Mr. Puckford, previous to returning home, called on Mr. Simpson. He found him in a state of great excitement, which, however, gradually calmed down after Mr. Puckford's solemn assurance, which he gave unhesitatingly, that the charming Mary Fortescue was certainly disengaged, and, in his opinion, by no means indisposed to entertain an eligible matrimonial proposition. All this was balm to the stricken Simpson; and after several failures, he at last succeeded in inditing a formal offer of his hand and fortune to the lady of his affection, of which impassioned missive Mrs. Puckford was to be the bearer, her husband undertaking that she would exert all her eloquence and influence to secure acceptance of the proposal.

"And now, Puckford," said Mr. Simpson, "we'll have a glass of wine, and drink the future Mrs. Simpson's health. What a charming ornament," he added, with a sort of rapturous sigh, as he placed the decanters on the table--"what a charming ornament she would be to this fire-place!"

"An odd expression that!" thought Mr. Puckford, forgetting that the speaker was an ironmonger, and dealt in such articles. In fact, from the way in which Simpson had been rapturizing upon Miss Fortescue's charms, a doubt of his friend's perfect sanity had sprung up in John Puckford's mind; and he shrewdly suspected that the affair would terminate in a *de lunatico inquirendo* instead of a licence.

"Do you know, Puckford," said Mr. Simpson, with

a benevolent, patronizing air, after the third or fourth glass—"do you know, I fancy there is a great likeness between you and Mary Fortescue?"

Mr. John Puckford, the reader must understand, was a handsome young man, with a brilliant, florid complexion, perfectly agreeing vision, and light-brown hair. No wonder, therefore, he was more startled than flattered by the comparison. The colour mounted to his temples, and a conviction of Simpson's utter insanity flashed across his brain. "Mad as a March hare!" he mentally ejaculated; at the same time resolving, should the paroxysm grow dangerously violent, to knock him down with one of the decanters, both of which, as two could play at that game, he drew, as if in doubt which wine he would take, to his own side of the table.

Mr. Simpson, mistaking the nature of his friend's emotion, added, " Don't suppose, Puckford, I intend any absurd flattery!"

" Not at all, Simpson ; I didn't suppose anything of the sort, I assure you."

" To be sure not; nothing is more contemptible. You are a good-looking fellow—very : but of course, I couldn't mean that you, a man, are to be compared to Mary Fortescue."

" I should think not!" drily responded the more and more mystified and bewildered Puckford.

" Exactly ; you do not resemble each other about the eyes, either in colour or expression."

" Oh ! "

" No : as to hair," continued Mr. Simpson meditatively, " yours, there can be no doubt, is decidedly the lightest."

" It's coming now," thought Mr. John Puckford, grasping at the same time one of the decanters, and eyeing his friend intently.

Mr. Simpson, quite misinterpreting the action added quickly, " Do, my good fellow, fill me a bumper, and we'll drink her good-looking friend's health—the lady, I mean, with the dark silky hair and brunette complexion. Do you know," continued the complacent Simpson, crossing his legs, throwing himself back easily in his chair, and hooking his thumbs to the arm-holes of his waistcoat—" do you know that, if Mary Fortescue had not been at your house yesterday evening, I might have——"

What the worthy ironmonger might, in the case supposed, have done or said, must be left to the reader's imagination, for on the instant a clerk hurriedly entered the apartment, to announce that an important customer awaited Mr. Simpson in the counting-house below. Hastily rising, Mr. Simpson shook hands with his friend, and both departed their several ways; Mr. Puckford bearing off the epistle addressed to Miss Fortescue, and musing as he went upon lover-madness, which, he fully agreed with Rosalind, deserved chains and a dark house quite as much as any other variety of the disease.

The next day Mr. Simpson received a note from Mary Fortescue, modestly and gracefully expressed, in which, with charming humility, and many expressions of gratified surprise, the offer of his hand was —on one condition, unexplained, but which rested altogether with himself—gratefully accepted.

Such was the state of affairs when, on the 1st of March, Mr. Simpson, as I have before stated, entered a brougham, and directed the driver to make the best of his way to Mile End. It was a fine bright and exceedingly cold day; but notwithstanding the nipping eager air, the love-lorn ironmonger, as he approached the house which contained his charmer, was in a state of profuse perspiration and high nervous excitement. Once more he drew from his pocket the fairy-note, and glanced over the modest, grateful, delicately-feminine expressions. " Dear lady," he audibly exclaimed, as he finished about the five-hundredth perusal of the familiar lines—" dear lady, she will be all tears and tenderness !"

About a minute after giving utterance to this consolatory reflection, Mr. Simpson found himself in Mrs. Puckford's presence, who, congratulating him on his punctuality, and pointing to the door of the front apartment, said, " There is only *one* lady there, and you know *her*." Mr. Simpson's heart leaped and thumped, as if desirous of bursting through his green velvet waistcoat. He stepped desperately towards the door, and essayed to turn the brass-handle; but so profusely did the bashful man's very fingers perspire, that they slipped round the knob without turning it. The second trial, with the help of his cambric-handkerchief, was more successful, and the lover was in the presence of the lady.

Certainly it was she! Mrs. Frazer, the hapless Simpson's Mary Fortescue, was there in bodily reality. But the grateful humility, the "tears and tenderness," prefigured by the charming note!——Oh Alfred Gray!

The unruffled ease, the calm, reserved politeness with which Mrs. Frazer received him, chilled his enthusiastic fervour wondrously. His perspiration became a cold one, and in a few moments he felt as if enveloped in coatings and leggings of Wenham-Lake ice. Recovering himself as speedily as he could from the shock of this unexpectedly-chilling reception, Mr. Simpson stammered forth something about his extreme good fortune in having obtained a favourable response from so amiable a person, *et cetera*.

"Certainly," replied the lady, "I think you are *very* fortunate, Mr. Simpson." And then, by way of saying something particularly civil, and to relieve the modest man's embarrassment, she added, "But few men have, like you, sufficient discrimination to discern and appreciate attractions which lie hidden from the merely superficial observer."

Poor Simpson gasped for breath! He was literally dumfoundered! Here was modest gratitude, to say nothing of "tears and tenderness," with a vengeance! Miss Fortescue, with a precarious salary of some twenty pounds per annum, exclusive of bread and butter, was, in her own opinion, conferring a tremendous obligation upon a civic dignitary worth at least twenty thousand pounds, by accepting him for a husband! That was quite clear; and although Mr. Simpson was too much in love to deny such a proposition in the abstract, still it was, he thought, scarcely consistent with maiden modesty to state it so very broadly.

Notwithstanding his amazement, Mr. Simpson, as soon as he recovered breath, contrived, so well had he studied for the occasion, to get out a sentence or two about the superiority of connubial to single blessedness. This sentiment also met with ready acquiescence.

"Oh! dear, yes," said Mrs. Frazer; "I would not have been an old maid for the world!"

"Well," thought the astonished admirer of feminine reserve, almost doubting the evidence of his ears, "this is certainly the frankest maiden I *ever* conversed with!"

A considerable pause followed. Mrs. Frazer, seated upon a sofa, played with the luxuriant auburn—really auburn—tresses of her nephew Alfred.

"A handsome boy," at length remarked Mr. Simpson. "It's a pity that he hasn't different coloured hair!"

"A pity!" exclaimed the lady; "I think it beautiful! And," added she, looking the astonished man somewhat sternly in the face, "I should be well pleased if all *our* children had hair of the same colour!"

This was a climax! Simpson leaped to his feet as if impelled by the shock of a galvanic battery. "*Our* children! Well, after that! But I must be dreaming," thought the fastidious ironmonger, as he wiped the perspiration from his teeming forehead; "labouring under some horrid enchantment."

Dreaming indeed, and to be swiftly and rudely awakened. The door opened, and a gentleman entered, whom Mrs. Frazer immediately introduced with—"Mr. Simpson, my husband, Mr. Frazer!"

The blow was terrific! Simpson staggered back as if he had been shot. He glared alternately at the husband and wife for a few seconds; then, pale as his shirt-collar, tottered to a chair, and sinking into it ejaculated with white lips, "Oh!"

"What is the matter, sir?—you look ill," said Mr. Frazer.

The bewildered man made no reply. His brain was whirling. "Who on earth, then, *had* he been courting?"

A loud knock at the street-door somewhat aroused him. "My sister, I dare say," exclaimed Mrs. Frazer.

"Her sister! Possibly *his* Mary might be the brunette ; and yet—— There were but three females present on that fatal evening, besides Mrs. Puckford, that he distinctly remembered ; and perhaps——" Vain hope! the door opened, and the brunette and two gentlemen entered—"Mr. and Mrs. Holland, and Mr. Alfred Gray."

All illusion was now over. He, Robert Simpson, wealthy tradesman, respected fishmonger, and common-councilman, was the betrothed husband of a red-haired damsel with a decided cast, with whom, moreover, he had never exchanged a sentence ! His first impulse, as the certainty of his miserable fate flashed upon him, was to strangle Alfred Gray out of hand as the author of his destruction, when fortunately another *rap-tap* arrested his fell intent.

"Miss Fortescue at last!" cried Mrs. Frazer, as if announcing glad tidings.

"Oh!" ejaculated the accepted suitor, dropping nervelessly back into the seat from which he had just risen—"Oh !"

He was seized with a sort of vertigo ; and what occurred, or how he behaved for a considerable interval, he never distinctly remembered. He was, however, soon seated at table by the side of his affianced bride, Mr. Puckford saying grace. This was the *actual* state of affairs; but poor Simpson's impression at the moment was, that he had been led out to sudden execution by an enormous Jack Ketch with red hair and a frightful squint, and that his friend Puckford was the chaplain reading the funeral service. Gradually, however, his brain cleared, and he grew cooler and more collected. Upon reflection, his position did not appear so *very* desperate. As to Mrs. Frazer, all that was of course over, past praying for, and he must dismiss it from his mind as speedily as possible. The lady beside him, who he could see was almost as discomposed as himself, was, he had no doubt, a sensible person—her letter was sufficient evidence of that—and when he had explained the unfortunate mistake that had occurred, which he would by-and-by take a quiet opportunity of doing, would no doubt release him from an engagement he had never intended to contract. He would, moreover—Simpson was anything but a churlish or ungenerous man—bestow upon her a marriage-portion of, say, four or five hundred pounds, which would doubtless enable her to marry respectably, and thus console her for her present disappointment. Thus philosophizing and reasoning, Mr. Simpson's spirits, considering the suddenness of the shock he had endured, rallied wonderfully, and he was enabled to address a few words of course to Miss Fortescue in almost a cheerful voice and manner. The lady's answer was uttered in the gentlest, sweetest tones he had ever listened to; and Mr. Simpson was a connoisseur in voices. The conversation continued—became general; and the dinner, commenced so inauspiciously, passed off, considering all things, remarkably well. After dinner, Miss Fortescue—her friends, who greatly esteemed her, generously drawing forth her powers—appeared to great advantage. Her mind, of a superior order, had been well cultivated, and her conversation was at once refined, sparkling, and sensible. Mr. Simpson was surprised, pleased, almost charmed. Music was proposed, and she sang several songs admirably. Mr. Simpson determined to postpone his explanation—necessarily an unpleasant one—till the next day, when he would do it by letter. The party separated about nine o'clock, long before which hour it had several times glanced across the ironmonger's mind, that a dislike of any particular coloured hair was, after all, a very absurd prejudice: as to the *cast*, that, he was satisfied, was so slight as scarcely to deserve the name. It had been arranged that they should all dine with the Frazers the day after the next; and as Mr. Simpson handed Mary Fortescue into the cab, in which Mrs. and Mr. Frazer were already seated, she whispered, " Oblige me by coming on Sunday half an hour before the time appointed: I have something of importance to say to you." Mr. Simpson bowed, and—how could he do less?—raised the lady's hand to his lips. The carriage drove off, and the worthy

man was left in the most perplexing state of dubiety
and irresolution imaginable. He began to think he
had gone too far to recede with honour; and, what
was very extraordinary, he felt scarcely sorry for it!
At all events, he would not act rashly: Sunday was
not far off: he would defer his explanation till then.

Mr. Simpson, punctual to his engagement, found
Miss Fortescue awaiting him alone. He felt on this
occasion none of the violent emotions he had experienced on the previous Friday. His heart, instead
of knocking and thumping like a caged wild thing,
beat tranquilly in his bosom; yet it was not without
a calmly-pleasurable emotion that he met the confiding, grateful smile which beamed on his entrance
over the lady's features. Seating himself beside her,
he, with respectful gentleness, requested her to proceed with the matter she wished to communicate.
She blushingly complied, and speedily beguiled him,
if not of his tears, which I am not quite sure about,
of something, under the circumstances, far more
valuable. "Her family, not many years before in
apparently affluent circumstances, had been, by re-
verses in trade, suddenly cast down into extreme
poverty. The only surviving members of it, her
mother and youngest sister, had been long principally dependent on her exertions for support. The
assistance she had fortunately been able to render
had hitherto sufficed them; but of course, if she
married, that source of income must fail; and she

never *would* marry—indeed, she had never, till surprised by his generous offer, contemplated marriage—but she was even now fully resolved never to do so unless—unless——" Mary Fortescue paused in her narrative, and her timid, inquiring glance rested anxiously upon the varying countenance of her auditor.

Mr. Simpson was not made of adamant, nor of iron, though he traded in the article; and no wonder, therefore, that the graceful manner, the modest, pleading earnestness, the gentle tones, the filial piety of his betrothed, should have vanquished, subdued him. Her features, plain as they undoubtedly were, irradiated by the lustre of a beautiful soul, kindled into absolute beauty! At all events Mr. Simpson must have thought so, or he would not have caught the joyfully-weeping maiden in his arms and exclaimed, in answer to her agitated appeal, " Unless your home may be theirs also? Be it so: I have, thank God, enough and to spare for all."

Thus was oddly brought about, and finally determined on, one of the happiest marriages, if Mr. Simpson himself is to be believed—and he *ought* to know—that holy church has ever blessed. Should he attain, of which there is every reasonable prospect, the dignity of Lord Mayor, he will, I am quite sure, attribute that, as he now does all fortunate events, to his supreme good-luck in having unwittingly fallen in love with another man's wife !

THE BEAUTY OF BARBICAN

THERE is a story current in the neighbourhood of
St. Giles's, Cripplegate Without, in connection with a
headstone, now only about a foot above the surface of
the crowded churchyard of that parish—the church
itself, by the bye, was Milton's burial-place—on which
may still be faintly discerned, that the name of the
tenant below was Charles something, beginning with
a P.   This tale seems to me of sufficient interest and
significance to warrant its being introduced to a wider
circle.

Michael Benson, a tin-plate smith, drove, it appears,
a thriving trade in Redcross Street, Barbican, about
the middle of the eighteenth century, and ultimately
amassed considerable wealth. He was reputed a
somewhat odd, eccentric, hard-grained man, whose
bark, however, was much worse than his bite, which
mood of mind was ascribed by elder gossips to his
having been "crossed in love" by one Lucy Andrews,
the daughter of a plumber and glazier, and popularly
known, in the days when the second George was
king, as the Beauty of Barbican. This fascinating
damsel unhappily preferred the showier attractions

of a non-commissioned cavalry officer to the less
glittering though far more solid pretensions of the
industrious and thriving smith; and the Mars and
Vulcan story of classical antiquity had its Cripplegate
version by the union, in the church of that name, of
the fair and faithless Lucy with the dashing sergeant
of dragoons. Honest Michael was at first greatly
staggered by this heavy and, it seems, quite unexpected blow; but he soon recovered his equilibrium,
addressed himself with heartier zeal than ever to
his forge and anvil, and, as previously stated, so successfully, that compassionate candidates for the office
of healing the wounds inflicted by the fickle Lucy
were by no means wanting; but Michael Benson
would have none of them. Perhaps the treachery of
the Beauty of Barbican had inspired him with a
general distrust of the deceptive sex; or, which is
likelier, her image still lived in his memory with a
freshness beside which their feebler charms showed
dim and pale. This last was the conclusion arrived
at by those more intimate friends of the smith, who
knew how, at convivial and unguarded moments, his
heart would leap to his lips; and this opinion received, in the autumn of 1745, a striking confirmation.
Following close upon the news of Johnny Cope's
brilliant battle with the Highlanders at Prestonpans,
there came news of Lucy's husband, Colour-Sergeant
Haselgrove, having been killed there, and that the
Barbican beauty, now a forlorn widow, with a young

family, was temporarily sojourning in the neighbourhood of Carlisle. Michael Benson for some time
appeared to treat this intelligence with contempt or
indifference—in reality, with mistrust and disbelief.
It was not very long before he changed his tone.
Confirmation of the tidings must have reached him
from a reliable source, for in February, 1746, he
suddenly disappeared from Redcross Street, and did
not show again for nearly three weeks. His trip to
the north—whither it was soon ascertained the steps
of the stalwart and faithful swain had been directed—
had, everybody admitted, greatly improved him both
in looks and temper. His morose manner fell off like
a garment ; and reverting to the other extreme, he
grew languishingly eloquent upon connubial felicity,
and the inexpressibly forlorn condition of wretched
bachelors. His house, too, was newly fitted and
furbished up, as a suitable residence for a man of
family and substance ; and, finally, he admitted, in
whispered confidences to his cronies, that the ensuing
month of merry May would see him united in holy
wedlock to the bereaved widow of the slain dragoon.
Vanity of vanities—all is vanity ! Fate had de-
creed that that barbarous beauty should be Michael
Benson's death or ruin. Whilst assisting to fix a
new and flaming sign over his shop, the ladder upon
which he stood slipped, and he was precipitated with
stunning violence to the pavement. It was at first
believed that he was mortally hurt, and this, it was

subsequently manifest, must have been his own impression upon recovering consciousness ; but ultimately skilful surgery and a good constitution brought him through ; and by the time bright-eyed, bliss-bringing May was at hand, he had almost recovered his health and vigour—only to encounter a severer stroke than he had yet suffered. A letter reached the impatient Benedict-expectant one morning, with the intelligence that Sergeant Haselgrove had never been dead at all!—that he had been severely wounded only, and taken prisoner, in General Cope's illustrious campaign, and detained, without the power of communicating with his sorrowing wife and friends, till released by the catastrophe of Culloden ! Poor Michael was flung back upon a sick-bed again ; but this hurt, like that caused by the fall from the ladder, was found to be curable ; and false-promising May had not departed, when his restrung energies were once more concentrated upon the solid realities of life and business. And herein, at least, fortune did not jilt or play the fool with him : year after year found him wealthier, stouter, jollier ; and he had not yet lived half a century, when he was elected to the civic common council for the ward of Cripplegate. This elevation proved an unfortunate one, by stimulating a for some time growing taste for the pleasures of the table ; and corpulence, gout, and incipient apoplexy soon displayed their fatal ensigns Business becoming distasteful, he determined on resigning it in favour of his orphan nephew, Charles Passmore, who had been for some time the managing-man of his establishment, and retiring for the remainder of his days to the sweet rurality of Islington—in which then sylvan parish he possessed considerable property—as soon as a house he had commenced building, near the spot where the Angel Tavern now stands, should be completed.

Man proposes; God disposes. Michael Benson was sitting alone one evening after the close of the day's business, revolving this and other pet projects in his mind, when a letter was brought him, with a message that the bearer, a young woman in deep mourning, waited for an answer. He snatched the letter, muttering as he did so a peevish expression of annoyance at being disturbed; but no sooner had his glance fallen upon the superscription, than a flash of wild surprise broke over and crimsoned his countenance. Eagerly he tore it open, and read with swimming eyes a touching appeal to feelings of langsyne, from his ever-beloved Lucy, in behalf of her only remaining child, who would only deliver it after the writer's death. Mrs. Haselgrove's husband had preceded her to the tomb, to which she herself was then fast hastening—a dark and awful passage, but cheered and illumined by the certainty she felt, that for her sake Lucy would find a home with the good Michael, whose honest worth and deep affection the writer had learned rightly to value when too late.

The perusal of this letter profoundly agitated Michael Benson, and it was some time before he could master himself sufficiently to ring the bell, and direct the bearer of the note to be shown in. He had extinguished the candles, probably to mask from the young girl thus solemnly committed to his charge, the emotion which almost convulsed him ; and it was by the softening light of the moon and stars, which streamed in through the uncurtained window, that he silently perused her features, and recognized in them the image of the Lucy of his love. The timid, trembling girl seemed to quail before his eager, scrutinizing gaze ; but when he presently found words to assure her that the request of her dying parent should be sacredly, religiously fulfilled, she threw herself, in an ecstasy of sorrow and thankfulness, into his outstretched arms ; whilst he, utterly overwhelmed, wept and sobbed with an equally passionate vehemence.

This unexpected and charming addition to his household quickened for a time the sluggish pulses of the civic counsellor with a more healthy life ; but habits of indulgence are seldom permanently eradicated in elderly persons. They gradually regained their wonted ascendancy ; and Lucy Haselgrove had only been about three months with him, when a lightning stroke of apoplexy revealed how nearly they had already brought him to the tomb. Surgical aid having been promptly obtained, he was for this time quit for the fright, and an ever-present dread of a second visitation. "It was very lucky," remarked the surgeon, addressing Charles Passmore, "that I was within call; for even a brief delay in such cases is a pretty sure passport to another world." The nephew made a cold, matter-of-course reply, which it struck the medical gentleman at the time contrasted oddly with the quick bright flush that at the same moment suffused his pale features. No further comment was, however, made, and the conversation terminated.

Charles Passmore is described as a bold, stubborn, unprincipled, yet withal specious young man, precocious alike in ambition and avarice, which master-passions, it will be seen, he hesitated at no means, however base, to gratify. Michael Benson, it seems, at first cherished a hope that a mutual liking might spring up between his nephew and adopted daughter; but this, he early found, was out of the question. Charles Passmore had views in a far higher quarter, which he doubted not the possession of his uncle's property would enable him to realize; and gentle, retiring, sensitive Lucy Haselgrove could feel no sympathy for the rude, irascible person who, from the first day of her abode in Redcross Street, had manifestly regarded her with extreme and, of late, quite savage dislike This feeling was, no question, excited by the apprehension, soon converted into certainty, that a considerable share of the wealth to which he considered himself exclusively entitled, would be bequeathed to her. Two legacies, amounting to £1000, divided between Guy's and Bartholomew's Hospitals, in a will otherwise exclusively in his favour, executed by Mr. Benson some five or six years previously, had greatly offended him; and how much was this ire inflamed when, in addition to that deduction from his coveted inheritance, he heard his uncle express his determination to secure Lucy a handsome maintenance, and this, too, without delay!

This resolution was stated in his presence to Mr. Aspern, an attorney of Coleman Street, whom Michael Benson had hastily sent for, warned, probably, by internal premonitions, that the night in which no man can work was at hand. The instructions given were brief and emphatic—£5000 to Lucy Haselgrove; £1000 to the hospitals, as aforesaid; and the residue, estimated with the business at about £12,000, to his nephew; and the will to be ready for execution on the following day. Mr. Aspern promised compliance, and took his leave, followed a few minutes afterwards by Charles Passmore.

It was rather late that evening when the nephew returned home. Mr. Benson had finished his supper, and was sitting alone, imbibing, in defiance of all warning, a few more of the "night-caps" which were so materially assisting him to his long last sleep. The young man's steps were unsteady, and his angry eyes sparkled with ill-repressed rage. Unaccustomed drink had washed away the mask which he had hitherto worn in his uncle's presence, and his true character was for the first time revealed to his astonished and indignant relative. A fierce altercation relative to the proposed will immediately commenced, and went on with increasing violence, till the insolence of the nephew had risen to such a pitch as to embolden him to hazard a base, exasperating imputation upon the characters of both Lucy and her mother.

"Lying, ungrateful scoundrel!" thundered Michael Benson, as he sprang with passionate energy to his feet, and menaced the slanderer with clenched fists; "but for your mother's sake, I——." He stopped abruptly, and clasped his forehead with both hands, whilst a mighty change fell like a thick pall over his inflamed countenance. A moment, and the words—"The surgeon—quick!" gurgled from his throat; his head fell on his chest, and, blindly staggering a few paces in the direction of the door, he fell with a deep groan on the floor.

Charles Passmore looked eagerly in the face of the helpless man. Assistance, he clearly saw, to be effectual, must be very speedy, and he stepped mechanically towards the bell. His fingers clutched the rope, but were instantly withdrawn; and he once more paced softly towards his prostrate relative, and gazed with earnest, fearful scrutiny on the convulsed features of the dying man. As he did so, the eyes slowly unclosed, and addressed him with so reproachful and ghastly an expression, that he turned hastily away, and again moved towards the bell. Three or four precious minutes passed, and then the bell was rung with furious violence.

"Fetch a surgeon!—quick! quick!" exclaimed Charles Passmore to the servant who answered the bell. "My uncle has fallen down in a fit."

Mr. Rymer was quickly on the spot, and instantly opened a vein. Too late! The sluggish blood yielded a few drops only, and it was plain that life was over. "A few minutes earlier might have made all the difference," remarked the surgeon; "but your uncle, Mr. Passmore, is past help now."

An hour afterwards, Charles Passmore was seated in his bedroom, alone with conscience. His face was white as stone, and his whole frame trembled with terror. There was brandy on the table beside him, of which he freely partook; but it required repeated draughts to still the gnawing of the awakened worm within. Slowly, however, the white race acquired colour; the troubled, shrinking eyes grew bold and steady; the palsied limbs ceased to shake and quiver, and articulate utterance was not impossible.

"Visitation of God!" he muttered. "To be sure— what else? Rymer is a conceited ass to suppose he could have afforded effectual aid, even had he been present at the moment of attack. Fortunately timed,

too, since it was to be. And now I think of it, there
is an important matter, the saving or throwing away
of a thousand pounds, which must neither be forgotten nor delayed. Well remembered!"

Thus speaking, Charles Passmore seized the candle,
listened for a moment on the landing to make sure
the house was quiet, and then crept stealthily down-
stairs. He returned in about ten minutes with a
folded parchment in his hand, which, after locking
the door, he eagerly addressed himself to read.

"Yes, this is it: 'My last Will and Testament;'
the date, June, 1765. 'All my property, real and
personal, to my dear nephew, Charles Passmore'—
with the exception of a thousand pounds to the two
hospitals. Eh? what's this?—'And two thousand
pounds to Lucy Haselgrove, or her children in
equal proportions ! Upon my word, this is pretty
well. *Three* thousand pounds sliced off instead of
one, as I understood; but, as I am the undoubted
heir-at-law, I shall take the liberty of doing, what I
heard the testator tell Mr. Aspern *he* should do—burn
this atrocious will."

A momentary doubt of the perfect prudence of the
act flashed across his excited brain, and he hesitated
to commit the important instrument to the flames.
But his uncle had no relative so near as himself
by many degrees; there could not be the slightest
danger, therefore, and the gain—three thousand
pounds—was certain and enormous ! The will was

then consumed by small slips at a time, in order that no unusual light might attract the attention of passers-by.

Early on the morning of the funeral, Mr. Aspern, the attorney, called at Redcross Street.

"Golding," he said, "of Basinghall Street, your uncle's lawyer in former days, has been to my office making inquiries about the will made in 1765. I told him it could not be found, and that there could be no reasonable doubt that it had been destroyed by the testator, in fulfilment of his declared intention to do so. He appeared hardly satisfied, and I said he had better call here after the funeral. He is acting, I presume, for some relative or other of your deceased uncle's."

"A very distant relative, then, he or she must be," replied Passmore. "Mr. Golding is quite welcome, however, to institute as rigorous a search as he pleases. My uncle himself told me that he had destroyed the will."

"So I informed Golding; but he insists upon an investigation, and will be here about three o'clock. I will take care to be present Good-day, Mr. Passmore.

Besides Lucy Haselgrove—who, in compliance with a note marked "private and confidential," from Mr. Golding, had delayed leaving Whitecross Street, her home, alas! no longer, till he should see her after the funeral—calm, composed, but exceedingly pale,

Mr. Charles Passmore, and Mr. Attorney Aspern, there were several mourners, friends of the deceased, present in the first-floor front-room, when the solicitor of Basinghall Street was announced. Golding was a thin, wiry little man, with the eyes of a lynx, which, when he had made his general bow, glanced from the fortunate and decorous nephew to the unfortunate and weeping Lucy Haselgrove, with piercing, arrow-like scrutiny.

"The will made in 1765," began Mr. Golding, "has been, I understand you to say, destroyed by the deceased's own act?"

"Yes," replied Charles Passmore; "my lamented uncle told me so himself more than forty-eight hours before his death."

"And that which was to have replaced it has not been drawn up, much less executed?"

"Exactly," said Mr. Aspern.

"Still, I can have no doubt—I am acting, I may as well tell you, in the interest of this young lady, Miss Lucy Haselgrove, though not directly instructed by her—I can have no doubt, I say, that the heir-at-law will carry out his uncle's clearly-expressed intentions, though not legally compelled to do so?"

The heir-at-law coloured, and looked annoyed, but promptly answered, "I shall most assuredly do no such thing. Your client, Miss Lucy Haselgrove, is no relative of mine, and can have no claim, equitable or otherwise, to any portion of my lawful inheritance."

"And that is your fixed determination?" said Mr. Golding, with a sort of stern exultation in his tone and manner.

"Certainly it is. The prime duty of every man is to look after his own interest; that of his relatives demands his next care."

"Very prettily said indeed! and it happens, too, that *I* have just now a prime duty to perform. Mr. Michael Benson's last will has been destroyed—of that fact I have not the slightest doubt—and, *you say*, by the testator's own act, about which there may be two opinions. Be that, however, as it may, I have the honour to inform you that, by a will *not* destroyed, and now in my possession, dated April 7, 1746—at which time, it may be remembered, Mr. Benson's life was for a time considered in danger, in consequence of a fall from a ladder——"

"I remember it well," interrupted one of the mourners present; "the more by token—— But I beg pardon."

"By that will, now the *last* will of my then client, Michael Benson," continued Mr. Golding, with his keen eyes fixed upon the ashy countenance of the heir-at-law, "all the property, real and personal, of which the testator might die seised and possessed, was bequeathed to Lucy Haselgrove, formerly of Barbican, and then of Carlisle, and after her to her children in equal proportions. Lucy Haselgrove, therefore, here present, being, as I am instructed, the only surviving child of Lucy Haselgrove, formerly Lucy Andrews of Barbican, is the sole legatee under this will, and owner of the entire realty, as well as personals, left by the said Michael Benson. I——'

A cry of desperation from Charles Passmore, accompanied by a frantic effort to seize the fatal document—by his own act rendered fatal—interrupted Mr. Golding. Foiled in his maniacal attempt, the infuriated young man reiterated his inarticulate shriek of rage, and turned revengefully towards the bewildered and now terrified Lucy Haselgrove, lost his balance before he could reach her, reeled, and fell without sense or motion on the floor.

Thus essentially concludes a story still current in the parish of Cripplegate Without, London. It is only necessary to add, that much of the foregoing detail was gleaned from the ravings of Charles Passmore during his confinement in Bethlehem Hospital as a confirmed lunatic, which lasted till his death and burial in Cripplegate churchyard, as recorded by the nearly sunken gravestone before spoken of; that Lucy Haselgrove was put into peaceable possession of the property of Michael Benson; and that one of the handsomest and most popular lady-mayoresses that flourished at the close of the eighteenth century, was the fortunate daughter of the Beauty of Barbican.

AN OFFER OF MARRIAGE.

Never had the ancient and quiet village of Westford been so flustered, mystified, and altogether put out, within the memory of the oldest inhabitant—and folk, as the grave-stones testify, live to a great age there—as during the spring of last year. From time immemorial, everybody had known everybody in Westford—their pedigree, birth, parentage, education, past, present, and probable fortunes and condition ; and now a family whom nobody knew, had ever heard of, or could obtain any information about, had settled down in the heart of the place, under venerable Dr. Irwin's very nose, as it were, for Laurel Villa was but a stone's-throw from the vicarage. The house had been taken by a London solicitor, well known to its proprietor, deaf old Mr. Digby, who had not very distinctly heard, or at all events did not clearly recollect even the name of his new tenants—a widow-lady and her daughter, it was supposed. His attention was no doubt engrossed at the moment by the six months' rent paid down in advance—for Laurel Villa had been empty for a long time. Digby, however, had a dim notion that the name had an out-

landish sound with it; and this was more than likely,
inasmuch as the two servants, a man and wife, were
strange olive-coloured creatures, hardly capable of
speaking a word of honest English. This circumstance it was, I believe, which caused one of ours—
a serious young gentleman, melancholy, gentleman-
like, and pale as a turnip from overstudy of philosophy, it was said—Sawkins by name, and of perfect
respectability—to hint in his dark, oracular way, that
the strangers were possibly Jesuits in disguise—a
suggestion which sent a thrill through Westford, that
is, the spinster and wedded portion of it; for the
bachelors of the place, among whom I still unhappily
count myself, stoutly affirmed, after but one or two
brief glimpses of the younger lady, that she was far
more like an angel than one of the dreadful people
alluded to by Sawkins. The discovery of how charming a youthful face and figure had dropped suddenly
among us—out of the skies, as it were—added of
course greatly to the excitement, and, in the eyes of
numerous dames and damsels, invested the event
with a highly-dangerous character, as affecting the
peace of Westford. They foreboded rightly, as we
shall presently see, though it did not at first strike
me that the lady's beauty was of that perfect and
dazzling kind which such mischievous Helens are
usually supposed to possess: certainly, as was soon too
manifest, one of the most lovable faces ever seen.
taken altogether. One might call it a sunny face,

gaily lit up and tinted as it was by the dancing light
of the soft brown eyes; but I doubt whether the
complexion, clear and exquisitely fair as it was, would
be pronounced decidedly brilliant; or whether the
nose—a rather small, but charming one, nevertheless,
ever so slightly turned up, *retroussé* as the French
say—was of orthodox mould or symmetry. The
mouth, to be sure, was unexceptionable, if a rosebud
fresh with dew and fragrant with perfume be unexceptionable; and the hair, of the colour of the eyes,
was glossy, soft, and entangling. Her figure——
But I had better not proceed further : I will only say,
that one of our damsels, who stands five feet ten
inches in her satin slippers, pronounced her decidedly
short; and another, whose favourite apophthegm is
that very precious things are wrapped in very small
parcels, as confidently declared her to be far too
tall.

This is the best sketch, poor and imperfect as it
is, which I can give of the youthful, elegantly-attired,
and graceful lady who, on the first Sunday morning
after her arrival in Westford, walked up the aisle of
the parish church just as the service was about to
commence, and asked the grey-haired sexton to place
her in a seat. He was about to do so, when the
stranger said softly, and with some hesitation : " Lady
Greville and family are not, I believe, at home, and
you will perhaps allow me to sit in their pew ?"

Now, this was altogether an astounding proposition.

The seat in question was emphatically *the* pew of the church—an enclosure sacred for centuries to the use of the great patrician family of the neighbourhood, the Grevilles, who were and are baronets, lords of the manor, and of thousands of fertile acres. Lady Greville, a very stately personage, and her two daughters, were indeed absent on the continent, and not expected to return for some weeks; and her son, Sir Henry Greville, when he attended church, always, in the absence of his own relatives, sat with the family of his intimate friend, Arthur Raymond, the only son of a retired merchant-prince, who, a few years before, had purchased a large estate in the neighbourhood, and was now second only to the Grevilles in local rank and importance. The pew was consequently unoccupied; but one of the aborigines of Westford would as soon have dreamed of mounting the pulpit, and asking permission to preach in the place of the Rev. Dr. Irwin, as of entering it. The surprise of the sexton was, it may be supposed, extreme. He hesitated, and repeated what the stranger had said, as if in doubt that he could have heard aright. The request was again made, and with so charming, so graceful a tone and manner, that the ancient servitor, before he had time to comprehend perfectly what he was about, unlocked the seat-door, and, to the indescribable astonishment of the congregation, admitted the audacious intruder! This was not all—very far indeed from being all, as the Misses Dorothea and

Jane Austin, who sat in an adjoining pew, and who had unquestionably the sharpest eyes and longest necks in Westford, saw the stranger, after hastily drawing a curtain, which, however, but partially concealed her from the two ladies I have named, stoop down towards a lidded oak receptacle containing the Greville books of devotion, as if she had been familiar with it all her life, seize upon an old family Bible, undo its silver clasps, turn at once to the fly-leaf, where, as it seemed, she hastily perused some lines in a female hand, whilst tears, unmistakable tears, filled her eyes! What on earth could be the meaning of it? asked all Westford, especially when, on coming out of church, they positively beheld the strange lady drive off to Laurel Villa in Sir Henry's carriage, placed at her service by that gentleman in consequence of a heavy shower of rain which had suddenly come on, and from which the umbrella, brought by the olive-faced servant, would hardly have effectually shielded her. The perfect ease, too, with which the offer was accepted, and the gracious smile that she bestowed upon the handsome young baronet, who with his friend, Arthur Raymond, remained behind in the damp church-porch till the carriage should return! "Did you ever?" asked matrons and maidens of each other in blank wonderment; but nobody ever did, and that was all that could be said on the matter.

On the following evening, the Misses Austin, Miss

Rawson—all three spinsters of an uncertain age—and Miss Mary Foster, a slim young lady in short curls and very low tucker, contracted, it was said, to Mr. Richard Austin, the brother of the first-named ladies, were seated at tea—self-invited, by the way—with the vicar's lady. The truth was, it had become known that the Rev. Dr. Irwin was paying a visit to Laurel Villa—a very lengthened one—and the company assembled were waiting with almost desperate impatience for his return.

"Quite a foreign name," remarked Miss Rawson: "Mal something; but I could not quite hear what the dark-looking servant said."

"Mal!" said Miss Dorothea Austin—"Mal! that is French—one of the words of the motto on the Queen's ——h-e-e-m!" This pause of the fair Dorothea was occasioned by the sudden entrance of Mr. Sawkins.

"The Queen's garter!" suggested the young lady in curls. The other ladies, with the exception of Mrs. Irwin, seemed quite scared, and looked steadily out of the window at the vicar's carved yew-trees. "Bold thing!" they appeared to be thinking; "but then what can be expected after a year in a London boarding-school!"

"I think," said Mr. Sawkins, resuming the conversation which he had partially overheard—"I think the name of the strangers is Malleville: at least it is so given by the servants."

" That is simply a mispronunciation of the English name of Melville. A Mrs. Melville it is who has taken Laurel Villa," observed the vicar's lady.

" Melville ! "

" Yes. I was just thinking," continued Mrs. Irwin, as she poured out the tea, " that this is not the first time a strange mystery, or interest rather, has attached to Laurel Villa. You, my dear Dorothea, no doubt remember that about five-and-twenty years ago——"

If Miss Dorothea's violent start, as this shocking insinuation escaped Mrs. Irwin's lips, had caused her to let fall the cup she held in her hand, instead of only spilling a portion of its contents on the carpet, the merry twinkle in the venerable lady's bright gray eyes would have been properly punished, for it belonged to her best Dresden set. The eloquent blood flamed in Dorothea's cheeks, and her voice quavered with indignation as she burst out with: " I remember nothing about Laurel Villa, and desire to remember nothing about it or its inmates ! "

" Well, well, don't be angry. *I* remember," continued Mrs. Irwin, with an accent of sadness—" I remember well Major Conway, who once dwelt there, and his marriage with Rosamond Tarleton, Lady Greville's sister."

" They went abroad soon afterwards, did they not ? " asked Miss Rawson.

" Yes. Lady Greville was bitterly opposed to the connection, and would never afterwards hold any communication with her sister, by letter or otherwise. Yet her death, about four years ago, greatly affected her ; and she would give much, the vicar thinks, to recall the past."

" Is Major Conway yet living? "

" I do not know. Nothing, I believe, has been heard of him at Greville House since his lady's death."

The entrance of the vicar—a silver-haired, but still bluff, hearty gentleman — interrupted the conversation. The expression of sober gladness, so to speak, which beamed in his eyes, caused Mrs. Irwin to say quickly in an under-tone : " It is as I supposed ? "

" Yes. Mr. Sawkins," added the vicar, as he seated himself at the tea-table, " can you tell me if the intention of Arthur Raymond and Sir Henry Greville still holds as to their continental trip ? "

" Up till yesterday morning it certainly did ; but I heard a hint dropped about an hour since, that the impatience of one if not both of the gentlemen to be gone has suddenly cooled."

" Ah ! I hoped so !" The reverend doctor looked pleased, and instantly and pertinaciously turned the conversation to other subjects. Vainly did his visitors strive to extract something relative to the tantalizing mystery over the way: the vicar was inflexible; and they at length gave over the effort in despair, took grimly-ferocious leave, and departed homewards.

The information imparted by the reverend gentleman to Mrs. Irwin, as soon as they were alone, was in substance as follows:—The young lady, as they had surmised, was Gertrude Conway, the only surviving child of Major and Rosamond Conway. Mrs. Melville was a widowed sister of the major, who had died about two years before in the south of France, where he had long resided. Mrs. Melville's income —not a large one—would die with her; and as her health also was declining, she had determined upon making one more attempt at placing Gertrude under Lady Greville's protection. She had a fixed idea, that the only mode likely to effect this object was to introduce her suddenly, and without notice, into the presence of her stately aunt, when her great resemblance to her mother would, Mrs. Melville trusted, soften the obdurate lady's heart in her favour. Mrs. Melville also believed, that, if warned of what was intended, Lady Greville would peremptorily refuse to see her; and moreover, could not be reasoned out of her belief, that Sir Henry Greville must have been prejudiced by his mother against the Conway family. Her plan then was—and the vicar, though somewhat contrary to his own judgment, for he hated plots and concealments, yielded his assent, and promised his assistance—that during the five or six weeks still expected to elapse before Lady Greville's return, the cousins, Gertrude and Sir Henry, should be permited, encouraged rather, in habits of friendly intimacy, by meeting occasionally at the vicarage, Mrs. Melville shrewdly concluding that Gertrude's remarkable style of beauty, and the grace and elegance of her manners, would at least make such an impression upon her cousin, as to insure her his powerful intercession when the decisive moment should arrive.   In the mean time, she would be known as Gertrude Melville only.   The vicar promised inviolable secresy, and the very next evening contrived a meeting with the young people at his house. After this, there were few evenings that Sir Henry and his inseparable friend and companion, Arthur Raymond—whose family, by the way, were also absent from their seat near Westford—did not pass in the reverend doctor's drawing-room. It soon, consequently, became a settled conviction in every person's mind, that Dr. and Mrs. Irwin were bent on helping the young and obscure stranger to perhaps the best match, both as regarded wealth and birth, to be found in the county.

If this were so, the worthy gentleman must have been a good deal startled by a brief scene which occurred one evening a day or so only before Lady Greville was expected home. When the vicar entered the drawing-room, the young lady was seated at the pianoforte, trying over a number of songs, at the suggestion of Sir Henry, who turned the leaves assiduously. The aspect of the two—the admiration visible upon the gentleman's countenance, and the bright joyousness of the lady's features—was satisfactory enough, until a sound, faint as a sigh, sad as a groan, caught her ear—*her* ear, not Sir Henry's—when the tone of the rich silver voice faltered, and the time of the song was increased to a galop. The baronet made no remark, but continued to turn the music-leaves as delightedly as before. The vicar had looked in the direction of the singer's momentary furtive glance, but would scarcely have recognized Arthur Raymond, in the obscure corner where he sat, but for his dark flashing eyes. Dr. Irwin was about to speak when Gertrude suddenly rose from the piano, complained of headache, and asked Mrs. Irwin to accompany her over to Laurel Villa, and stay supper there. This request, at a sign from the vicar, was immediately complied with, and in a few moments they were gone.

Sir Henry continued to turn over the songs that had been sung, humming as he did so a few favourite bars now and then; and Arthur Raymond remained in the same motionless attitude, and with the same fierce expression flashing from his singularly expressive eyes. The worthy doctor was at a loss what to do or say. He felt a presentiment that something was wrong; that an unfortunate, perhaps perilous game of cross-purposes was in progress; and how had it happened, was his painful self-question, that this palpable danger had never before struck him? The two friends, though both of about the same age—in their twenty-sixth year—of similar tastes and pursuits in many respects, were the very opposites of each other in temperament and original cast of mind. Sir Henry, always perfectly master of himself, calm, reflective, unimpassioned, lively and gallant in female society, greatly resembled his lady-mother in decision and firmness of disposition. Arthur Raymond, on the contrary, was of an impulsive, enthusiastic temperament, and impressionable in a high degree.

"Come, Raymond," said Sir Henry, suddenly breaking in upon the vicar's reverie, "it is time we were off." His friend rose, and after exchanging brief adieus with the agitated doctor, they left the house. The reverend gentleman, after a few minutes' cogitation, took up his hat with the intention of following them, though with scarcely any defined purpose in doing so ; but by the time he reached the outer gate, they were already out of sight ; and he, sadly perturbed and apprehensive, walked slowly over to Laurel Villa.

I do not remember if I have before remarked, that Westford is a beautifully-situated village ; but if not, in now stating that it lies contiguous to an abbey at present in ruins, but rich and flourishing in the olden time, the reader will at once understand that it was exquisitely so. The good monks were gifted with unerring instinct for searching out pleasant pastures by abounding rivers, and sunny sheltered aspects. It was along such a river, winding in the moonlight like a silver riband through copse and meadow, that, after exchanging one or two sharp, strange sentences, the young men strode quickly in the direction of the abbey ruins.

These sentences were overheard by Richard Austin, whose name has been mentioned before. He was a person of some property, the only encumbrance on which were his two sisters, who lived with him. Austin was a sort of country buck, one of the vainest coxcombs alive, and mischievous and spiteful as a monkey. People said he was contracted to Mary Foster ; but if this were so, the charms of Gertrude Melville had rendered him, temporarily at least, unfaithful ; and he had made shy, blundering, awkward advances towards that lady, so contemptuously repulsed as to excite in him the deadliest animosity and spite. The words he had overheard, and the excited demeanour of Arthur Raymond, determined him to follow and watch what might be the upshot.

He had walked about half a mile, when he observed them turn, and he presently perceived that they were walking arm in arm, and that it was probable, therefore, that the cause of disagreement had passed away. Austin, however, walked on, shielded from their observation by intervening copsewood. Just as he drew near, they stood still, as if about to separate, and Austin came stealthily within earshot.

Something was said by Sir Henry Greville about the beauty of the night, and then the full, manly, but now somewhat tremulous tones of Arthur Raymond, were heard.

"You have made me strangely happy, Greville; and yet may not you be deceived?"

"My life upon it, no! I am a keen student of the hidden meanings of women."

"I was so differently impressed: and so wonderful too," continued Raymond, in a half-abstracted manner, as if recalling some fresh, delightful dream, and uttering it aloud—"so wonderful that you should have been so often in Gertrude Melville's society, and felt towards her merely as a brother—as an affectionate relative."

"Nothing more, I assure you; besides, from some half-words dropped by the good vicar's lady, I had early reason to believe that—— But we will speak further on the matter hereafter. It is getting late; and it is quite possible Lady Greville and my sisters have arrived—if so, will you look in and dine with us to-morrow?"

"I hardly know how I can, for my father has brought down with him half a regiment of male friends. But shall we have a run with the hounds in the morning?"

"I cannot promise, as I have some business to arrange to-morrow; but I will send you an early note; and if not, I dare say I shall be able to spare time to come over and breakfast with you. If I do, I shall bring Collier with me: he will be glad to see your father."

"Do. Good-bye!" and the friends parted.

All this was poison to the skulking, envious man who overheard it. A cruel, dastardly thought shot through his mind and gleamed across his sallow face. " I think I could," he muttered, " let down the strings that make this music, as the man says in the play. Sir Henry is, I am sure, mistaken in the lady's sentiments; but he, it is plain, would not marry *her*. Now, if she could be made to believe that the young baronet had sent a proposal for her hand, the secret of her preference would be betrayed, herself exposed to the bitterest mortification, and all chance of her entering the wealthy family of the Raymonds destroyed. By Jove! I see how it could be easily managed, for his writing I can imitate to a nicety." Thus musing, the miscreant slowly wended his way homewards ; and it was late that night before his self-imposed task was completed to his satisfaction— assisted, as it has always been said he was, by his sisters ; but this, I hope, for the honour of womanhood, is an error, though in Westford a prevalent one.

The next morning, Richard Austin was early at Greville House. The porter who admitted him was desired to ask if Sir Henry hunted that day, and he left the hall for that purpose. The moment his back was turned, Austin placed a letter quickly in the wired box on the table, in which there were already several others. He had scarcely done so when the servant, whose duty it was to take the letters to their several addresses, entered the hall, placed them in his leather-bag, and forthwith departed. Sir Henry's answer, that he did not hunt that day, quickly followed; and Austin, in high glee, rode off.

Arthur Raymond had been still earlier abroad ; he had not, indeed, slept at all during the night. Not yet could he yield to sleep—oblivion—a moment of the new and rapturous life beating at his heart! But he could not remain in even bodily repose. In the abbey woods he could run, leap, shout--give physical play to the joyous tumult in his throbbing veins. And when had morn risen radiant and glorious as now, even upon Westford, so calmly, so beautifully bright? When before had the air been so exhilarating, the flowers exhaled such perfume, the birds warbled such music? When had the silver river so leaped and sparkled to meet the golden kisses of the sun? Never, in his remembrance—never ! It was a changed world! Thus raved the fond madman, still, as he did so, drawing nearer and nearer to the magnet which compelled his steps. The inmates of Laurel Villa were, he well knew, early risers. He should perhaps obtain a glimpse of Gertrude in the front flower-garden, screened from the public path by flower-bushes and a light iron fence. He was right. Although it was scarcely eight o'clock, she was there watering some plants. The lady must have read aright the expression of his excited features, for her eyes fell timidly before his, and the fair cheek glowed with a deeper crimson than before, whilst the smile about the charming mouth, as she invited him to walk in, had, he thought, a character of archness about it, never previously observed.

He *would* walk in; but the liveried letter-carrier from Greville House was coming towards them: he, Arthur Raymond, expected a note from Sir Henry, and the man had doubtless recognized him. The messenger quickly approached, drew up at the gate, placed in Arthur Raymond's hand *two* letters, and then rode over to the vicarage. Has a serpent stung Arthur Raymond, that he starts so wildly? "For you—for you," he gasped, "and from Sir Henry Greville!"

The lady, divining with woman's quickness the cause of his agitation, said instantly : "A letter for me, from your friend Sir Henry! Pray open it, then, and read me its purport; for my hands, you see, are full." Arthur Raymond did not require to be twice told. He tore off the envelope, and, confusedly running over the contents, shrieked out the following fragments of sentences: "Beloved Gertrude—the rapturous conviction that—that mutual sympathy— Raymond's scarcely concealed advances—compel me to hesitate no longer "——"Ah God!"

The suddenness of the blow paralyzed the unhappy

young man, and he sank down as if smitten with sudden death. Terribly alarmed, the lady called loudly for assistance, which soon arrived in the shape of the two foreign servants. Leaving him to their care, she seized the astounding letter, and hastened to seek Mrs. Melville; but before they could return to where Gertrude had left Arthur Raymond, he had not only been restored to consciousness, but had burst away with a wild passionate cry from his attendants, and at so fierce a speed that he was already out of sight.

Dr. Irwin was immediately sent for; and on being shown the letter, he instantly pronounced it—from internal evidence of the style, matter, mode of expression, admirably as the handwriting had been imitated—to be a malicious forgery. The result of the conference was, that the reverend gentleman's four-wheeled chaise was got ready with all possible despatch, and the two ladies with himself set off at once for Greville House, where, as the vicar heard, Lady Greville and family had arrived late the previous evening. It was felt to be of the last importance to prevent a meeting of the young men whilst one of them laboured under so exasperating a delusion.

Whilst this was passing, Arthur Raymond was down upon his face in the dark wood. He had just strength to reach it, to feel that he was alone, concealed from all the world, and the next moment fell prone on the dank grass, totally insensible. How long he thus remained, he knew not. The cold dew helped at length to revive him ; and as the agonizing memory of what had occurred came darkly back, a fierce, unreasoning aspiration for immediate vengeance usurped and dominated every function of his mind. An unopened letter was by his side. It was torn open, and read eagerly : " My mother and sisters arrived late last evening, and Collier and I intend taking an early gallop by Somerton, reaching Marston Hall, through the abbey wood, in time for breakfast." One loud, vengeful shout burst from the maniac, and he went off at headlong speed towards home.

He was not long in reaching Marston Hall, in hurriedly acquainting Lieutenant Barlow—a young dashing officer of dragoons, who had arrived the day before on a visit—with the deceit and insulting treachery of Sir Henry Greville ; and then, provided with a case of duelling pistols, powder, ball, and so on, they both left the house, and hastened towards the abbey wood. Lieutenant Barlow, so incoherent and wild were Arthur Raymond's words, could only understand that his companion had been grossly and insultingly betrayed by the person they were going to meet ; and he was beginning to think whether it might not be as well to have a clearer, more distinct idea of the cause of quarrel, before he irretrievably engaged himself in it, when Sir Henry Greville and Major Collier, an old Indian veteran, came in view, leisurely cantering along. A yell of passion burst from Arthur Raymond, and he was

I

springing madly forward, but was forcibly restrained by Lieutenant Barlow. "Stay here, my dear fellow; I must first speak to these gentlemen."

The two horsemen reined quickly up as they came near enough to read the expression of the lieutenant's face. "What is the matter?" asked Sir Henry.

"You had better dismount, sir. We must speak together: here, throw the bridle over this branch. Your services also, major, will, I fear, be required."

"Arthur," exclaimed Sir Henry quickly, as the infuriated young man, unable to restrain himself, came fiercely up—"what is the meaning of this——"

"Damnable, treacherous scoundrel!" broke in Raymond.

"Ha!"

"You had no thought, not you, of Gertrude Melville—villain! traitor!"

"I neither had nor have," rejoined Sir Henry, who plainly perceived that some terrible misapprehension existed.

"Liar, too, as well as villain!" shouted Raymond, beside himself with rage. "A coward too, perhaps. Well, then, take that!" and he struck the baronet a violent blow on the face.

Sir Henry appeared about to return it, when Major Collier arrested his arm. "A blow, Sir Henry, cannot be avenged in that way. Barlow, since this must be, give me the pistols, and do you measure the distance —twelve steps, and place your man: we stand here.'

Little further was said: the pistols were loaded, the ground paced off, and the young men placed opposite each other

"Hark!" said Lieutenant Barlow; "there is a sound of carriage-wheels approaching."

"No, no, no!" cried Raymond, with frantic vehemence, observing the seconds hesitate. "One of you give the word as agreed; and quick."

The sound had ceased. Either their ears had deceived them, or the grass deadened the noise of the wheels.

"I will give the word," said the veteran. "Greville," he added in a low tone to his friend, "do not throw away a chance; your antagonist, I see, means mischief. Now then," he continued, "ready—present—fire!"

The reports of the pistols were simultaneous; and now, plainly enough mingling with the ringing echo of the explosion, was heard the gallop of horses, and the sound of wheels, intermingled with the screams of women. In another moment, Lady Greville's carriage, in which were her ladyship, Mrs. Melville, Gertrude Conway, and the reverend vicar, came in sight. The smoke had whirled off, and both the combatants were standing. Arthur Raymond had dropped his pistol on the ground, once convulsively tossed his arms in the air, and was now gazing, as if fascinated, in the direction of the open carriage, which rapidly approached. For a few moments only did he so gaze ; the, for a time, will-constrained muscles suddenly relaxed, and he fell to the ground, to all appearance wounded to death.

It did not, happily, prove so ; though the passage of the rash young man through the Valley of the Shadow of Death was long and painful. The bullet, which had lodged in the right side, was extracted without difficulty ; but brain-fever subsequently came on, and nothing, it was all along plain, but a remarkably vigorous constitution, could have brought him through.

There are a few brief points to notice, and one act of scanty justice to record, and I have done. Lady Greville had received her niece with the greatest cordiality ; and Mrs. Melville was fain to admit, that her cautious plotting and contriving had been productive only of confusion, sorrow, and danger. Just as frankly and heartily did Arthur Raymond confess the rash violence of which he had been guilty towards his old friend and companion ; the injustice of his doubts of Gertrude's preference, which the cooler and more clear-headed Sir Henry had assured him of—a preference confirmed and sealed beyond question on New-Year's Day last past. at one of the most magnificent weddings our county has ever witnessed ; the lady being given away by the baronet, and her cousins, the Misses Greville, assisting as bridesmaids. It really seemed that his long illness must have improved the bridegroom's health, for assuredly Arthur

Raymond never, everybody said, looked half so handsome and happy before. As to the bride's appearance—— But there—it's of no use trying.

Richard Austin's authorship of the forged letter was fully established, partly in consequence of flurried words that had fallen from Miss Dorothea at the time of the supposed fatal termination of the duel. No legal punishment could, however, it appeared, be inflicted; and except one of the soundest horse-whippings administered by Sir Henry which ever man had, and a capital ducking in the horse-pond by one of the most unanimous of small mobs I have ever seen, the fellow skulked out of Westford scot-free, and was soon afterwards followed by his sisters. The young lady with the brief curls did not share his fortunes. She remains with us, and, it is but common justice to say, is greatly improved in all respects —partly owing to the quiet steady examples by which, since her return from London, she has been surrounded, and partly, no doubt, to a thumping legacy devised to her some seven or eight months ago by an octogenarian aunt. So entirely am I, for one, convinced of this that—that—— But no; I merely took up my pen to relate what I knew concerning " An Offer of Marriage ; " and that which Mary Foster must have received full a quarter of an hour ago, is undoubtedly a genuine one.

THE CADET BRANCH.

Two of the cheeriest, blithest ladies of my acquaintance were the Misses Tabitha and Deborah Darvill, who, with their long-widowed, grey-haired mother, resided, a few years ago, in one of the pleasant semi-rural cottages the neighbourhood of London is so thickly studded with, upon an income which, to persons unfamiliar with the magic of a minute and judicious economy, might appear barely sufficient for the mere necessaries of life, but which *they* made amply suffice for most of its modest luxuries. Guileless, cheerful-hearted maidens! who that witnessed with what a gentle loving-kindness you

> " Rocked the cradle of declining age"—

how gaily you gossiped, how prettily you played and sang—how sensibly, when you had nothing better to do, you discoursed—could have thought otherwise than contemptuously of the venerable fallacy which connects misanthropy with elderly-maidenhood, and invariably associates singleness at forty with crabbedness and an evil disposition ? For myself. I beg to express a firm belief that if Tabby and Debby—familiar domestic brevities these, permitted, be it understood, only to a favoured few—I say, I firmly believe that if Tabby and Debby had each blessed three husbands, and been surrounded by a dozen or more cherubs in bibs and pinafores, they could scarcely have been more gentle, obliging, and thoroughly amiable than they actually were. This, I repeat, is my solemn opinion. But coming as it does from a confirmed old bachelor, it must of course be taken *cum grano salis*. One weakness, besides tea, these ladies confessed to: they loved, with an enthusiasm unsurpassed by that of the celebrated Mrs. Battle, a sound, quiet rubber of whist— good old constitutional whist, mind; none of your *short* heresies—with its illustrations, " a clear fire, a clean hearth, and the rigour of the game." Fortunately they lived in a thoroughly whist neighbourhood. The two semi-detached cottages that, with their own, constituted the chief street of that young locality were occupied by two staid widowers, with whom, since the death and burial of their wives, whist seemed the one cherished object of existence; and hundreds of rubbers were valiantly fought out in that pleasantest of pleasant parlours between the mature maidens and their somewhat ancient neighbours—Mr. Peter Danby, and Mr. John Dusatoy.

Yes. Peter Danby and John Dusatoy are the names

of the gentlemen ; but if the reader is to understand clearly this charming little "histoirette"—that is, if I do not mar it in the telling—something more of introduction than the mere announcement of their names is essentially necessary. Mr. Peter Danby— a man of singularly-expressive silence—may be dismissed after his own manner in a very few words. He is a retired drysalter, living physically and morally upon the accumulations, material and mental, of former exertions. The first—the material—are decidedly the most tangible, consisting as they do of between five and six thousand pounds in sundry solid securities, national and joint-stock. The mental capital, though not perhaps so accurately set down, nor so easily reckoned up as consols and debentures, must necessarily be considerable ; as, without having added one single item to it within the memory of the oldest inhabitant of the street— who is unquestionably the old lady yonder, nodding so comfortably in her arm-chair over her knitting— he has for many years enjoyed, and still continues to enjoy, a daily reputation from it: a man of powerful action, I have no doubt, but of marvellous few words. Many a brave talker, I am told, he has in his time listened down : kept steadily at it, in fact, till the fountain was thoroughly run out. Shortly, to sum him up, and give his brief-total, he is a kind of drysalter-illustration of Mr. Carlyle's somewhat paradoxical apophthegm in his Hero as Poet :

"Speech is great, but silence is greater." His tremendous superiority at whist may be imagined.

Mr. John Dusatoy, on the other hand, is essentially a man of words; but unfortunately of such small ones, that a shower of them produces the faintest imaginable impression. A decent, quiet, well-meaning little man, nevertheless, is John Dusatoy. Dusatoy, I repeat, is a very quiet, respectable person; wears a carefully-kept flaxen wig, and has everything handsome and comfortable about him; and, to crown all, a daughter, who——

Yes, sir; positively the young lady seated at the rosewood work-table, with the beautifully-moulded Grecian head, raven tresses, dark full brilliant eyes —and now, as she rises to snuff the candles for the absorbed whist-players, you perceive, of queenly figure and graceful, elastic carriage—is the little flaxen wig's heiress and only daughter, Geraldine Dusatoy. Well, sir, what of that? I maintain that it is a soap and candle dealer's birthright— his and every man's inalienable, constitutional privilege—to have his daughter christened by any name he pleases. You admit it? That being the case, I don't mind still further enlightening you. But in order that I should be enabled to do so, you must, if you please, step back with me to just seventeen years ago last Monday evening. A long distance! And now we have got to it, only look what a dark, gusty, sleety, plashy, disagreeable evening it is!

Well, on this very evening Mr. John Dusatoy was belated at a distance of something more than six miles from his lawful home and wife, situated both of them in one of the large manufacturing towns of the north of England. It was entirely his own fault, I must tell you, that he was thus belated. He might have been home hours before, had he not been fascinated, juggled out of his usual prudence, by a troop of spangled vagabonds, with a black-eyed gipsy-girl for their prima donna, who were exhibiting their tricks and tumblings at the " Golden Fleece," whither Mr. John Dusatoy had betaken himself by appointment early in the afternoon, for the settlement of a rather heavy account. When he at last rose to depart, he found that he had awfully overstayed his time; and direful were the forebodings which filled his mind as to the reception he should meet with from Mrs. Dusatoy—a respectable, but altogether over-eloquent lady, who, John instinctively felt, as he glanced at the hands of his watch, had already heaped up abundant treasures for him. " Nearly seven miles by the road," soliloquized the repentant, self-accusing soap-dealer: " bless me, I shall be two hours or more getting home that way. Through the wood saves nearly three miles; but then it is so plaguy dark; I might miss my way." He nevertheless resolved to venture. The brandy-and-water he had swallowed rendered him unusually valiant; and on he desperately staggered, through marsh, and brake,

and brier. Rash, rarely successful men are they who
wander from beaten paths in search of short cuts to
desired havens ; and honest Dusatoy proved no exception to the rule. For more than two mortal
hours did he wander to and fro in the dark, marshy,
perplexing wood ; till, worn out, bewildered, terrified
almost to death, he sat down upon a damp, uncomfortable stump, fairly overcome with fright and vexation. The imminence of the peril roused him to
renewed exertion. "Man lost !—man lost !—man
lost !" he shouted, jumping up, and raising his voice
to a dreadfully-cracked pitch, in the desperate hope
of attracting assistance. The strange sounds echoed
through the stillness of the forest ; but no sympathizing voice responded to the agonized appeal.
"Man lost !—man lost !" reiterated the perturbed but
persistent oilman with quavering vehemence. This
time there was an answer. "Who—o—o—o—o ?"
came distinctly down the wind. "Poor Johnny
Dusatoy !" he replied with deprecatory supplication ;
"as honest a man as ever broke a bit of bread !"
"Who—o—o—o—o ?" again returned the sympathizing stranger. Johnny eagerly repeated his description, baptismal, patronymic, and moral, and
still the same query replied to his frantic asseverations. On, however, he pressed in the direction of
the voice ; and, as he conjectured, was not more than
a quarter of a mile from the cold-blooded questioner,
when, emerging from the tangled darkness into a

somewhat clear opening in the wood, he was startled out of his few remaining wits by the apparition of an enormous gipsy suddenly confronting and striding towards him. No wonder his jaws rattled like a pair of castanets, and that he shook in every fibre of his little body: it was—no doubt about it, considering the hour and the locality—a most unpleasant meeting.

"Who is that?" demanded the grim vagabond; "who is that dialoguing with the owls at this time of night?"

"I—I—I, p-o-o-o-r Jo-ohnny Du-u-u-satoy, as ho-o-o-nest a ——"

"Oh, it's you, is it? I'm glad of it, for I thought I had missed you. You are the very man I want."

"A-a-a-am I?"

"Yes: you are rich and childless; and you must take this one, and bring it up as your own. The girl you saw at the inn has preserved it during the last five or six days at the hazard of her life. The band, for various reasons best known to themselves, will have it destroyed and buried snugly out of the way. I have undertaken the job; but at the request of that girl have promised to deliver it to you; with this distinct understanding, that you bring it up as your own; and above and before all, that you never breathe a word to one living soul as to how you came by it."

"Ye-e-es."

"You consent: I am glad of it, as it may save trouble. Now, then, here's a Bible: look and see that it is a real one. Good. Now place your hand upon it, and repeat after me." Mr. John Dusatoy stretched forth his hand, and mechanically repeated the words of an awful oath binding him to secresy. He then, at the command of the gipsy, kissed the book.

"It is well. Now mark: if ever you reveal to a single human being what has passed to-night, you will be a dead man before twenty-four hours are over. Come, this is your path."

Five minutes afterwards, Mr. John Dusatoy found himself upon the high road, within ten minutes' distance of his home, with a lusty infant of about two years of age in his arms. His mind was in a state of complete confusion. He certainly had seen such things done in a play, and had read of them in circulating romances, but that a respectable man and a rate-payer should be served a trick of the kind in actual real life seemed utterly absurd and incredible. He, however, moved mechanically homewards, holding the babe nearly at arm's length, something after the manner in which people carry joints of meat to a bake-house; and had arrived within a yard of his domicile before a thoroughly full sense of the utter desperateness of his condition flashed upon him. If he had before dreaded encountering his amiable partner, how on earth was he to face that determined woman with such a present as *that* in his arms? The very idea of it turned him up and down; and cold and sleety as it was, he perspired like a roasting-cook in the dog-days. Long, long he stood irresolute; but at length nerving himself to desperation, he rang the bell. Quickly a well-remembered step was heard upon the passage floorcloth, and a well-remembered voice exclaimed—"Oh, there you are at last! Upon my word this is very pretty—remarkably so indeed. Aint you ashamed of yourself?" continued Mrs. Dusatoy, fairly boiling over, and at the same moment throwing open the door. "Aint you ashamed——"

The current of her eloquence was checked at once. I give you my word, sir, that a company of grenadiers charging into that passage with fixed bayonets and bear-skin caps could not have so scared that remarkable woman, as did the blessed babe sustained upon her husband's outstretched arms. She started back dumfoundered, paralyzed! Johnny, profiting by the momentry panic of his better half, darted by her, rushed frantically into the parlour, and deposited the infant on the table, exclaiming, as he wiped his teeming forehead, "There! I swore a dreadful oath I would do it, and I *have* done it. There!"

The scene which followed must be left to the imagination, which, if a very brilliant one, may possibly do it justice. I can only relate the fag-end of the fray, after the storm had spent itself, and John Dusatoy had escaped to bed, "Well, Sally," said the mistress of the house, addressing her confidential maid-of-all-work, " we cannot throw the brat into the street, so you had better take it and let it sleep with you to-night ; " and Mrs. Dusatoy, who had been engaged for the last two or three minutes in an unsatisfactory voyage of discovery over the baby's features, endeavoured to transfer it to the arms of her hand-maid. But the child would not be so shifted. It clung perversely, but most endearingly, round Mrs. Dusatoy's neck, pressing its coral mouth upon her lips, and peremptorily refusing to depart. The good woman's better nature was awakened by the child's appeal. Thoughts of the one, only one sweet bud of promise that had briefly blessed her life, swelled her heart and filled her eyes. " Never mind, Sally, she shall remain with me to-night at all events." The next morning, after patiently listening to her husband's explanation, Mrs. Dusatoy agreed to adopt the child. It soon secured a firm hold on the affections of both husband and wife ; and as the Dusatoys were even in those days comparatively rich, a liberal education was ungrudgingly bestowed upon the beautiful Geraldine—this name was found marked upon a portion of the infant's dress, and was of course retained— and possessed as she was of great natural capabilities, she speedily reflected credit on her instructors. Her birth, or rather her rescue and adoption, Mrs. Dusatoy a few weeks before her death, unreservedly communicated to the sorrowing adopted daughter. That knowledge has not, as you perceive, in the slightest degree abated the affectionate respect which she has constantly manifested towards her kind, well-meaning reputed father.

And now, sir, having, as I trust, fully satisfied your curiosity respecting the young lady at the work-table, you will, if you please, allow me to continue my story without interruption.

The whist-players, then, on the evening in question, were not, it was quite clear, in harmonious accordance. Both Tabby and Debby seemed fidgety and nervous, strangely forgot what cards were out, and altogether played abominably. Twice Mr. Dusatoy, as fresh hands were in course of distribution, had querulously remonstrated with Debby upon not leading the right suit at the right time ; and once Mr. Peter Danby, after enduring much unwincingly, paused in the midst of the play, laid his cards emphatically on the table, raised his spectacles from his eyes to his forehead, and glared solemnly in fair Tabitha's face with a look which said as plainly as look could, " Remember, madam, you are losing *my* money as well as your own." There were four sixpences, I should state, under one of the candlesticks. This done, he replaced his spectacles, resumed his cards, and steadily continued the game.

"Well," said Miss Deborah at the conclusion of

the hand, "we *are* playing shockingly; but the truth is, we have been a good deal flustered this afternoon by a letter from General——"

"*Lieutenant*-General D'Harville," interposed Tabitha, at the same time volunteering the orthography of the general's name.

"Yes, Lieutenant-General D'Harville," resumed Deborah; "and that, it seems, is the correct mode of spelling *our* name, which has been somehow shortened and vulgarized by dear papa's connection with the city. The general reminds us that we are a cadet branch of the family tree. Now what, for mercy's sake, *is* a cadet branch?"

"It's people that go to the East Indies to serve their queen and country in the capacity of gentlemen," replied John Dusatoy with confident alacrity.

"Nonsense, Mr. Dusatoy. How can Tabby and I, or dear mamma, be people of that sort?"

Mr. Peter Danby paused for an instant in the act of shuffling the cards for a fresh deal, and looked with much intelligence at Miss Deborah; he then favoured Mr. Dusatoy with another emphatic glance, easily translatable into "You're a donkey;" he, however, only *said*, as he placed the pack before him, "CUT!" Everybody felt that Mr. Danby *knew* what a cadet branch was, but that he for the moment declined imparting his knowledge. This was a favourite trick; and indeed one of the chief modes by which he raised and sustains his great reputation.

"I believe," said Geraldine, coming, as usual, to the rescue, "that a cadet is a younger brother, and I suppose his family might be called the cadet branch of the house?"

"That explains it, dear Geraldine," cried the spinsters both in a breath. "Quite. Well, who *would* have thought it?"

General Sir Frederick D'Harville had in fact written a curt stately note, informing Mrs. D'Harville—corruptly spelt Darvill—that having lost his only son about a twelvemonth previously in one of the great Indian battles, he and Lady D'Harville had determined to adopt one of their nieces, and bestow her handsomely in marriage, in order, as better could not be, that the ancient family might be continued and perpetuated through the cadet branch. He would call, for the purpose of escorting his niece to Maida Hall, on the morrow about noon.

For obvious reasons, the entire contents of this strange missive were not communicated to the company; but enough transpired to convince the widowers that a dreadful blow had been aimed at the peace of the card-table; and that, moreover, any further play even on that evening was out of the question. Mr. Peter Danby rose, quietly placed his broad-brimmer on his deliberate head, drew on his gloves, buttoned up his coat, bowed comprehensively, and stalked forth in accusing silence. Mr.

Dusatoy and his adopted daughter departed half an hour later.

Alas! there was more, much more in danger than the whist-table! Pope was quite right; in these days the evil one tempts, not by poverty, but riches. For the first time Tabby remembered with bitter malevolence that Debby was three years her junior; and Debby, for the same reason, exulted ungenerously over her sister. Twelve hours before, neither of them would have believed in the possibility of such feelings arising within their gentle bosoms; so sad was the change wrought by the glittering bait, present and prospective, set before them by their crafty uncle the lieutenant-general.

The general arrived the next morning in great state. He was a fine military-looking man, and was indeed possessed of many admirable qualities; but all dimmed and obscured, to the superficial observer at least, by overweening pride of birth and lineage, and haughty superciliousness of manner. He was ushered into the front parlour by the awe-struck maid-servant; and a minute afterwards, Geraldine Dusatoy, blushing and somewhat embarrassed, but losing nothing of her native grace and dignity of manner, entered to apologize for the momentary absence of Sir Frederick's nieces.

The instant the general's eye fell upon the form of the beautiful girl, he started from his chair with strange emotion; and advancing rapidly towards her with extended hands, exclaimed in a tone of joyful surprise, "My niece!" Geraldine explained, and Sir Frederick's countenance immediately fell. He did not, however, relinquish her hand, and continued to gaze at her with a troubled, inquisitive glance. Presently the door opened; "Miss Deborah D'Harville," said Geraldine, very much embarrassed, and anxious to divert the general's attention from herself.

" It is very strange," muttered Sir Frederick, gently yielding Geraldine's hand, and turning mechanically towards Deborah ; " who is this young lady ?"

"Geraldine Dusatoy—a neighbour."

Tabitha now entered ; and Sir Frederick's attention being necessarily given to the sisters, Geraldine Dusatoy adroitly slipped away, much wondering at the general's strange behaviour.

General D'Harville's reception of his nieces, as soon as he recovered his rarely-disturbed self-possession, was kind and courteous. It was soon arranged that Deborah, as the youngest, should succeed to the vacant niche of heiress to the house of D'Harville ; and preparations for immediate departure were at once commanded. I will not say that the general's hopes and anticipations were not somewhat damped by the perusal of the record of mature age stamped upon the countenance even of his youngest niece ; but he by no means despaired of the stability of his ancient house. He was a man of singularly sanguine temperament, and had in his youth led two forlorn-hopes.

Arrived at Maida Hall, Deborah was introduced to her stately aunt, Lady D'Harville—a tall, splendid, but apparently a grief-stricken woman. "Surely," thought Deborah, "I have seen that face before. Oh, to be sure! If she were twenty years younger, and happier-looking, she would be the very image of Geraldine."

Lady D'Harville received her niece with a cold, sad smile; and Deborah, after a few frigid words of course, was consigned to the care of her appointed attendants.

"Your niece's education, Sir Frederick," said Lady D'Harville as soon as Deborah had left the apart-ment, "has, I fear, been sadly neglected. You will have enough to do to render her presentable at the next drawing-room."

"Yes; there is no time to spare either. At all events, she has good blood in her veins. We must make up for lost time as well as we can."

The result of the general's resolution to make up for lost time is very clearly set forth in the following epistle received by Miss Tabitha about a fortnight after her sister's departure :—

"Maida Hall.

"DEAR TAB,—If you still feel any desire to be a great heiress, and live in state, get your things packed up ready; for, please goodness, I'll put up with the life I'm leading here no longer; no, not to be cadet branch to Queen Victoria! The general comes home to-morrow evening; and if he won't take me back in the carriage, I'll run away! Why, Tabby dear, you can have no conception of the torments and martyrdoms I have been made to endure, in the hope of transmogrifying me into a fine lady. But it's no use, Tabby dear, not the slightest: it's not in me, and that's the honest truth. First of all, as early as seven in the morning, I'm drilled for three-quarters of an hour by Sergeant Pike, in order to make me keep my shoulders back; after breakfast, my French and Italian masters take me in hand for an hour each: then come the piano and harp professors, and I am made to thump and twang away till luncheon-time: directly that is over, Monsieur Pirouette, the dancing-master, exercises me for two mortal hours; and when *he* has concluded, it is time to surrender myself into the hands of Mademoiselle Angélique, to be screwed up, frizzed, and plaited for dinner. Ah, Tabby, if I could once see that dear Angélique upon the bare back of our donkey, and I behind with a good switch in my hand, *wouldn't* I —— But no matter, here I wont stop, that's poz! The cadet branch and posterity may shift for themselves for what I care; I'll have no more of it, and so you may tell dear mother; and believe me, Tabby, your affectionate sister in affliction,   " DEBORAH DARVILL.

"Yes, Darvill! good, honest, downright Darvill! The deuce take their H's, and their E's, and their apostrophes, say I, for ever and amen!"

Tabitha and Geraldine Dusatoy were still occupied on the following morning commenting upon this portentous letter, when the general's carriage was seen to drive furiously up to the garden gate, and presently out sprang Deborah, before the door was well opened, and came running frantically up the gravelled path towards the cottage. In she burst, hot, panting, and impatient.

" God bless you, Tabby; here's an uproar, and all of my making! Geraldine, don't be frightened, there's a dear; but as sure as you're alive, you are an elder branch, or worse. Turn down your left shoulder, and you'll see. The general had been talking to his lady about your uncommon likeness— but there, poor soul, you don't know anything about it—and I happened to let out that you were a ' babe in the wood,' suckled by gipsies seventeen years ago, and that your name was Geraldine; and if Lady D'Harville hasn't been going on distractedly ever since, wringing her hands, and walking in her sleep, like the lady in the play. Oh! here she is."

Lady D'Harville, supported by her husband, here entered the room in a terrible state of agitation. The instant she saw Geraldine she sprang wildly towards her, and, clasping her in her arms, exclaimed in a choking voice, and with frenzied eagerness, "It is she!—I know it—feel it! Oh! God would not so deceive a mother! Quick, quick, if you would not see me die! Her left shoulder—three moles triangularly placed!"

"It is she!—look here!" shrieked Sir Frederick with wild excitement, and at the same time seizing the astonished Geraldine in his arms. Lady D'Harville slid down on her knees, and, with clasped hands and streaming eyes raised towards heaven, ejaculated in broken accents, " Thanks, Father of mercies, thanks!"

The explanation which, as soon as the excitement had in some degree subsided, was gone into, proved perfectly satisfactory. Maida Hall had been broken into and plundered, a few days previous to the night on which John Dusatoy had duetted with the owls, by a band of gipsies, and the child carried off, in the expectation, it was conjectured, of obtaining a reward for its restoration. The pursuit, however, was so hot, that the band must have feared to afford any clue to the detection of the authors of the burglary by any negotiation of the sort; and hence doubtless their resolution to put the child out of the way, a design happily frustrated by the compassion of the gipsy-girl, and the opportune appearance of Mr. John Dusatoy at the " Golden Fleece."

Matters were speedily arranged: Mr. Dusatoy parted regretfully with Geraldine ; but both were consoled by the frank and cordial invitation the honest man received from Sir Frederick and Lady D'Harville to visit Maida Hall as frequently as he found it convenient and agreeable to do so. A large addition to the income of Mrs. Darvill and her daughters was also spontaneously offered by the general, and of course gratefully accepted.

Sir Frederick, Lady, and Geraldine D'Harville departed just as the shades of evening began to fall. Half an hour afterwards the candles were lighted, the card-table again set out, Mrs. Darvill was wheeled closer to the fire, and the accustomed four once more seated themselves at their beloved board of green cloth. Deborah, enfranchised Deborah, all smiles and sunshine, having shuffled the cards, waved them in the air with a gesture of exuberant triumph, and then, bringing them down with a flourish, plump before Mr. Peter Danby, exclaimed, "Cut!" "With all my heart," rejoined Mr. Danby, suiting the action to the word. "Hurrah!" This unwonted outburst added of course considerably to the excitement, which, however, completely subsided during the progress of the deal. "Play!" cried Tabitha. Deborah played, and on went the solemn game; and on it is going to this day, as any lady or gentleman who can procure an introduction may easily satisfy him or herself on any evening during the week, "Sundays excepted."

ESTELLE ST. ANGE.

Philippe Armand, a Paris notary, and probably the youngest man of the ancient and honourable fraternity to which he belonged—for he had but lately succeeded to his father's business—entered late one evening, during one of the most terrific phases of the first French Revolution, a back sitting-room in the house of Madame Colardeau, a court *modiste*—when there was a court—established for many years in the Palais Royal. The year was waning towards its close, and the weather was cold, wet, and gloomy—the time itself was out of joint; but, spite of all depressing exterior influences, Monsieur Philippe Armand—a handsome, but somewhat pale and delicate-looking young man—appeared, very contrary to his wont, in exuberant spirits.

"Ah, Madame Colardeau, I am delighted to see you. You look charmingly; and Mademoiselle Estelle ?——"

"Is quite well, Monsieur Armand; and you, too, seem to have wonderfully recovered from the despair with which you pretended to be overwhelmed but a

few weeks since. I expected every day to hear you
had been fished out of the Seine; and here you are,
not only very well alive, but apparently as merry as a
Savoyard. Oh, you men—you men!"

" Times are changed, madame. Events ripen
quickly in the wondrous days in which we live."

" Oh, *par exemple!*" rejoined Madame Colardeau;
" there is nothing surer than that. It required
twenty years under the old *régime* to establish this
business ; but your charming Republic has thoroughly
demolished it in less than as many months."

" Courage, Madame Colardeau—courage! Better
times than you have ever known are coming, rely
upon it. A tempest is unpleasant, dangerous even
while it lasts, but it clears and purifies the air. I
have news for you."

" News for me?"

" For you and Mademoiselle St. Ange. Eugène
Duvernay, son of ci-devant Count Duvernay, is,
thanks to my assistance, safe across the frontier."

" *Comment!*" screamed Madame Colardeau, turning pale as death. " Eugène Duvernay left France,
and without us?"

" Certainly he has left France, and evidently without you; but I do not understand——"

" Oh, Monsieur Armand, you do not know—you
were not told. *Mon Dieu*, can it be possible? But
I have had my suspicions. The count's son gone!
What will become of us—of Estelle especially?"—

and the excited *modiste* paced up and down the apartment in an agony of grief and terror.

The countenance of Philippe Armand lost in an instant its joyous expression, and his white lips quivered with ill-defined apprehension as he demanded the meaning of so strange an outburst.

" We are undone, ruined, lost!" sobbed Madame Colardeau. " Unhappy, deceived Estelle ——"

" Who is ruined, lost, deceived?" interrupted the notary, fiercely. " You must have lost your senses. In what manner can the enforced departure of so light, so worthless a coxcomb as Eugène Duvernay, permanently affect the peace of Mademoiselle St. Ange, or your welfare?"

Madame Colardeau continued to wring her hands, and utter broken exclamations of grief and passion, but vouchsafed no other answer.

" Hark you, madame," cried M. Armand, grasping her rudely by the arm, and forcing her into a chair, " by all the saints in heaven, but you *shall* answer me! What, I insist upon being told, is the meaning of these frantic outcries?"

" Oh, Monsieur Philippe," whimpered the startled *modiste*, " Estelle should have told you—should **have** explained—I cannot, must not. If what you say is true, there is no faith, no honesty in man."

" I think I comprehend you," rejoined the notary, in a calmed voice. " I trust, at least, that I do; and if so, you must permit me to view the event which has so much discomposed you in a very different light and aspect. Now, listen as patiently as you can whilst I relate to you what Estelle *did* confide to me, and then tell me if I have anything yet more sad and terrible to learn."

" Go on, monsieur; go on—I listen."

" It is now about six weeks since I sought a decisive interview with your niece, Mademoiselle St. Ange; not for the mere purpose of revealing to her, in coloured phrase and words of passion, the deep, heart-seated devotion which, for long, patient years, I had cherished for her—with woman's ready quickness she had long since divined that secret—but to offer her, then for the first time in my power, an honourable home, a position in the world, to be rendered daily brighter, more enviable, by the exertions of a brave, honest, respected man. Estelle listened to me with sympathy, with tears, with almost tenderness; but at the same time confessed a preference for the son of Count Duvernay, to whom she said her faith was plighted. I was stunned, bewildered, almost mad! I knew the man upon whom she had lavished the priceless treasure of her love; and after passionately warning her—vainly I could see—against trusting in the promises or oaths of one of the basest, the most specious hypocrites that ever brought contempt and scorn upon high station, left her presence, as you know, in a frenzy of despair. Now tell me, madame," added the notary, after slightly pausing, and in a voice which, spite of his efforts to speak calmly, quivered with emotion, "can you have a revelation more terrible than that to make?"

"Go on, monsieur," sobbed Madame Colardeau; "you said he was gone—had passed the frontier?"

"After parting from Estelle I endured an age of grief, anxiety, and despair, until last Thursday evening, when Eugène Duvernay suddenly presented himself in my apartment."

"Monsieur Duvernay visited you?"

"Yes; he was pursued, and in imminent danger of the guillotine, or he might not perhaps have so greatly condescended. You are aware that he and his father, like many others of their class, have all along affected acquiescence in the new order of things, and were in some sort pets of the 'Gironde.' Their friends themselves, being just now in imminent peril of Samson's terrible axe, could of course no longer afford them protection: an order for their arrest had been issued, and Eugène Duvernay, and his equally estimable sire, had been for several days lurking in obscure hiding-places from the agents of the *Salut Public.*"

"That accounts, then, for his strange absence," interjected Madame Colardeau, somewhat reassured.

"He threw himself for protection upon my honour and generosity; at the same time declaring that he had for some weeks withdrawn all pretension to the hand of Mademoiselle St. Ange, who, moreover, knew of his application to me, and had expressed a confidence that I would, for her sake, aid him to escape the bloody doom which awaited him."

"*Ciel!*" exclaimed Madame Colardeau, with much emotion. "Can it be possible?"

"It is true as heaven! I consented, so adjured, to assure his safety at the risk of my own. I immediately procured passports in a feigned name for him of course, and to make all sure saw him on his road till danger of pursuit or recognition was over. At parting, he presented me with this ring, as a token to Estelle that I had vindicated the confidence she had reposed in my devotion to her wishes, and that he thereby resigned in my favour all claim or pretension to her hand."

"Claim!—pretension! But, *mon Dieu*, Monsieur Armand, they are married!"

"Married!" echoed the astonished notary with frenzied vehemence. "Married! But no, no; you are jesting: he could not be so utterly a villain!"

"I repeat to you, Maître Philippe Armand, that Eugène Duvernay and Estelle St. Ange were married a month ago at the Hôtel Duvernay, in the Faubourg St. Germain, by the Abbé Boujeau—he who was arrested and executed but last week."

Whilst Madame Colardeau was speaking, the door leading to the interior of the house was gently opened, and Mademoiselle St. Ange, death-white, affectedly calm, but evidently struggling with frightful emotion, glided into the apartment.

" Estelle ! " exclaimed Philippe Armand in a voice broken by grief and indignation, and approaching as if to take her hand.

" The ring—the ring ! " gasped Mademoiselle St. Ange, waving him from her with an expression of passionate disgust. " I have heard all : the ring— where is it ? "

The notary placed it on the table ; she seized it eagerly, and, after minutely examining it, murmured, " It is indeed my father's ring—the troth plight which Eugène vowed never but with life to part from. And so, monsieur," continued the unfortunate girl, turning her beaming, tearless glance upon Philippe Armand, " you are come to claim as a bride the woman you have widowed? This ring is part of the spoils of the accursed scaffold where my husband has, I doubt not, by your contrivance, perished."

" What is it you say ? " interrupted the notary, aghast with surprise and indignation. " I swear to you, Estelle, by all that men hold sacred, that Eugène Duvernay placed that ring voluntarily in my hands, with the message —— "

" Peace ! " broke in Estelle ; " peace, audacious slanderer of the illustrious dead, with whom, in life, you could no more compare than might the wayside weed with the stately monarch of the forest. My husband was the very soul of faith and honour. But hark you, Philippe Armand," she added with passionate bitterness, "even if it were as you assert, were the lying fable you have concocted as true as it is false, I would not, in the veriest extremity of want, of despair, having been once so honoured, stoop to a churl like you."

The notary reeled and staggered beneath her words as if they had been blows, or rather burning arrows piercing through his brain. "Estelle," he at last mournfully exclaimed after a brief pause, during which Mademoiselle St. Ange, with sudden revulsion of feeling, had thrown herself, in an ecstasy of tears, into the arms of her aunt—"Estelle, unhappy girl, the time will come when you will recognize, and, I trust, repent the falsehood of the hideous charge you have, in your unreasoning frenzy, brought against me. And now, Estelle, hear from me in this extreme hour, which sunders the sole link which bound me to earth, to life, one solemn word of truth, and, it may be yet, of helpful warning: but for your mad ambition, stimulated and flattered by her who now holds you in her embrace, to ally yourself far above your sphere and honest state, the anguish, the despair which now wring your heart would have been spared you. Farewell! Never more will my presence irritate or disgust you."

It must be remembered, in extenuation of the unjust violence displayed by Estelle, that the young wife had idolized her husband, and, with woman's

L

frequent blindness in such cases, believed him, as she said, to be the very soul of truth and honour. So impressed, it was no marvel that she should suspect Philippe Armand of having invented the story he had related, in order to profit by the death of a rival he had himself denounced to the revolutionary tribunal—a deed, by the way, of no unfrequent occurrence in the palmy days of Terrorism. Spite of the solemn denial of the notary, she continued firm in this belief, and, mourning her husband as dead, resolved to cherish his memory, as that of one whom, when this transitory existence was past, she was destined to rejoin in that better world where life and love are both eternal.

When Philippe Armand again left his apartment, where he had been confined for several days after his last interview with Mademoiselle St. Ange, or, more properly, Madame Duvernay, he was a changed man. The fire of sanguine youth, strong hope, high courage, had passed away; his step was feeble, his eye dull, and but for the calm, gentle smile which accustomed greetings of familiar voices had still at times power to call forth, it might have been thought that his spirit had utterly died within him, so purposeless, so sad, so utterly desolate did he appear. Estelle St. Ange had been the earliest, the only being that had caught his boyhood's fancy; and each succeeding year had only the more deeply stamped her peculiar and subduing beauty—a mild appealing loveliness, tinted with rainbow smiles, and tremulous with changeful light and tears—upon his heart. A rash, inexperienced player at the game of life, he had staked his all upon one chance, and lost it. He did not feel the slightest resentment towards Estelle after the first angry emotions excited by her cruel injustice had subsided. She, too, he felt, had built her house upon the sand; and a profound pity for the desolate lot which must await the worse than-widowed wife of Eugène Duvernay. mingled with, and heightened and purified, the sentiment he still cherished for Estelle St. Ange. To baffle the heartless husband at the iniquitous game he had been playing, would, he felt, almost repay him for his own withered hopes and blighted life; but how, in an affair so adroitly managed, to effect that object? Time, the unthanked and patient solver of all difficulties, was speedy with his answer.

The last day of the devoted Girondists, or at least of all that had remained to brave their fate in Paris, had arrived, and the notary found himself suddenly and inextricably entangled and borne along by the eager crowds who were hastening to witness the closing scene in the lives of the young, the eloquent, the brave, who had sought to govern France by rounded periods and choice moral maxims; and to hear them, in imitation of the Indian of the American prairies, sing their defiant death-song in half-real, half-simulated scorn of their merciless foes. so soon themselves to tread the same dark path to a **yet** darker eternity! Philippe Armand, though heart-sick at the sad spectacle, remained spell-bound to the spot till the last head of that day's batch of victims had been shorn away by Samson's dripping knife; and then, dizzy and faint with horror and excitement, moved hastily away. His sudden move-ment, as he turned, displaced the hat and wig of a man standing close behind, and, like himself, ap-parently absorbed, fascinated, by the terrible drama which had just been enacted. As the man quickly withdrew his attention from the reeking scaffold to readjust his hat and wig, their eyes met, and a glance of mutual recognition was instantaneously ex-changed. The countenance of the stranger changed in a moment to a chalky whiteness, and it seemed that he would have fallen, had not the notary, with ready presence of mind, passed his arm through his, and said, "Come, let us walk home together."

Not another word passed between Armand and the stranger till they had gained the former's do-micile, and then, having carefully shut the door, the notary abruptly addressed his trembling com-panion.

"That displacement of your wig, Count Duvernay, was awkward, and might have been fatal."

"True, Monsieur Armand. I was involved in the crowd, and forced, much against my will, to witness that scene of unutterable horror, fearing as I did to attract attention by very strenuous efforts to escape. But why have you brought me here?"

"Listen, Count Duvernay: I can save your life, and *will*, on one condition."

"Name—name it!" gasped the count.

" I am about to do so.   Last Tuesday evening five weeks the Abbé Bonjeau married, at your residence, Eugène Duvernay to Estelle St. Ange of the Palais Royal."

"But Eugène is a minor: the marriage was an illegal one—— "

"I am quite aware, Count Duvernay," interrupted the notary in a peremptory tone, "that chicanery may hereafter avail to annul the marriage ; and that result I am determined, for reasons of my own, to prevent if possible."

"Oh, my son informed me that you and Mademoiselle St. Ange were—— "

"Never mind what your son informed you.   Here are, in a word, my terms : I will procure you a passport, furnish you with a supply of money—in short, enable you to leave France—on condition that you immediately sign a formal declaration, which I will draw up, reciting the date, names of the priest and witnesses, and that the marriage was celebrated with your full knowledge and consent."

"But, Monsieur Armand—— "

"It is useless to waste words. Either your attested signature to such a paper, or the guillotine: take your choice. I *know* you connived at your son's baseness; and either I will foil you both, or you touch on your last hour. You consent? It is well."

The notary seated himself at his desk, and for the next quarter of an hour was occupied in drawing up a formal document to the effect he had indicated.

" At what hour did the marriage take place?"

" About seven in the evening."

The notary rang a bell which stood on the table, and a clerk appeared at the door. "Call Henri: I wish you both to witness this gentleman's signature."

In a few minutes the necessary formalities were completed, and the clerks retired.

"Which route do you propose to take?"

" That of Rouen: I have friends in the neighbourhood, who would favour my embarkation for England."

" You shall have a passport for that place. In the mean time take this rouleau of gold."

" How shall I express my thanks—my gratitude?

" You owe me none. Be careful not to stir out of this apartment till I return: I shall not be long."

The necessary papers were, by the notary's influence at the Hôtel de Ville, speedily procured; Count Duvernay reached Rouen in safety, and, after some delay, embarked in the night for England, where, however, he was destined never to arrive. A few weeks afterwards, it was ascertained that he had perished at sea.

Madame Colardeau, whose utterly ruined business left her indeed no choice, gathered together the scanty wrecks of her property, and, with Estelle, engaged lodgings at a respectable farmhouse distant about seven miles from Paris; and there her niece was in due time confined of a daughter. Of her husband Estelle heard nothing directly; but just previous to leaving Paris, a sum of eight hundred francs in gold was left at Madame Colardeau's, directed to her as Madame Duvernay, accompanied by a written intimation that the same sum would be supplied quarterly, provided no attempt was made to ascertain the name of the sender, whom, it was stated, a discovery might seriously compromise.

Estelle and her aunt—who had by this time ascertained that Eugène Duvernay had not, as his abandoned wife at first suspected, perished on the revolutionary scaffold—beheld in this anxious provision for their needs a conclusive proof that the charge of repudiating or ignoring the marriage, brought against him by Philippe Armand, was thoroughly false; and with a spirit fortified by the sweet consciousness of being still hedged in and sheltered by the tutelary care of him to whom she had given her heart, Estelle awaited with patient resignation the coming on of the happy time which should restore her husband to his family and his country.

Many wearing years had passed away; her aunt's

locks were white with age, and the little Estelle had grown up into a graceful, intelligent girl, when a note arrived by post at Sans-Souci farmhouse, informing Madame, now Countess Duvernay, that her husband, Count Duvernay—the father, it was stated, had been long since dead—had accepted the Emperor's permission to return to France ; and had, in fact, arrived and retaken possession of the Hôtel Duvernay. The handwriting of the note was evidently that of the person who transmitted their quarterly stipend ; and the writer suggested the necessity of the Countess Duvernay presenting herself, accompanied by her aunt, to her husband on that very evening.

Flurried, bewildered, terrified, hoping, yet dreading, to verify the announcement so suddenly made, Estelle, arrayed in her richest attire, and accompanied by her daughter and Madame Colardeau, set off about evening in a hired *fiacre* towards Paris.

Count Duvernay was seated in a magnificent drawing-room of the Hôtel Duvernay, laughing and chatting with some military friends on the subject of his return, of the restoration of his property—which, luckily for him, had escaped being "nationalized" —the apparent favour of the Emperor, and the rich and handsome wife already selected for him, when the door of the apartment flew open, and "Madame la Comtesse Duvernay" was loudly announced.

"*Comment!*" exclaimed the count, jumping up. "What is the meaning of this ?"

"It is I—it is Estelle, dear Eugène," said his wife, staggering forwards, and scarcely able to stand; "and this is our daughter!"

The count started back in dismay and confusion. "You—I—wife! The woman must be mad," he added, regaining by a powerful effort his self-control. "Who admitted this person?" he sternly demanded of the bewildered servants. Estelle stood for an instant as if unconscious of, or rather as if unable to comprehend, the meaning of his words; and then, as if the full sense of the count's perfidy had suddenly struck, as with a dagger, to her heart, uttered a piercing scream, and would have fallen prostrate on the floor but for the supporting arms of a gentleman who had followed her into the room.

"Take her, good madame," said the gentleman, addressing Madame Colardeau; "I cannot now sustain even her slight burden. Place her on the sofa."

"And who, in the devil's name, are you?" demanded the count fiercely.

"Philippe Armand, public notary, at your service," quietly replied the gentleman, as he turned and confronted the enraged nobleman.

The count's eye quailed before the steady gaze of the notary, and he muttered something about remembering that a silly, illegal ceremony had in his boyhood passed between the lady and himself.

"You mistake, Count Duvernay," coolly replied

Philippe Armand; "it was a perfectly legal marriage, as this copy of a formal declaration made by your estimable father, and supported by the evidence of Madame Colardeau, will amply testify."

The rage of the count, after perusing the paper presented to him, was terrific; and a violent altercation, to which Estelle, who had speedily recovered consciousness, listened with breathless attention, ensued between him and the notary. The film by which she had been so long blinded fell gradually from her eyes, and Eugène Duvernay and Philippe Armand stood at last plainly revealed in their true colours.

"Let us leave this house," she exclaimed, rising from the couch, and, though pale as marble, and trembling convulsively, speaking in a firm voice. "Come! God bless and reward you, Philippe," she added, seizing his hand, and wringing it with passionate energy; "and if you can, pity and forgive me."

The gossips of Paris had full employment for several succeeding days with the numerous versions of the sudden discovery of a Countess Duvernay, which flew from mouth to mouth. The count consulted men of law, and, to his infinite chagrin, was informed that the marriage could not be impugned. The affair, favourably, because truly represented, reached the ear of the Empress Josephine, and, through her influence, Napoleon issued a command in the guise of counsel, that the matter should be at once equitably arranged. Estelle of course declined living with a husband who had endeavoured to repudiate her, and a division of the count's property was made, by which affluence was secured to herself and a splendid succession to her daughter, whose guardianship she was permitted to retain. The count served several years in the French armies, and rose to high rank. He was killed at Montereau; and Estelle took possession of the Hôtel Duvernay, where she long resided with her early-widowed daughter and amiable grandchildren.

About a fortnight after the return of Count Duvernay to Paris, and consequent legal confirmation of his marriage with Estelle St. Ange, Philippe Armand lay upon his bed a dying man. The last rites of the church had been administered, the priest had retired, and the flagging pulse of life, rapidly becoming feebler and more indistinct, falteringly announced that a spirit chastened by affliction was about to return to God who gave it.

"It is growing late and dark," he faintly muttered, "and still she does not come."

The darkness was in his own eyes, for the autumn sun was still high above the horizon.

"It is but three o'clock," answered the attendant in a low soft voice; "and there has been scarcely time since your message reached her."

The sound of carriage-wheels arrested the words

of the speaker; presently, light, hasty steps ascended the stairs, and Estelle, her daughter, and Madame Colardeau, entered the death-chamber.

" Philippe, best, kindest, truest friend," exclaimed the Countess Duvernay, clasping his white, thin hand, and bathing it with tears, " would I might bid you live for me!"

" Beloved Estelle," murmured the dying man, and a smile, as of parting sunlight, irradiated his pale features, " I *have* lived for you, and, that life-task accomplished, am now well content to die. Farewell, beloved, till we meet in heaven!" He was gone.

THE CAPTAIN'S STORY.

In the neighbourhood of the Haymarket, London, there are several minor chess, whist, and gossip clubs, held principally at cafés, in an apartment which, for club evenings, is sacred to the members, consisting chiefly of superannuated clerks, actors, and other professional mediocrities, with a sprinkling of substantial, steady tradesmen. In one of these modest gatherings Captain Smith, an extremely communicative and anecdotical gentleman, may occasionally be met with, surrounded by an attentive circle of admiring friends, listening with all their ears to one of the many marvellous adventures it has been his lot to encounter during a wandering and varied life. He is not a frequent visitor; his tastes inclining him to scenes of more boisterous conviviality than cigars and coffee, with a seasoning of theatrical and political gossip, can afford or supply; and he accordingly uses these, to him hum-drum assemblies, only as resting or halting-places between more exciting orgies; valuable chiefly for affording him listeners, much more easily amused and astonished than men of larger life-adventure and experience. He is, however, a *real* captain, and I fancy something of a hero too, in the conventional use of the term, as he seems to have very different, and, I believe, much truer notions of war and glory, than gentlemen who shout about " bright swords," and dilate with periphrastic unction of "red battle-fields." A lithe active man is he; and stiff as a ramrod withal. His harsh stubbly hair is brushed in one particular direction with parade precision; and his high bald forehead, when in convivial mood, glistens as brightly as his sharp grey eyes, which, one can see with half a one, have been wide open all his life. He rose, it is understood, though he never mentions it himself —perhaps from a feeling of modesty, a quality, albeit. in which, like most field heroes, he is somewhat deficient—from the ranks. From his perfect knowledge of the Spanish tongue (he passed his youth at Gibraltar, with occasional trips to the Spanish coast with his father, who turned an honest penny in the smuggling line), he was frequently employed during the Peninsular war by the British commanders in the very necessary, but extremely ticklish, duty of making himself *personally* acquainted with the state of the French camps and fortresses—in other words, as a *spy;* an exceedingly uncomfortable office for any gentleman troubled with " nerves." Captain Smith frequently thanks God he never had any, to his knowledge, in his life; no more, he sometimes says, after reading the debates—no more than a member of Parliament.

Thus much premised, suppose we step in for a minute, and make his acquaintance. That is the captain with his back to the fire. The gentleman who has just handed him a cigar, and is addressing such martial queries to the old campaigner, is a neighbouring haberdasher. Just before we entered, he inquired, as is his nightly wont, if the waiter was sure the clock was quite right. He is always a little nervous about the time, as his spouse is apt to be unpleasantly lively for a lady of her colloquial and other prowess, if he is not at home at half-past ten precisely. He loves peace " at home," as much as he seems to delight in war " abroad," and is consequently extremely punctual. But see, Tape is tapping the captain again. The veteran cannot fail to flow forth presently; at first, perhaps, a little jerkingly—*glug, glug, glug*—but, after a little coaxing, in the freest, easiest style imaginable.

" A splendid march, Captain Smith, that of Wellington upon Ciudad Rodrigo ?"

" Sloppy, Mr. Tape, sloppy; nothing but mud, and snow, and slush. Winter-time; I remember it well," replied Captain Smith.

" Beautiful account Napier gives of it," rejoined the martial Tape. " Wellington," he says, "jumped on the devoted fortress with both his feet!"

" Does Napier say that?" demanded the veteran,

knocking the consumed ashes off the end of his cigar on the mantelpiece. "*Does* Napier say that?"

"Yes, indeed he does."

"Then Napier tells what is——" replied the matter-of-fact captain. "The lightest, longest-legged of the 'Light Bobs' couldn't have done it, much less the duke. The duke's short in the legs—sits high in the saddle, though—long body, dumpy legs. Could no more do it than he could fly; didn't try either. All a flam!"

Mr. Tape explained that the jumping was metaphorical; and after a time, Captain Smith seemed to have acquired a misty notion of what was meant. Still, it was, he said, a very bad way of writing "history;" which species of composition should, he emphatically observed, be all facts, and no mistakes.

"The retreat from Burgos was a masterly affair," persisted warrior Tape; "masterly indeed—uncommon!"

"I dare say it was; and as you seem to admire it so much, I wish you had been one of the 'prentices under the master, just to see how it was done, and how agreeable and pleasant such a masterly job is to the people that do the work. I was one of them; and I declare to you I had much rather have been in this café, smoking this abominable cigar which *won't* smoke"—and the captain threw the unsatisfactory weed into the fire; immediately, however, accepting another from the ready hand of the obsequious Tape.

That, fortunately, drew uncommonly well; the spiral columns ascended with the fulness and freedom in which the veteran loved to luxuriate. He swallowed his *demi-tasse* at a gulp; and his sharp grey eyes, twinkling with fresh lustre, said—"It was in coming from Burgos that I got into one of the miserablest scrapes I ever experienced in my life; and all owing to my tender-heartedness, the very worst thing for a campaign a man can carry about him."

"Tell us, captain! What was it? How was it?" cried half-a-dozen voices.

Two elderly gentlemen, who had been playing draughts for the previous four or five hours, finding it impossible, amidst so much clamour, to bestow the requisite attention on their extremely intellectual game, also drew near to listen, as the very best thing, after draughts, they could do.

Captain Smith smiled graciously, seated himself, indulged in a few prefatory whiffs, and proceeded :—

"During the many journeys I at different times made through the province of Leon in Spain, I fell in with a very worthy couple, whom I took a great liking to. Pedro Davila was by trade a cooper: he made all the casks and tubs for miles round the little town near which he lived, which was situated, I should tell you, a good deal out of the direct road, or rather the nearest road—for there is nothing very direct in that country—from Burgos to Astorga. For my part, I preferred roundabout ways at that time to straight ones; I found them safer. Pedro had a nice garden, too, beautifully cultivated, and the prettiest little black-eyed Andalusian wife—Pedro was also a native of the south of Spain—a man's eyes ever lighted upon. Pedro in his youth had taken service with a Spanish grandee, who, being compelled to fly his country—a common, every-day thing abroad—took up his abode in Paris; and there Pedro got rid of his fine old constitutional prejudices against foreigners, and obtained in exchange some modern universal philanthropy—about the most dangerous article to go to market with in Spain it is possible to imagine. And sure I am that if Pedro had known what a dreadful mess his turning philosopher would get *me* into, to say nothing of his wife, he was far too good a fellow to have done anything of the sort."

"But what on earth, Captain Smith," interrupted Tape, "could philosophy, Pedro's, or any one's else, have to do with you?"

"You will hear, Tape: it was his liberal-mindedness and my tender-heartedness joined together that played the mischief with us both. An excellent fellow, notwithstanding," continued the captain, after a brief pause, "was Pedro Davila; *too* good for a Spaniard, much: one could hardly believe it of him. I was going to say he was equal to an Englishman; but that, perhaps, would be pushing it *too* far. Many a skin of wine have we emptied together:

none of the sloe stuff you get here, but the genuine juice of the grape itself."

The captain smacked his lips at the pleasing reminiscence, and then, to reward them for the exercise, imbibed a portion of another *demi-tasse*, craftily qualified to his taste.

"At the time I speak of, it was highly dangerous to harbour, succour, or conceal any French man, woman, or child. Death, or worse punishment, was pretty sure to be the doom of any one offending against the law of vengeance; and it happened that one of the most ferocious of minor guerilla leaders, a relentless hunter and slayer of miserable fugitives, was Ramez, a native of the village or town near which Pedro lived. He was seldom long absent from home, and was, in fact, the real governor of the place.

Well, it chanced one unfortunate day that a wounded French officer, who had been chased for several days by Ramez and his fellows, crawled into Pedro's cottage, and implored shelter and succour. His request was, as you may anticipate, after what I have told you of Pedro's notions of philosophy, granted; and the hunted man was successfully concealed, carefully tended, and restored to health. The day of his departure had arrived; he was carefully disguised, mounted on Pedro's mule, and was just bidding his benefactor good-bye at the garden gate 'Marietta, fortunately, as it turned out, was not at home), when who should poke up his diabolical snout from the other side of the hedge but Ramez! The ugliest rascal, gentlemen," continued Captain Smith, with violent emphasis, " the most ill-favoured scoundrel I ever saw in my life was Ramez; and that from a man who has been twenty years in the army, and who has lived upwards of twenty in London, is saying a great deal."

This was quite cheerfully assented to. The ugliness that after such a lengthened and first-rate experience bore off the palm, was pronounced necessarily incomparable by the entire auditory.

" He gave poor Pedro," continued the captain, "one most diabolical look (I'll be bound the streaks from his eyes—he always squinted both sides inwards when he was in a passion—crossed each other within an inch of his nose), then rushed forward, and bawled lustily for help. The Frenchman spurred furiously into the adjoining forest, and escaped. Pedro was seized, and the alpha and omega of it, as the chaplain of the old half-hundredth used to say, was, that he was lugged to prison, tried a few hours afterwards, and condemned to death as a traitor. It was a wild time in Spain then : most places managed their own affairs in their own way, and this was Master Ramez' and the alcalde's way. Pedro was to have been strangled, *garrotted* they call it, but there was no apparatus handy, and nobody that particularly liked the job; so, as a particularly heavenly grace to him, the alcalde said, it was determined he should be shot on the third day after his arrest.

" It happened," resumed the captain, after again refreshing himself, " that I was, on the very day after Pedro's arrest and condemnation, returning from Burgos to General Picton's head-quarters, a good way beyond Astorga ; and being near, and in no very particular hurry, I turned out of my road to visit Pedro. When I arrived at the cottage, I found things, as you may suppose, in a very different state from what I had been imagining for the last hour or so. Instead of wine, there was hysterics ; and for an omelette and salad, shrieks and faintings. Marietta clung round my neck with tremendous energy—I should not have thought, if I had not experienced it, that a pretty woman's embrace could have been so very unpleasant—frantically beseeching me to send for the British army to liberate her Pedro. Extricating myself from her grasp as speedily as possible, I began to cast about in my mind as to what could be done ; but I could not at all clear up my ideas. Remembering that I never had been able to do so on a lean stomach, I suggested that we should first dine, and then, perhaps, I might hit upon something for poor Pedro's benefit. Marietta agreed with me ; and we had, considering that her husband and my dearest friend was to be shot the day after the next, a very nice comfortable dinner indeed—very—and some capital wine afterwards; and then, gentlemen, the father of mischief, or the wine, or Marietta's black eyes, I don't know which, perhaps all together, induced me to make as spoony a proposal as ever fell from the lips of a green cockney."

"There are clever, sensible men in the city," interjected Tape, as the captain paused an instant to supply himself with a fresh cigar.

"Perhaps so, Mr. Tape, but those gentlemen seldom volunteer into the army, I believe. I knew," said the veteran, continuing his narrative, "that I might as well whistle jigs to a milestone, and expect it to get up and turn partners, as ask the general in command of the division, about forty miles off, to rescue Pedro from the grasp of the Spanish authorities. The British generals never meddled with the administration of Spanish justice under any pretence whatever; but I also knew that if he received a message stating that *I* was in danger, he was bound by general orders to afford me every assistance in his power. 'Marietta,' said I at last—the wine *must* have been unusually strong—'I have hit upon it. We'll save Pedro yet, in spite of them all!' The pretty creature jumped up, clapped her hands, and, sobbing, laughing, and talking all in a breath, exclaimed, 'Dear Inglese, I knew you would!' 'You, Marietta,' said I, as soon as she was sufficiently calm to listen, 'go to Ramez and the alcalde, and tell

them you will deliver into their hands the famous
Afrancesado spy, Henriquez Bajol, on condition of
their releasing Pedro. If they consent, denounce
me.' 'You, Henriquez?' said she, staring bewilderedly. 'Never you mind,' I replied: 'a note to
General Picton—I'll write it at once—will soon get
me out of their clutches, whoever I am.' I wrote the
note and gave it her. 'Now mind, Marietta,' said I,
solemnly, 'that Pedro sets off with this note the
instant he is liberated. How soon can he reach
the general on foot?' 'By to-morrow night,' she
answered. 'Very well; and now then, about it at
once.' She was off in a twinkling, and I was at
leisure to reflect on what I had done. To tell the
truth, I did not, after a few minutes' quiet cogitation,
feel excessively comfortable. They would be certain
to believe the story; Henriquez being, I was sure,
known to none of them personally. I was a precious deal more like a Spaniard then than an Englishman; and I spoke the language so well—not alto.
gether grammatically, it is true, but so like a native
of the south of Spain—that I felt I should have some
difficulty, should occasion require it, to undeceive
them. Then they had such a pestilent way of making not only sure but *short* work with whoever they
suspected of commerce with the hated French, that
it flashed unpleasantly across my mind—the general's
help might, perchance, arrive too late! However, I
was in for it; and so, taking another draught of

wine, and refilling my pipe—there's great philosophy in a pipe, as we all know—I awaited the result of my charming scheme as calmly as I could.

"It was not long coming. About half an hour after Marietta's departure the door was slammed open, and I found myself sprawling and kicking, or rather sprawling and trying to kick, for they wouldn't let me, in the arms of five or six ugly rascals, who, showering upon me all the time the vilest abuse, hurried me off to prison. Into it they thrust me like a dog; and there, when I could recover breath and speech, I greeted Pedro, my fellow-prisoner. The alcalde and Ramez had only *promised* to release him, and of course, when the object was gained, refused to abide by the bargain. If I had not been the most consummate ass that ever browsed or brayed, I might have guessed as much. Ramez had now two victims, and that promised a *double* holiday.

"Well, gentlemen, this was, you may suppose, a very unpleasant situation to find myself in; but as, thank Heaven, I was never much troubled with nerves, I did not so much mind it after a bit. Marietta, I was sure, would be off to the general with her best speed when she saw the ugly turn matters were taking; so that, if my captors were not in a very patriotic hurry indeed, there was a chance on the cards yet. Pedro obtained some cigars of the jailor, an old acquaintance of his; they were first-rate, and we both became gradually calm and composed. Ah, gentlemen, I have often thought that if the moral observations I addressed that evening to my friend Pedro, upon the duty of respecting national prejudices, particularly with regard to sheltering wounded foreigners, and the shocking folly of making rash engagements with young women, especially after dinner, had been taken down by a short-hand writer, they would have raised me to the next rank after Solomon!"

"No doubt of it," said Tape, looking nervously at the clock: "but do get on, captain; don't stop, *don't!*"

"I will not, Tape; but don't you hurry me as they did. Well, the next day I was dragged before the alcalde and that rascal Ramez, where, to my very great and most unpleasant surprise, two men, guerilla soldiers, swore that they had frequently seen me in communication with the French outposts, and that they verily believed me to be no other than the infamous Henriquez. Vainly I protested, finding the thing was getting much too serious, that I was an English officer; my assertions were laughed at, and I was reconveyed to my dungeon, after having heard myself sentenced to be shot at the same hour which was to see the last of Pedro. Mr. Tape, please to touch the bell. I'll take another cup, for my tongue always feels dry and hot when I come to this part of the story."

Mr. Tape did as he was desired quickly, and bade the waiter who answered the summons "jump about." The anxious haberdasher had but just three minutes to spare.

"That, gentlemen," continued the captain, "was a very uncomfortable night. I was never, from a child, particularly fond of water-drinking; but I remember crawling off the straw many times during the night, and almost emptying *both* pitchers. At ten o'clock we were to suffer, to be shot to death by half-a-dozen rusty muskets. It was dreadfully aggravating! Day dawned at last; six, seven, eight, nine, *ten* o'clock tinkled through the jail; the door opened, and in stalked Ramez and the alcalde, followed by the rusty shooting-party. We were politely informed that 'time' was up, and that we must both come to the scratch at once, as the spectators didn't like to be kept waiting. They then kindly pinioned us, and away we marched. You never, perhaps, walked in your own funeral procession, Tape, did you?"

"Lord, Captain Smith, how can you ask such a horrid question?"

Well, if you ever should, you'll remember it, that's all. Seeing King Lear is nothing to it, though that's reckoned pretty deep. On we marched, the priests praying, the bells tolling, and the infernal musket-men eyeing us as if to make up their minds exactly where to have the pleasure of hitting us. One scoundrel with a short, ugly snub of an apology of a nose, meant, I could see, to send his bullet through my Roman. Altogether, it was the most disagreeable walk I ever took in my life. We soon arrived at the place of sacrifice, and were ordered to kneel down. 'Pedro,' said I, 'that jewel of a wife of yours has played us a sweet trick ; but perhaps she'll arrive in time, if she comes at all, to return thanks for all the good things we are about to receive ; and that's a consolation any way.' I then took another look in the direction in which the expected succour *ought* to appear, when I saw, and tried to rub my eyes with my elbows to make sure I saw, but couldn't, a horsewoman on the summit of the hill it *was* Marietta ! I roared out like a raging bull, and Pedro gave chorus. As soon as Marietta caught sight of what was going on, she curbed her horse sharply back, and beckoned with eager gestures over the hill. A minute afterwards the ridge was crowned by half a regiment of British dragoons. The instant they saw us, they gave one loud cheer, and came on like a whirlwind.

" ' A narrow escape, Smith,' said the commanding officer. ' But come, mount at once. There is a large French force in the neighbourhood, and the general's orders are not to halt an instant.' I was delighted to hear it. The less said was, I felt, the soonest mended. If the general, thought I, were informed *why* he had been put to this trouble and risk, our meeting would scarcely be a very amicable one.

'Who is this?' said the officer, pointing to Pedro, who, though he hallooed lustily, was by no means yet out of the wood. 'One of ours,' I boldly replied. 'Then mount, my good fellow, at once, replied he, motioning to one of the led horses. Pedro understood the gesture, though he didn't the language; and giving Marietta, who had unpinioned him, one hug, was in the saddle in a jiffy. 'Out of the way,' cried the commanding officer to the alcalde, who, instigated by Ramez, was approaching to claim Pedro at least as lawful prize—'out of the way, fellow!' and he struck him sharply with the flat of his sword. The frightened functionary tumbled out of our path; the bugle sounded, and we were off, safe, sound, and merry."

" Bravo!—hurrah!—hurrah!" resounded in irregular chorus through the room. Tape was off like a shot: the unfortunate man was full seven minutes behind his time.

" Gentlemen," said Captain Smith, after the applause had subsided, "do not, if you please, forget the moral of my story. Everything, the chaplain used to say, has a useful moral—even short rations —though I never could agree with him to that extent. The moral of this adventure I take to be this—*Never, under any circumstances, assume to be what you are not; for if shot or hanged in a wrong character, you will never be able to amend the 'errors of description.'*"

THE POINT OF HONOUR.

One evening in the autumn of the year 1842, seven persons, including myself, were sitting and chatting in a state of hilarious gaiety in front of Senor Arguellas' country-house, a mile or so out of Santiago de Cuba, in the Eastern Intendencia of the Queen of the Antilles, and once its chief capital, when an incident occurred that as effectually put an extinguisher upon the noisy mirth, as if a bomb-shell had suddenly exploded at our feet. But first a brief account of those seven persons, and the cause of their being so assembled, will be necessary.

Three were American merchants—Southerners and smart traders, extensively connected with the commerce of the Colombian Archipelago, and designing to sail on the morrow, wind and weather permitting, in the bark *Neptune*—Starkey, master and part owner—for Morant Bay, Jamaica; one was a lieutenant in the Spanish artillery, and nephew of our host; another was a M. Dupont, a young and rich creole, of mingled French and Spanish parentage, and the reputed suitor for the hand of Donna Antonia, the daughter and sole heiress of Senor Arguellas, and withal a graceful and charming maiden of eighteen—a ripe age in that precocious clime; the sixth guest was Captain Starkey, of the *Neptune*, a gentlemanly, fine-looking English seaman of about thirty years of age; the seventh and last was myself, at that time a mere youngster, and but just recovered from a severe fit of sickness which a twelvemonth previously had necessitated my removal from Jamaica to the much more temperate and equable climate of Cuba, albeit the two islands are only distant about five degrees from each other. I was also one of Captain Starkey's passengers, and so was Senor Arguellas, who had business to wind up in Kingston. He was to be accompanied by Senora Arguellas, Antonia, the young lieutenant, and M. Dupont. The *Neptune* had brought a cargo of sundries, consisting of hardware, cottons, *etcetera*, to Cuba, and was returning about half laden with goods. Amongst these, belonging to the American merchants, was a number of barrels of gunpowder that had proved unsaleable in Cuba, and which, it was thought, might find a satisfactory market in Jamaica. There was excellent cabin accommodation on board Captain Starkey's vessel, and as the weather was fine, and the passage promised to be a brief as well as pleasant one—the wind having shifted to the north-west, with the intention, it seemed, of remaining there for some time—we were all, as I have stated, in exceedingly good humour, and discussing the intended trip, Cuban, American, and European politics, the comparative merits of French and Spanish wines, and Havannah and Alabama cigars, with infinite glee and gusto.

The evening, too, was deliciously bright and clear. The breeze, pronounced by Captain Starkey to be rising to a five or six knot one at sea, only sufficiently stirred the rich and odorous vegetation of the valleys, stretching far away beneath us, gently to fan the heated faces of the party with its grateful perfume, and slightly ripple the winding rivers, rivulets rather, which everywhere intersect and irrigate the island, and which were now glittering with the myriad splendours of the intensely-lustrous stars that diadem a Cuban night. Nearly all the guests had drunk very freely of wine, too much so, indeed; but the talk, in French, which all could speak tolerably, did not profane the calm glory of the scene till some time after Senora Arguellas and her daughter had left us. The senor, I should state, was still detained in town by business which it was necessary he should dispose of previous to embarking for Jamaica.

"Do not go away," said Senora Arguellas, addressing Captain Starkey, as she rose from her seat, " till I see you again. When you are at leisure, ring the *sonnette* on the table, and a servant will inform me. I wish to speak further with you relative to the cabin arrangements."

Captain Starkey bowed. I had never, I thought, seen Antonia smile so sweetly; and the two ladies left us. I do not precisely remember how it came about, or what first led to it, but it was not very long before we were all conscious that the conversation had assumed a disagreeable tone. It struck me that possibly M. Dupont did not like the expression of Antonia's face as she curtsied to Captain Starkey. The after unpleasantness did not, however, arise ostensibly from that cause. The commander of the *Neptune* had agreed to take several free coloured families to Jamaica, where the services of the men, who were reputed to be expert at sugar-cultivation, had been engaged at much higher wages than could be obtained in Cuba. The American gentlemen had previously expressed disapprobation of this arrangement, and now began to be very liberal indeed with their taunts and sneers relative to Captain Starkey's "negro principles," as they pleasantly termed that gentleman's very temperate vindication of the right of coloured people to their own souls and bodies. This, however, would, I think, have passed off harmlessly, had it not been that the captain happened to mention, very imprudently, that he had once served as a midshipman on board the English slave squadron. This fanned M. Dupont's smouldering ill-humour into a flame, and I gathered from his confused maledictions that he had suffered in property from the exertions of that force. The storm of angry words raged fiercely. The motives of the English for interfering with the slave-traffic were denounced with contemptuous bitterness on the one side, and as warmly and angrily defended on the other. Finally —the fact is, they were both flustered with wine and passion, and scarcely knew what they said or did— M. Dupont applied an epithet to the Queen of England, which instantly brought a glass of wine full in his face from the hand of Captain Starkey. They were all in an instant on their feet, and apparently sobered, or nearly so, by the unfortunate issue of the wordy tumult.

Captain Starkey was the first to speak. His flushed and angry features paled suddenly to an almost deathly white, and he stammered out: "I beg your pardon, M. Dupont. It was wrong—very wrong in me to do so, though not inexcusable."

"Pardon! *Mille tonnerres!*" shouted Dupont, who was capering about in an ecstasy of rage, and wiping his face with his handkerchief. "Yes, a bullet through your head shall pardon you—nothing less!"

Indeed, according to the then notions of Cuban society, no other alternative save the duello appeared possible. Lieutenant Arguellas hurried at once into the house, and speedily returned with a case of pistols. "Let us proceed," he said in a quick whisper, "to the grove yonder; we shall be there free from interruption." He took Dupont's arm, and both turned to move off. As they did so, Mr. Desmond, the elder of the American gentlemen, stepped towards Captain Starkey, who, with recovered calmness, and with his arms folded, was standing by the table, and said, " I am not entirely, my good sir, a stranger to these affairs, and if I can be of service I shall——"

" Thank you, Mr. Desmond," replied the English captain ; " but I shall not require your assistance. Lieutenant Arguellas, you may as well remain. I am no duellist, and shall not fight M. Dupont."

" What does he say ? " exclaimed the lieutenant, gazing with stupid bewilderment round the circle. " Not fight ! "

The Anglo-Saxon blood, I saw, flushed as hotly in the veins of the Americans as it did in mine at this exhibition of the white feather by one of our race. " Not fight, Captain Starkey ! " said Mr. Desmond with grave earnestness after a painful pause ; " you whose name is in the list of the British royal navy, say this ! You must be jesting ! "

" I am perfectly serious—I am opposed to duelling upon principle."

" A coward, upon principle ! " fairly screamed Dupont, with mocking fury, and at the same time shaking his clenched fist at the Englishman.

The degrading epithet stung like a serpent. A gleam of fierce passion broke out of Captain Starkey's dark eyes, and he made a step towards Dupont, but resolutely checked himself.

" Well, it must be borne ! I was wrong to offer

you personal violence, although your impertinence certainly deserved rebuke. Still, I repeat, I will not fight with you."

"But you *shall* give my friend satisfaction!" exclaimed Lieutenant Arguellas, who was as much excited as Dupont; "or, by Heaven, I will post you as a dastard, not only throughout this island, but Jamaica!"

Captain Starkey for all answer to this menace coolly rang the *sonnette*, and desired the slave who answered it to inform Senora Arguellas that he was about to leave, and wished to see her.

"The brave Englishman is about to place himself under the protection of your aunt's petticoats, Alphonso!" shouted Dupont with triumphant mockery.

"I almost doubt whether Mr. Starkey is an Englishman," exclaimed Mr. Desmond, who, as well as his two friends, was getting pretty much incensed; "but, at all events, as my father and mother were born and raised in the old country, if you presume to insinuate that——"

Senora Arguellas at this moment approached, and the irate American with some difficulty restrained himself. The lady appeared surprised at the strange aspect of the company she had so lately left. She, however, at the request of the captain, instantly led the way into the house, leaving the rest of her visitors, as the French say, *plantés là*.

Ten minutes afterwards we were informed that

Captain Starkey had left the house, after impressing upon Senora Arguellas that the *Neptune* would sail the next morning precisely at nine o'clock. A renewed torrent of rage, contempt, and scorn broke forth at this announcement, and a duel at one time seemed inevitable between Lieutenant Arguellas and Mr. Desmond, the last-named gentleman manifesting great anxiety to shoot somebody or other in vindication of his Anglo-Saxon lineage. This, however, was overruled, and the party broke up in angry disorder.

We were all on board by the appointed time on the following morning. Captain Starkey received us with civil indifference, and I noticed that the elaborate sneers which sat upon the countenances of Dupont and the lieutenant did not appear in the slightest degree to ruffle or affect him; but the averted eye and scornful air of Donna Antonia as she passed with Senora Arguellas towards the cabin, drawing her mantilla tightly round her as she swept by, as if—so I, perhaps wrongfully, interpreted the action—it would be soiled by contact with a poltroon, visibly touched him—only, however, for a few brief moments. The expression of pain quickly vanished, and his countenance was as cold and stern as before. There was, albeit, it was soon found, a limit to this, it seemed, contemptuous forbearance. Dupont, approaching him, gave his thought audible expression, exclaiming, loud enough for several of the crew to hear, and looking steadily in the captain's face : "*Lâche !*" He would have turned away, but was arrested by a gripe of steel. "*Ecoutez*, monsieur," said Captain Starkey ; "individually, I hold for nothing whatever you may say ; but I am captain and king in this ship, and I will permit no one to beard me before the crew, and thereby lessen my authority over them. Do you presume again to do so, and I will put you in solitary confinement, perhaps in irons, till we arrive at Jamaica." He then threw off his startled auditor, and walked forwards. The passengers, coloured as well as white, were all on board ; the anchor, already apeak, was brought home ; the bows of the ship fell slowly off, and we were in a few moments running before the wind, though but a faint one, for Point Morant.

No one could be many hours on board the *Neptune* without being fully satisfied that, however deficient in duelling courage her captain might be, he was a thorough seaman, and that his crew—about a dozen of as fine fellows as I have ever seen—were under the most perfect discipline and command. The service of the vessel was carried on as noiselessly and regularly as on board a ship of war; and a sense of confidence that, should a tempest or other sea-peril overtake us, every reliance might be placed in the professional skill and energy of Captain Starkey, was soon openly or tacitly acknowledged by all on board. The weather throughout happily continued fine, but the wind was light and variable, so that, for several

days after we had sighted the blue mountains of
Jamaica, we scarcely appeared sensibly to diminish
the distance between them and us. At last the
breeze again blew steadily from the north-west, and
we gradually neared Point Morant. We passed it,
and opened up the bay at about two o'clock in the
morning, when the voyage might be said to be over.
This was a great relief to the cabin-passengers—far
beyond the ordinary pleasure to land-folk of escap-
ing from the tedium of confinement on shipboard.
There was a constraint in the behaviour of everybody that was exceedingly unpleasant. The captain
presided at table with freezing civility; the conversation, if such it could be called, was usually restricted
to monosyllables; and we were all very heartily glad
that we had eaten our last dinner in the *Neptune*.
When we doubled Point Morant, all the passengers
except myself were in bed, and a quarter of an hour
afterwards Captain Starkey went below, and was soon
busy, I understood, with papers in his cabin. For
my part I was too excited for sleep, and I continued
to pace the deck fore and aft with Hawkins, the first-
mate, whose watch it was, eagerly observant of the
lights on the well-known shore, that I had left so
many months before with but faint hopes of ever
seeing it again. As I thus gazed landward, a bright
gleam, as of crimson moonlight, shot across the dark
sea, and turning quickly round, I saw that it was
caused by a tall jet of flame shooting up from the

main hatchway, which two seamen, for some purpose
or other, had at the moment partially opened. In
my still weak state, the terror of the sight—for the
recollection of the barrels of powder on board flashed
instantly across my mind—for several moments completely stunned me, and but that I caught instinctively at the ratlines, I should have fallen prostrate
on the deck. A wild outcry of "Fire! fire!"—the
most fearful cry that can be heard at sea—mingled with and heightened the dizzy ringing in my
brain, and I was barely sufficiently conscious to discern, amidst the runnings to and fro, and the incoherent exclamations of the crew, the sinewy, athletic
figure of the captain leap up, as it were, from the
companion-ladder to the deck, and with his trumpet-
voice command immediate silence, instantly followed
by the order again to batten down the blazing hatchway. This, with his own assistance, was promptly
effected, and then he disappeared down the forecastle.
The two or three minutes he was gone—it could
scarcely have been more than that—seemed inter-
minable; and so completely did it appear to be
recognized that our fate must depend upon his
judgment and vigour, that not a word was spoken,
nor a finger, I think, moved, till he reappeared,
already scorched and blackened with the fire, and
dragging up what seemed a dead body in his arms.
He threw his burden on the deck, and, passing swiftly
to where Hawkins stood, said in a low, hurried whis-

per, but audible to me: "Run down and rouse the passengers, and bring my pistols from the cabin-locker. Quick! Eternity hangs on the loss of a moment." Then turning to the startled but attentive seamen, he said in a rapid but firm voice: "You well know, men, that I would not on any occasion or for any motive deceive you. Listen, then, attentively. Yon drunken brute—he is Lieutenant Arguellas' servant—has fired with his candle the spirits he was stealing, and the hold is a mass of fire which it is useless to waste one precious moment in attempting to extinguish."

A cry of rage and terror burst from the crew, and they sprang impulsively towards the boats, but the captain's authoritative voice at once arrested their steps. "Hear me out, will you? Hurry and confusion will destroy us all, but with courage and steadiness every soul on board may be saved before the flames can reach the powder. And remember," he added, as he took his pistols from Hawkins and cocked one of them, "that I will send a bullet after any man who disobeys me, and I seldom miss my aim. Now, then, to your work—steadily, and with a will!"

It was marvellous to observe the influence his bold, confident, and commanding bearing and words had upon the men. The panic-terror that had seized them gave place to energetic resolution, and in an incredibly short space of time the boats were in the water. "Well done, my fine fellows! There is plenty of time, I again repeat. Four of you"—and he named them—"remain with me. Three others jump into each of the large boats, two into the small one, and bring them round to the landward side of the ship. A rush would swamp the boats, and we shall be able to keep only one gangway clear."

The passengers were by this time rushing upon deck, half-clad, and in a state of the wildest terror, for they all knew there was a large quantity of gun-powder on board. The instant the boats touched the starboard side of the bark, the men, white as well as coloured, forced their way with fren-zied eagerness before the women and children— careless, apparently, whom they sacrificed so that they might themselves leap to the shelter of the boats from the fiery volcano raging beneath their feet. Captain Starkey, aided by the four athletic seamen he had selected for the duty, hurled them fiercely back. "Back, back!" he shouted. "We must have funeral order here—first the women and children, next the old men. Hand Senora Arguellas along; next the young lady her daughter: quick!"

As Donna Antonia, more dead than alive, was about to be lifted into the boat, a gush of flame burst up through the main-hatchway with the roar of an explosion; a tumultuous cry burst from the frenzied passengers, and they jostled each other with frightful violence in their efforts to reach the gangway. Du pont forced his way through the lane of seamen with the energy of a madman, and pressed so suddenly upon Antonia that, but for the utmost exertion of the captain's herculean strength, she must have been precipitated into the water.

"Back, unmanly dastard! back, dog!" roared Captain Starkey, terribly excited by the lady's danger; and a moment after, seizing Dupont fiercely by the collar, he added, "or if you will, look there but for a moment," and he pointed with his pistol-hand to the fins of several sharks plainly visible in the glaring light at but a few yards' distance from the ship. "Men," he added, "let whoever presses forward out of his turn fall into the water."

"Ay, ay, sir!" was the prompt mechanical response.

This terrible menace instantly restored order; the coloured women and children were next embarked, and the boat appeared full.

"Pull off," was the order; "you are deep enough for safety."

A cry, faint as the wail of a child, arose in the boat. It was heard and understood.

"Stay one moment; pass along Senor Arguellas. Now, then, off with you, and be smart!"

The next boat was quickly loaded; the coloured lads and men, all but one, and the three Americans, went in her.

"You are a noble fellow," said Mr. Desmond,

pausing an instant, and catching at the captain's hand; "and I was but a fool to——"

"Pass on," was the reply; "there is no time to bandy compliments."

The order to shove off had passed the captain's lips when his glance chanced to light upon me, as I leaned, dumb with terror, just behind him against the vessel's bulwarks.

"Hold on a moment!" he cried. "Here is a youngster whose weight will not hurt you;" and he fairly lifted me over, and dropped me gently into the boat, whispering as he did so: "Remember me, Ned, to thy father and mother, should I not see them again."

There was now only the small boat, capable of safely containing but eight persons, and how, it was whispered amongst us—how, in addition to the two seamen already in her, can she take off Lieutenant Arguellas, M. Dupont, the remaining coloured man, the four seamen, and Captain Starkey? They were, however, all speedily embarked except the captain.

"Can she bear another?" he asked, and although his voice was firm as ever, his countenance, I noticed, was ashy pale, yet full as ever of unswerving resolution.

"We must, and will, sir, since it's you; but we are dangerously overcrowded now, especially with yon ugly customers swimming round us."

'Stay one moment; I cannot quit the ship whilst there's a living soul on board." He stepped hastily forward, and presently reappeared at the gangway with the still senseless body of the lieutenant's servant in his arms, and dropped it over the side into the boat. There was a cry of indignation, but it was of no avail. The boat's rope the next instant was cast into the water. "Now pull for your lives!" The oars, from the instinct of self-preservation, instantly fell into the water, and the boat sprang off. Captain Starkey, now that all except himself were clear of the burning ship, gazed eagerly, with eyes shaded with his hand, in the direction of the shore. Presently he hailed the headmost boat. "We must have been seen from the shore long ago, and pilot-boats ought to be coming out, though I don't see any. If you meet one, bid him be smart; there may be a chance yet." All this scene, this long agony, which has taken me so many words to depict very imperfectly from my own recollection, and those of others, only lasted, I was afterwards assured by Mr. Desmond, eight minutes from the embarkation of Senora Arguellas till the last boat left the ill-fated *Neptune*.

Never shall I forget the frightful sublimity of the spectacle presented by that flaming ship, the sole object, save ourselves, discernible amidst the vast and heaving darkness, if I may use the term, of the night and ocean, coupled as it was with the dreadful thought that the heroic man to whose firmness and presence of mind we all owed our safety was inevitably doomed to perish. We had not rowed more than a couple of hundred yards when the flames, leaping up everywhere through the deck, reached the rigging and the few sails set, presenting a complete outline of the bark and her tracery of masts and yards, drawn in lines of fire! Captain Starkey, not to throw away the chance he spoke of, had gone out to the end of the bowsprit, having first let the jib and foresail go by the run, and was for a brief space safe from the flames; but what was this but a prolongation of the bitterness of death?

The boats continued to increase the distance between them and the blazing ship, amidst a dead silence broken only by the measured dip of the oars; and many an eye was turned with intense anxiety shoreward with the hope of descrying the expected pilot. At length a distinct hail—and I felt my heart stop beating at the sound—was heard ahead, lustily responded to by the seamen's throats, and presently afterwards a swiftly-propelled pilot-boat shot out of the thick darkness ahead, almost immediately followed by another.

" What ship is that ?" cried a man standing in the bows of the first boat.

" The *Neptune,* and that is Captain Starkey on the bowsprit ! "

I sprang eagerly to my feet, and, with all the force I could exert, shouted : " A hundred pounds for the first boat that reaches the ship ! "

"That's young Mr. Mainwaring's face and voice!" exclaimed the foremost pilot. "Hurrah, then, for the prize!" and away both sped with eager vigour, but unaware certainly of the peril of the task. In a minute or so another shore boat came up, but after asking a few questions, and seeing how matters stood, remained, and lightened us of a portion of our living cargoes. We were all three too deep in the water, the small boat perilously so.

Great God! the terrible suspense we all felt whilst this was going forward. I can scarcely bear, even now, to think about it. I shut my eyes, and listened with breathless, palpitating excitement for the explosion that should end all. It came!—at least I thought it did, and I sprang convulsively to my feet. So sensitive was my brain, partly no doubt from recent sickness as well as fright, that I had mistaken the sudden shout of the boats' crews for the dreaded catastrophe. The bowsprit, from the end of which a rope was dangling, was empty! and both pilots, made aware doubtless of the danger, were pulling with the eagerness of fear from the ship. The cheering among us was renewed again and again, during which I continued to gaze with arrested breath and fascinated stare at the flaming vessel and fleeing pilot-boats. Suddenly a pyramid of flame shot up from the hold of the ship, followed by a deafening roar. I fell, or was knocked down, I know not which; the boat rocked as if caught in a fierce eddy; next came the hiss and splash of numerous heavy bodies falling from a great height into the water; and then the blinding glare and stunning uproar were succeeded by a soundless silence and a thick darkness, in which no man could discern his neighbour. The stillness was broken by a loud cheerful hail from one of the pilot-boats : we recognized the voice, and the simultaneous and ringing shout which burst from us assured the gallant seaman of our own safety, and how exultingly we all rejoiced in his. Half an hour afterwards we were safely landed ; and as the ship and cargo had been specially insured, the only ultimate evil result of this fearful passage in the lives of the passengers and crew of the *Neptune* was a heavy loss to the underwriters.

A piece of plate, at the suggestion of Mr. Desmond and his friends, was subscribed for and presented to Captain Starkey at a public dinner given at Kingston in his honour—a circumstance that many there will remember. In his speech on returning thanks for the compliment paid him, he explained his motive for resolutely declining to fight a duel with M. Dupont, half-a-dozen versions of which had got into the newspapers. " I was very early left an orphan," he said, "and was very tenderly reared by a maternal aunt, Mrs. ——." (He mentioned a name with which hundreds of newspaper readers in England must still be familiar.)

" Her husband — as many here may be aware—fell in a duel in the second month of wedlock. My aunt continued to live dejectedly on till I had passed my nineteenth year ; and so vivid an impression did the patient sorrow of her life make on me—so thoroughly did I learn to loathe and detest the barbarous practice that consigned her to a premature grave, that it scarcely required the solemn promise she obtained from me, as the last sigh trembled on her lips, to make me resolve never, under any circumstances, to fight a duel. As to my behaviour during the unfortunate conflagration of the *Neptune*, which my friend Mr. Desmond has spoken of so flatteringly, I can only say that I did no more than my simple duty in the matter. Both he and I belong to a maritime race, one of whose most peremptory maxims is that the captain must be the last man to quit or give up his ship. Besides, I must have been the veriest dastard alive to have quailed in the presence of — of—that is, in the presence of—circumstances which—in point of fact—that is——" Here Captain Starkey blushed and boggled sadly : he was evidently no orator ; but whether it was the sly significance of Senor Arguellas' countenance, which just then happened to be turned towards him, or the glance he threw at the gallery where Senora Arguellas' grave placidity and Donna Antonia's bright eyes and blushing cheeks encountered him, that so completely put him out, I cannot say ; but he continued to stammer painfully, although the company cheered and laughed with great vehemence and uncommon good-humour in order to give him time. He could not recover himself; and after floundering about through a few more unintelligible sentences sat down, evidently very hot and uncomfortable, though amidst a little hurricane of hearty cheers and hilarious laughter.

I have but a few more words to say. Captain Starkey has been long settled at the Havannah; and Donna Antonia has been just as long Mrs. Starkey. Three little Starkeys have to my knowledge already come to town, and the captain is altogether a rich and prosperous man; but though apparently permanently domiciled in a foreign country, he is, I am quite satisfied, as true an Englishman, and as loyal a subject of Queen Victoria, as when he threw the glass of wine in the Cuban creole's face. I don't know what has become of Dupont; and, to tell the truth, I don't much care. Lieutenant Arguellas has attained the rank of major: at least, I suppose he must be the Major Arguellas officially reported to be slightly wounded in the late Lopez buccaneering affair. And I also am pretty well now, thank you!

THE DARK CHAMBER.

Not very long ago there dwelt at Brookdale, a sunny spot of Warwickshire, one of the prettiest, merriest maidens, Phœbe Morris by name, that ever danced upon a green sward, or broke the susceptible hearts of a quiet pastoral and agricultural village. The neatest, smartest, handiest dairymaid in the county, she nevertheless created at times such dire confusion, heart-burnings, and jealousies amongst the somewhat numerous operatives on the farm, that Farmer Gadsby would frequently threaten to discharge her if she did not leave off playing the mischief with his young men. To all which good-humoured objurgation Phœbe would demurely reply, " that it was no fault of hers ; goodness knows, she gave the 'jackan apes' no encouragement, and should be heartily glad to be rid of the whole pack of them !" Honest Farmer Gadsby, a man of peace, though wearing buttons, seldom pursued the colloquy much further ; consoling himself as he walked off with a quiet reflection that had been framed and glazed in his

family for several generations, to the effect—I am
not able to quote the precise words—" That a maiden
is a riddle, the true solution of which is seldom discovered till after marriage." Phœbe, moreover, from
being an orphan, " who had seen better days "—that
indefeasible claim to forbearance and consideration
with all unsophisticated people—was a privileged
person both with the farmer and his dame; and it
was therefore with no little satisfaction, both as regarded the peace of the farmstead, and the comfortable settlement in life of the light-hearted, well-
meaning, though somewhat skittish maiden, that the
worthy couple observed after a time symptoms of a
serious intimacy growing up between her and William
Bayfield, the steady, thriving master-wheelwright of
Brookdale. Young Bayfield was quite a catch, as regarded circumstances, for a dairymaid, however smart
and well-featured; and innumerable—in a village
sense—were the exclamations of contempt and wonder indulged in by maids and matrons of the small-
farmer and shopkeeper class at the *mésalliance* of a
prosperous tradesman with a mere milkmaid. Little
recked, however, it soon became manifest, the object
of these ill-natured strictures the displeasure of
his critics; and so spirited and successful was the
wooing, that the banns between William Bayfield,
bachelor, and Phœbe Morris, spinster, were published
within one little month of the day which witnessed
the first appearance of the enamoured wheelwright

in the list of Phœbe's miscellaneous admirers; converting into certainty the apprehensions suggested by the arrival at William Bayfield's dwelling, the very day before, of an eight-day clock, a mahogany chest of drawers, a gilt pier-glass, and a carpet—positively a Brussels carpet! The spinsterhood of Brookdale had no patience—how could they have?—with such airs, and indignantly wished it might last, that was all!

Alas! it soon became extremely doubtful whether the modest housekeeping so sharply criticized would ever commence! The rustic incense so long and profusely offered to the pretty Phœbe had not, it may be easily imagined, tended to diminish the stock of vanity with which the merry maiden was naturally endowed. She was unfortunately far too fond of exhibiting the power which she possessed, or fancied she did, over her humble admirers. The true affection which she felt towards her affianced husband did not suffice to shield him from her coquettish, irritating arts; and just three days previous to the expected wedding, a violent quarrel between the lovers, threatening to end in a total rupture of the proposed alliance, had taken place. The cause of quarrel will be best understood by the dialogue which took place between them on the following afternoon. Bayfield, who had not slept a wink all night, nor been able to settle himself to anything during the morning, had sent a message, through kind Dame

Gadsby, that he wished to speak to Phœbe, and was waiting for her by the chestnut-trees. Phœbe had herself been in trouble all day, fearing she had carried matters too far; but this message at once reassured her, and she determined, foolish wench, to make no concession whatever to the wounded pride and self-esteem of her lover.

" Well, Mr. Bayfield," said she, approaching him after a purposely protracted delay, " what have you to say to me? I understood you had resolved never to speak to me again !"

" Well, Phœbe, I *did* say so, and meant it too at the time; but you well knew I was too much in love to be able to keep my word." Phœbe laughed. " Come now, let us be friends again; there's a good girl."

" Oh, I dare say; and so give you leave to show off your jealous airs again with impunity? No indeed !"

" Nay, Phœbe, it was partly, at all events, your own fault. You tried me sadly; but come, let bygones be bygones. As to young Gaythorpe, of course he thinks nothing of you; so that——"

" Don't be too sure of that, Mr. Bayfield," interrupted Phœbe, tossing her head, and pouting her pretty lip. " Edward Gaythorpe has eyes in his head, I suppose, as well as other folk."

" I dare say he has," replied Bayfield, his jealousy reawakening; " and if you prefer him to me, even so let it be; I'll not stand in his way."

Phœbe angrily retorted, and the result was a more vehement quarrel than before; and they at last separated, both avowing a fixed determination never to see or think of each other again. After striding nearly to the end of the long lane in which they had been standing, William Bayfield turned round, half-repentingly, just at the moment, as ill fortune would have it, that Edward Gaythorpe, who had been observing the pair from the covert of the chestnut-trees, joined his mistress, and officiously walked by her side as she proceeded homewards. Her soft eyes were suffused with tears, and she replied only by curt monosyllables to the soothing blandishments of the young farmer. Of this poor Bayfield was necessarily unaware; he saw only the ill-timed, suspicious *rencontre*, and, his heart overflowing with rage and grief, strode fiercely away towards the village. Instead of proceeding to his own dwelling, he entered (a most unusual thing for him to do, especially in the daytime) the principal tavern of the place, and, seating himself in the parlour, called hastily for brandy-and-water.

It unfortunately happened that Sergeant Crump, a zealous recruiting officer in the service of the Honourable East India Company, and indefatigable trumpeter of the manifold virtues, civil and military, of that distinguished corporation, was, at the moment of Bayfield's entrance, haranguing the two or three persons present upon the brilliant advantages proffered by his lavishly-generous employers to all heroic spirits desirous of obtaining fame and fortune, glory and prize-money, where alone those desirable articles *could*, in the present stagnant state of the world, be with certainty attained—namely, in the delightful, dazzling East! The magniloquent oratory of the sergeant, hot and glowing as it was, altogether failed of kindling the cold clods he so pathetically addressed; and he would probably have soon ceased his funning in despair, had not his practised eye discerned in the countenance of the new-comer indications of a state of mind extremely favourable to a proper appreciation of recruiting eloquence. He consequently persevered, and by the time William Bayfield had poured the third tumbler of brandy-and-water down his throat—he could hardly be said to *drink* the liquor—had the satisfaction of perceiving that he was listened to with a sort of moody desperation and half-scornful approval. More liquor was called for; and finally Bayfield, maddened by potations to which he was unaccustomed, acting upon his previously exasperated state of mind, accepted with reckless idiocy the Company's shilling, and was at once enrolled in the sergeant's memorandum-book as a full private in one of the East India Company's cavalry regiments! As it was quite out of the question that a man in the position of William Bayfield would, whatever his present frenzy might prompt, think seriously of enlisting, a night's rest, and two or three pounds by way of "smart-money," would probably have terminated the affair, when, just as the orgie was at its highest, Edward Gaythorpe entered the room. It required but this to raise the excitement of the new recruit to downright madness. Furious taunts and menaces were quickly exchanged; Bayfield sprang wildly up, seizing at the same time, and drawing, the sergeant's sheathed sword, which lay on the table; Gaythorpe caught hold of the poker, and a desperate struggle ensued. Bayfield received a heavy blow on his left shoulder, and at the same instant thrust the sword through the body of his antagonist. The outcries of the sergeant—the company had departed some time before—quickly brought the landlord and two or three others into the room; Bayfield was first, with much difficulty, secured; and then Gaythorpe was conveyed to bed, and a surgeon sent for. William Bayfield, thoroughly sobered by the tragic issue of the fray, was, a few hours afterwards, escorted by the entire constabulary of the place to the nearest borough town, about six miles distant, and there securely lodged in jail.

Such a catastrophe had not occurred in quiet pastoral Brookdale within the memory of the oldest inhabitant; and dire was the tumult and the tossing to and fro of the bewildered mind of that small public. Phœbe Morris was in despair; her silly, coquettish behaviour had, she felt—though few others suspected it—occasioned all the mischief; and fervent were her vows of future amendment should this peril pass away. After a day or two, the excitement of the good folks began to gradually calm down. Young Gaythorpe's wound was found to be merely a flesh one, the sword having barely grazed his ribs, and consequently not at all dangerous. He was a good-natured young man, and, though somewhat smitten with Phœbe's pretty face, was not at all disposed, upon calm reflection, to avenge his fanciful disappointment upon his rival. His father, too, a rather wealthy yeoman, having, reasonably enough, much higher views for his son, was very anxious that nothing should occur to prevent Phœbe's union with Bayfield. No wonder, therefore, that under these circumstances a rumour speedily gained ground that the Gaythorpes did not mean to prosecute; and that, moreover, the wounded man had no distinct recollection as to who began the fight—whether he first assailed Bayfield with the poker, or Bayfield him with the sword. It seemed, therefore, more than probable that the at one time ugly-looking affair would end after all in mere smoke.

There was apparently but one obstacle to this much-desired consummation; but that was a formidable one. The sergeant, who, in the struggle to disarm Bayfield, had received a slight cut on the cheek, which, in the owner's opinion, somewhat marred its martial comeliness, persisted that the prisoner had committed an entirely unprovoked and intendedly deadly assault upon Edward Gaythorpe, whom he had, moreover, repeatedly menaced with the direst vengeance previous to his entering the room. This evidence, it was felt, would entirely change the complexion of the case, and have the effect, if deposed before a magistrate, of consigning the unhappy wheelwright to prison, there to await his trial on something very like a capital charge at the next assizes.

The hearing of the charge had been adjourned from the following Thursday, to which day Bayfield had been first remanded, till Saturday at ten o'clock, in order to compel the attendance of Edward Gay-thorpe, who had declined to obey the mere summons of the magistrate. On the Friday evening, discon-solate Phœbe Morris arrived at the Falcon Inn, an old-fashioned, straggling hostelry, in which the obdu-rate sergeant, accompanied by a newly-entrapped recruit, had taken up quarters for that night only, in order to be present in time at the next morning's investigation. Phœbe's purpose was to essay what effect " beauty in tears " might have upon his iron nature. Vainly, however, did beauty, not only in tears, but pretty nearly in fits, plead to the recruiting rhinoceros; he was inexorable. " He had," he said, " one duty to perform towards society, which had been outraged; and another," glancing grimly at his plastered cheek reflected in the glass over the mantel-piece, " towards himself, who had been injured; and those two duties he was determined to fulfil." Phœbe was at her wits' end; and but for some very strong consolation whispered in her ear by the chambermaid of the Falcon, who had assisted at the conference, and felt greatly irritated at the sergeant's flintiness, would probably have gone off into permanent hysterics. As it was, she contented herself with one or two reproachful sobs, and indignantly withdrew from the presence of a monster whom smiles could not soften nor the tenderness of tears subdue. "A perfect brute!" said the chambermaid, as soon as she was out of the sergeant's hearing; "but never mind, Miss Phœbe, there's more ways to kill a mad dog besides hanging the creechur!" With which enigmatical illustration Margaret Davies—so was the angry lady named—dismissed the subject; and Phœbe found herself shortly afterwards jogging sorrowfully, yet hopefully, homewards in Farmer Gadsby's taxed cart, much musing on the possible events of the morrow. Margaret Davies, I should mention, had nursed Miss Phœbe, as she persisted in calling her, in those "better days" to which I have alluded, and thence doubtless arose her sympathy with the afflicted fair one.

The sergeant had walked a long distance that day, and, feeling more than ordinarly tired, regretted, as he undressed himself in the double-bedded room he had bespoken for himself and his recruit, that he had not desired Boots to call him. "Never mind," thought he, "I shall be sure to wake by 10 o'clock, and that will be quite early enough." So thinking, he tumbled into bed, and slept without rocking.

The next morning William Bayfield was brought before a bench of magistrates, and Mr. Gaythorpe, junior, being in attendance, the charge against him was proceeded with; and it was soon apparent that if no other evidence than that of the unwilling prosecutor could be obtained, nothing but a common assault arising out of chance-medley, would be substantiated. The name of Mr. Crump was bawled out with immense emphasis, both inside and outside the hall of justice, by the bustling town-sergeant; but, much to the astonishment of those familiar with the precise habits and punctilious attention to orders of that rigid soldier, no Crump answered to the summons. The zealous functionary was directed to proceed to the Falcon in quest of the missing witness; and after about a quarter of an hour's absence, he returned with the tidings that "No. 24, Sergeant Crump and another," had left the Falcon at daybreak, and had not been since seen or heard of. This intelligence the town-sergeant had received from the respectable landlady's own lips. The attorney employed to defend Bayfield urged an immediate adjudication upon the evidence already heard as a matter of right; but the magistrates finally determined upon waiting for Crump till 4 o'clock in the afternoon, the usual hour for closing the office; when, if no additional evidence appeared, they would deci e the case.

Poor Phœbe's heart sank within her. Still her friend the chambermaid had spoken so confidently of "all day," that after a minute or two she rallied amazingly, and bestowed such a shower of gracious and encouraging smiles upon the penitent prisoner, as would, if, as those story-telling poets tell us, imagination possessed wings, have raised him from the dock up to the seventh heaven. As it was, his mortal part—whatever flights the ethereal essence indulged in—remained in durance vile, tremblingly apprehensive of the arrival of Crump.

And where was that dexterous snapper-up of youthful heroism all this anxious while? Alas! himself could scarcely have answered the question.

Sergeant Crump, as I have before mentioned, feeling unusually fatigued, was soon in a state of the profoundest slumber. Not less intense was the drowsiness of the jolter-headed recruit, who snored in the adjoining truckle-bed, and whose natural heavy-headedness had been considerably increased by copious draughts of malt-liquor. Long and sweetly did they slumber; till at last the sergeant, after a few preliminary twists and turns, started hastily up in his bed, impressed with a strong conviction that he had sadly overslept himself, and forthwith began rubbing his eyes. This he did partly from habit, and partly to rub out the darkness which still—fully awake as he deemed himself—seemed strangely to encase them. "Very odd," growled Sergeant Crump; "it *is* dark! Well, if I couldn't have sworn I had slept twelve hours at least!" Sergeant Crump was quite right; it *was* dark, one of the darkest nights, especially for summer time of year, as it then was, either he or any other gentleman had perhaps ever experienced. Mr. Crump tried to remember if there was a moon, or at what time that luminary went down, or rose up, but could not for the life of him determine; his last and present night's experience suggesting such totally different conclusions. "I cannot have been in bed anything like the time I supposed," he soliloquized. "It must be so; but it's very odd." Diggins, the recruit, was snoring away as vigorously as if he had only just begun the exercise; and the sergeant, convinced at last that, contrary to his usual habit, he had awoke before his time, again addressed himself to sleep. By dint of perseverance he managed to doze off again, and had remained in a state of semi-somnolency for perhaps three or four hours, when he again bolted upright in his bed, thoroughly wide awake and thoroughly bewildered! It was still as dark as before; and a horrible surmise crossed Mr. Crump's mind, that possibly the mechanism of the universe had somehow got out out of order, and that the sun might consequently never again rise upon a benighted world!

The fact was, No. 24, "Soldiers' Rooms," to which, wilfully misunderstanding the landlady's directions, the sympathizing chambermaid had directed the under-bedmaker to convoy the sergeant and his man, was an inner apartment in a distant part of the rambling old inn, the windows of which, as well as those of the rooms surrounding it, had been closed up, to mitigate the pressure of the window-tax, and was of course nothing more than a large roomy dark closet, to which even air obtained access only through the chimney. The sole window left was at the top of a wooden partition dividing the sergeant's room from the next, and had in its time done duty as a "borrowed light;" but inasmuch as the adjoining rooms were also hermetically sealed from the glare of day, was now at best but a "borrowed darkness." These rooms were usually reserved for soldiers of marching regiments occasionally billeted on the Falcon: a compelled entertainment by the way, which is seldom of a very superior character. The reader will now be able to comprehend the cause both of Phœbe Morris's nervous anxiety and of the sergeant's perplexity.

He was indeed perplexed in the extreme. At last, jumping angrily out of bed, he groped his way, after several mishaps in which both feet and shins suffered abominably, to the door, the key of which he remembered to have left in the lock. In his haste to find and grasp it, he struck it unawares, and out it flew from its shallow, ill-fitting receptacle to the floor; and all Mr. Crump's efforts to find it were unavailing. Had he been able to open the door, he would not have been much the better for it, as it merely led into another dark room, the outer key of which, for fear of accidents, provident Margaret Davies had taken care to secure. The sergeant next bethought him of the window; there must be, he argued, a window; and by means of a tentative process round the walls with his cane, he at last managed to discover its whereabout. The outside shutter was, he conjectured, closed; but how to reach it? Rousing the recruit, who by this time had pretty well slept off the effect of his previous evening's potations, he proposed to mount upon that worthy's shoulders. This was agreed to, and with some diffi-culty accomplished; but the sergeant, even on that ticklish eminence, could scarcely reach above the bottom of the narrow casement; and the fastenings were, he concluded, considerably higher up. In order to obtain the necessary altitude, Diggins drew his truckle-bedstead—a narrow fold-up affair, steady enough when a person was lying on it, but miserably unfit as a base for a man to stand upon, especially with another mounted on his shoulders—close to the wall; and after several unsuccessful efforts, the sergeant at last stood once more upon Diggins's shoulders, and was enabled to grope gingerly over the surface of the casement in search of shutter-bolts, of course without success. In his wrathful energy, Crump, for a moment oblivious of the precarious nature of the base upon which he was operating, pushed angrily at the window-frame, and at once overset the equilibrium which Diggins had till that moment with so much difficulty maintained. The folding bedstead heeled suddenly over; Diggins caught instinctively at the sergeant's legs; and the sergeant, in his turn, made a desperate snatch at the casement, sending in the effort his hand clean through one of the squares, clearly but painfully demonstrating, to himself at least, the absence of shutters; and then down came Crump and Diggins with stunning violence, and mutual execrations and discomfiture. Bruised, bleeding, and incredibly savage, the sergeant, having first helped to replace the bedstead of his equally savage companion, once more resigned himself to his pillow, persuaded, in his own despite, that it could not yet be day. Hour after hour they lay watching for the dawn, the faintest streak of which would have been unspeakably welcome. At last, his patience utterly exhausted, Crump sprang up, and kicked and bawled for help with all the power of his feet and lungs, in which exercise he was zealously aided by Diggins, whose appetite had by this time become ravenously sharp. Long and fruitlessly had they raved and thumped, and were just on the point of abandoning their efforts in despair, when a step was heard evidently approaching their dormitory. Presently a light shone through the crevices of the door, and the voice of the chambermaid, Mrs. Margaret Davies, was heard generously demanding who it was making that disturbance at nearly 10 o'clock at night, when quiet folk were just going to bed? "Going to bed!" Crump huddled on his clothes; and having, by the aid of the light, espied the key, opened the door with a bounce. "Going to bed!" he shouted distractedly as he glared upon the chambermaid—"going to bed!" No sooner did that amiable damsel catch sight of the haggard features and bloodstained hands and linen of the sergeant, than she plumped down in a chair, and set up a succession of the dismallest shrieks that ever disturbed and dismayed a Christian household. "Murder—fire—thieves—robbers!" resounded through the house with an effect so startling, that in a trice hostlers, porters, waiters, with a plentiful sprinkling of female helps, came rushing hurriedly to the rescue. Nobody either could or would recognize the culprits, spite of their energetic asseverations, till the arrival of the pursy, slow-moving landlady. The screams, which had gradually diminished in intensity, then altogether ceased; and in echo, as it were, of the ejaculation of her mistress, "Sergeant Crump and the recruit, as I'm alive!"

Mrs. Margaret Davies naïvely exclaimed; "Mercy upon us! Sergeant Crump! Why, so it is! Then you did *not* go away this morning without paying your last night's score?"

The sergeant, who dimly suspected the jade's trick which had been put upon him, only glared frightfully at her, and hastened his toilet.

"Margaret, I thought I told you to put Mr. Crump into No. 24?"

"Certainly, ma'am, you did; and I told Susy the same; but it appears she must have understood it to be No. 24, 'Soldiers' Rooms." Dear me, whoever would have thought it? And, bless me, what a dreadful situation for two gentlemen in her gracious Majesty's service to have been in so long! It's quite shocking to think of really!"

The suppressed tittering of the other servants—all of them, I suspect, more or less in the secret—here burst into uproarious merriment; the sergeant, almost choking with fury, looked round for some safe object to vent it upon, but finding none, wisely kept it corked for future use.

"And to think, ma'am," continued Phœbe's friend, "that in consequence of this *uncommissioned* officer's long nap, that scapegrace of a Bayfield should have got off this afternoon with only a trumpery fine of five pounds; not more than half the amount of the *recollections* which the sergeant has forfeited for not being at the hall to give evidence."

"What is that you say,—— woman?" exclaimed Crump, using the most vituperative epithet he could at the moment think of.

"Why, I say," meekly replied Margaret, "that your ten-pound *recollections*, which you gave the magistrates to appear, is declared forfeited; and that the town-sergeant is below with a warrant for the amount in case you should return to the Falcon this evening."

The exasperation of the sergeant was unbounded. The landlady, thinking probably that mischief might come of it, drove off his tormentors; and he was left to finish his ablutions in peace.

"Oh, Sergeant Crump!" exclaimed Mrs. Margaret Davies, returning at the end of two or three minutes, and holding the door ajar in her hand, "if you please, missus wishes to know if you mean to bespeak a bed for to-night?"

Crump darted towards the door; but the playful damsel was too nimble for him, and the long corridors and staircases echoed again with her joyous merriment as she skipped away.

The account given by the chambermaid of the result of the inquiry before the magistrates was quite correct. William Bayfield was fined five pounds, or, in default, to suffer two months' imprisonment for a common assault, *without* intent, *et cetera.* The fine was at once paid, and the certificate of adjudication of course barred any further proceedings. On the next bench-day, Crump having related, amidst shouts of laughter, the trick he had been played, asked to be excused payment of his forfeited recognisance. This, under the circumstances, was, after some demur, agreed to; but he was unable to obtain even "smart money" from Bayfield, he having been, upon the sergeant's own admission, inebriated when he accepted the Company's retainer.

The imminent peril in which her criminal coquetry had involved her affianced husband proved a salutary lesson to Phœbe, who has settled down into one of the discreetest, as well as prettiest and cheerfullest, wives in Warwickshire. Bayfield is now a prosperous man; and has recently purchased, at his wife's suggestion, the Falcon Inn, which the sudden death of the fat landlady had thrown into the market, chiefly for the purpose of assuring the succession of the business to Margaret Davies, to whose good offices he was on a very critical occasion so largely indebted. Sergeant Crump, disgusted with England, which in his indiscriminate wrath he rashly confounded with its chambermaids, betook himself with all convenient despatch to the gorgeous clime whose glories he had so frequently described; and if report speaks sooth, has discovered a still darker chamber than that of the Falcon beneath the towers of fallen Moultan.

THE UNLAWFUL GIFT.

THE chastened glory of a bright autumnal evening was shining upon the yellow harvest fields of Bursley Farm, in the vicinity of the New Forest, and tinting with changeful light the dense but broken masses of thick wood which skirted the southern horizon, when Ephraim Lovegrove, a care-cankered, worn-out, dying man, though hardly numbering sixty years, was, at his constantly and peevishly-iterated request, lifted from the bed on which for many weeks he had been gradually and painfully wasting away, and carried in an arm-chair to the door. From the cottage, situated as it was upon an eminence, the low-lying lands of Bursley, and its straggling homestead, which once called him master, could be distinctly seen. The fading eyes of the old man wandered slowly over the gleaming landscape, and a faint smile of painful recognition stole upon his harsh and shrivelled features. His only son, a fine handsome young fellow, stood silently, with his wife, beside him—both, it seemed, as keenly, though not perhaps as bitterly, impressed

with the scene and the thoughts it suggested; and
their child, a rosy youngster of about five years of age,
clung tightly to his mother's gown, frightened and
awed apparently by the stern expression he read
upon his father's face. A light summer air lifted the
old man's thin white locks, fanned his sallow cheeks,
and momently revived his fainting spirit. "Ay,"
he muttered, "the old pleasant home, Ned, quiet,
beautiful as ever. It's only we who change and pass
away."

"The home," rejoined the son, "of which we have
been robbed—lawfully robbed."

"I'm not so clear on that as I was," said Ephraim
Lovegrove, slowly and with difficulty. "It was partly
our own want of foresight—mine I mean of course:
we ought not to have calculated on——"

The old man's broken accents stopped suddenly.
The strength which the sight of his former home and
the grateful breeze which swept up from the valley
awakened, had quickly faded; and the daughter-in-
law, touching her husband's arm, and glancing anxiously at his father's changing countenance, motioned
that he should be reconveyed to bed. This was done,
and a few spoonfuls of wine revived him somewhat.
Edward Lovegrove left the cottage upon some necessary business; and his wife, after putting her child
to bed, re-entered the sick-room, and seated herself
with mute watchfulness by the bedside of her father-
in-law.

"Ye are a kind, gentle creature, Mary," said the dying man, whose failing gaze had been for some time fixed upon her pale, patient face : " as kind and gentle—more so, it seems to me, in this poor hovel than when we dwelt in yon homestead, from which you, with us, have been so cruelly driven."

" Murmuring, father," she replied in a low sweet voice, " would not help us. It is surely better to submit cheerfully to a hard lot than to chafe and fret one's life away at what cannot be helped. But it's easy for me," she hastily added, fearing that her words might sound reproachfully in the old man's ear—" it's easy for me, who have health, a kind husband, and my little boy left me, to be cheerful, but it is scarcely so for you, suffering in body and mind, and tormented in a thousand ways."

" Ay, girl, it has been a sharp trial; but it will soon be over. In a few hours it will matter little whether old Ephraim Lovegrove lived and died in a pig-sty or a palace. But I would speak of you. You and Ned should emigrate. There are countries, I am told, where you would be sure to prosper. That viper Nichols, I remember, once offered to assist—I could never make out from what motive—from what —— A little wine," he added feebly. " The evening, for the time of year, is very chilly : my feet and legs are cold as stones." He swallowed the wine, and again addressed himself to speak, but his voice was scarcely audible. " I have often thought," he murmured, "as I lay here, that Symons, Nichols' clerk, from a hint he dropped, knows something of—of—your mother and—and——" The faint accents ceased to be audible; but the grasp of the dying man closed tightly upon the frightened woman's hand, as he looked wildly in her face as he drew her towards him, as if some important statement remained untold. He struggled desperately for utterance, but the strife was vain, and brief as it was fierce: his grasp relaxed, and with a convulsive groan Ephraim Lovegrove fell back and expired.

The storm which had made shipwreck of the fortunes of Ephraim Lovegrove had levelled with the earth prouder roof-trees than his. In early life he had succeeded his father as a tenant of a farm in Wiltshire. He was industrious, careful, and ambitious; and aided by the sum of £500, which he received with his wife, and the high prices which agricultural produce obtained during the French war, he was enabled, at the expiration of his lease in Wiltshire, to become the proprietor of the Bursley Farm. This purchase was effected when wheat ranged from £30 to £40 a load at a proportionately exorbitant price of £5000. His savings amounted to about one-half of this sum, and the remainder was raised by way of mortgage. Matters went on smoothly enough till the peace of 1815, and the subsequent precipitate fall in prices. Lovegrove showed gallant fight, hoping against hope that exceptional legislation would ulti-

mately bolster up prices to something like their former
level. He was deceived. Every day saw him sinking
lower and lower; and in the sixth year of peace he
was reluctantly compelled to abandon the long since
desperate and hopeless struggle with adverse fortune.
The interest on the borrowed money had fallen considerably in arrear, and Bursley Farm was sold by
auction at a barely sufficient sum to cover the mortgage and accumulated interest. The stock was similarly disposed of, and stout Ephraim withdrew with
his family to a small cottage in the neighbourhood of
his old home, possessed, after his debts were discharged, of about thirty pounds in money and a few
necessary articles of furniture. The old man's heart
was broken; he took almost immediately to his bed,
and after a long agony of physical pain, aggravated
and embittered by mental disquietude and discontent, expired as we have seen, worn out in mind and
body.

The future of the surviving family was a dark and
anxious one. Edward Lovegrove, a frank, kindly-
tempered young man, accustomed, in the golden days
of farming, to ride occasionally after the hounds as
well equipped and mounted as any in the field, was
little fitted for a struggle for daily bread with the
crowded competition of the world. He had several
times endeavoured to obtain a situation as bailiff, but
others more fortunate, perhaps better qualified, filled
up every vacancy that offered, and the almost despe-

rate man, but for the pleading helplessness of his wife and child, would have sought shelter in the ranks of the army—that grave in which so many withered prospects and broken hopes lie buried. As usual with disappointed men, his mind dwelt with daily-augmenting bitterness upon the persons at whose hands the last and decisive blows which had destroyed his home had been received. Sanders the mortgagee he looked upon as a monster of perfidy and injustice, but especially Nichols the attorney. who had super-intended and directed the sale of the Bursley home-stead, was regarded by him with the bitterest dislike. Other causes gave intensity to this vindictive feeling. The son of the attorney, Arthur Nichols, a wild, dis-sipated young man, had been a competitor for the hand of Mary Clarke, the sole child of Widow Clarke, and now Edward Lovegrove's wife. It was not at all remarkable or surprising that young Nichols should admire and seek to wed pretty and gentle Mary Clarke, but it was deemed strange by those who knew his father's grasping, mercenary disposition, that *he* should have been so eager for the match, well knowing, as he did, for the payments passed through his hands, that the widow's modest annuity termi-nated with her life. It was also known and wonder-ingly commented upon, that the attorney was himself an anxious suitor for the widow's hand up to the day of her sudden and unexpected decease, which occurred about three years after her daughter's marriage with

Edward Lovegrove. Immediately after this event, as if some restraint upon his pent-up malevolence had been removed, the elder Nichols manifested the most active hostility towards the Lovegroves; and to his persevering enmity it was generally attributed that Mr. Sandars had availed himself of the power of sale inserted in the mortgage deed to cast his unfortunate debtor helpless and homeless upon the world.

Sadly passed away the weary, darkening days with the young couple after the old man's death. The expenses of his long illness had swept away the little money saved from the wreck of the farm; and it required the sacrifice of Edward's watch and some silver teaspoons to defray the cost of a decent funeral. At last, spite of the thriftiest economy, all was gone, and they were penniless.

"You have nothing to purchase breakfast with to-morrow, have you, Mary?" said the husband, after partaking of a scanty tea. The mother had feigned only to eat: little Edward, whose curly head was lying in her lap as he sat asleep on a low stool beside her, had her share.

"Not a farthing," she replied mildly, even cheerfully, and the glance of her gentle eyes was hopeful and kind as ever. "But bear up, Edward: we have still the furniture; and were that sold at once, it would enable us to reach London, where you know so many people have made fortunes who arrived there as poor as we."

" Something must be done, that is certain," replied
the husband. " We have not yet received an answer
from Salisbury about the porter's place I have applied
for."

" No; but I would rather, for your sake, Edward,
that you filled such a situation at some place further
off, where you were not so well known."

Edward Lovegrove sighed, and presently rising
from his chair, walked towards a chest of drawers
that stood at the further end of the room. His wife,
who guessed his intention—for the matter had been
already more than once hinted at—followed him with
a tearful, apprehensive glance. Her husband played
tolerably well—wonderfully in the wife's opinion—
upon the flute, and a few weeks after their marriage,
her mother had purchased and presented him with a
very handsome one with silver keys. He used, in
the old time, to accompany his wife in the simple
ballads she sang so sweetly—and now this last me-
morial of the past, linked as it was with tender and
pious memories, must be parted with! Edward Lovegrove had not looked at it for months: his life, of late
so out of tune, would have made harsh discord of its
music; and as he took it from the case, and, from
the mere force of habit, moistened the joints, and
placed the pieces together, a flood of bitterness
swelled his heart to think that this solace of " lang
syne" must be sacrificed to their hard necessities.
He blew a few tremulous and imperfect notes which

awakened the little boy, who was immediately cla-
morous that mammy should sing and daddy play as
they used to do.

"Shall we try, Mary," said the husband, "to please
the child?" Poor Mary bowed her head: her heart
was too full to speak. The flutist played the prelude
to a favourite air several times over before his wife
could sufficiently command her voice to commence
the song; and she had not reached the end of the
second line when she stopped, choked with emotion,
and burst into an agony of tears.

"It is useless trying, Mary," said Edward Lovegrove soothingly, as he rose and put by the flute.
" I will to bed at once, for to and from Christchurch,
where I must dispose of it, is a long walk." He
kissed his wife and child, and went up stairs. The
mother followed soon afterwards, put her boy to rest,
and after looking wistfully for a few moments at the
worn and haggard features of her husband as he lay
asleep, redescended the stairs, and busied herself
with some necessary household work.

As she was thus employed, a slight tap at the little
back window struck her ear, and looking sharply
round, she recognized the pale, uncouth features of
Symons, lawyer Nichols' deformed clerk and errand-
man, who was eagerly beckoning her to open the
casement. This was the person of whom Ephraim
Lovegrove had spoken just previous to his death.
Symons, who had never known father or mother,

had passed his infancy and early boyhood in the parish workhouse, from whence he had passed into the service of Mr. Nichols, who, finding him useful, and of some capacity, had retained him in his employ to the present time, but at so bare a stipend, as hardly sufficed to keep body and soul together. Poor Symons was a meek, enduring drudge, used to the mocks and buffets of the world; and except under the influence of strong excitement, hardly dared to rebel or murmur, even in spirit. His acquaintance with the Lovegrove family arose from his being placed in possession of the furniture and stock of Bursley Farm under a writ of *fi. fa.* issued by Nichols. On the day the inventory was taken, in preparation for the sale, a heavy piece of timber which he was assisting to measure fell upon his left foot, and severely crushed it. From his master he received only a malediction for his awkwardness; but young Mrs. Lovegrove— not so much absorbed in her own grief as to be in- different to the sufferings of others—had him brought carefully into the house, and herself tended his pain- ful hurt with the gentlest care and compassion, and ultimately effected a thorough cure. This kindness to a slighted, deformed being, who before had scarcely comprehended the meaning of the word, powerfully affected Symons; and he had since frequently en- deavoured, in his shy, awkward way, to testify the deep gratitude he felt towards his benefactress, of whose present extreme poverty he, in common with every other inhabitant of the scattered hamlet, had of course become fully cognizant. Charity Symons—the parish authorities had so named him, in order, doubtless, that however high he might eventually rise in the world, he should never ungratefully forget his origin—beckoned, as I have said, eagerly to the lone woman, and the instant she opened the casement, he thrust a rather heavy bag into her hand.

"For you," he said hurriedly: "I got it for next to nothing of Tom Stares; but mind not a word! God bless and reward you!" and before Mrs. Lovegrove could answer a word, or comprehend what was meant, he had disappeared

On opening the bag, the surprised and affrighted woman found that it contained a fine hen-pheasant and a hare! No wonder she was alarmed at finding herself in possession of such articles; for in those good old days game could not be lawfully sold or purchased; and unless it could be distinctly proved that it came by gift from a qualified killer, its simple possession was a punishable offence. This pheasant and hare had doubtless been poached by Tom Stares, a notorious offender against the game-laws : but what was to be done? Spite of the laws that were enacted upon the subject, the peasant and farmer intellect of England could never be made to attach a moral delinquency to the unauthorized killing of game. A dangerous occupation, leading to no possible good, and eventually sure to result in evil to the trans-

gressor, prudent men agreed it was; but as for confounding the stealing of a wooden spoon, worth a
penny, with the snaring of a hare, worth perhaps five
shillings—that never entered anybody's head. And
thus it happened that Mrs. Lovegrove, though conscious that the hare and bird had been illegally
obtained, felt nothing of the instinctive horror and
shame that would have mantled her forehead had she
been made the recipient of a stolen threepennyworth
of cheese or bacon. She recalled to mind the journey
her husband must take in the morning—he weak,
haggard for want of food—of which here was an
abundant present supply: her boy, too, who had twice
at tea-time, ere he fell asleep, asked vainly for more
bread! As these bitter thoughts glanced through
her brain, a sharp double rap at the door caused her
to start like a guilty thing, and then hastily undo her
apron, and throw it over the betraying present. The
door was not locked, and the postman, impatient of
delay, lifted the latch, and stepped into the room.
Was he soon enough to observe what was on the
table? Mary Lovegrove would have thought so, but
for the unconcerned, indifferent aspect of the man as
he presented a letter, and said, "It's prepaid: all
right;" and without further remark, went away.
The anxious and nervous woman trembled so much,
that she could hardly break the seal of the letter;
and the words, as she strove to make out the cramped
hand by the brilliant moonlight, danced confusedly

before her eyes. At last she was able to read. The letter was from Salisbury, and announced that Mr. Brodie " regretted to say, as he had known and respected the late Ephraim Lovegrove, that he had engaged a person to fill the situation which had been vacant a few hours previous to his receiving Edward Lovegrove's application." That plank, then, had sunk under them like all the rest! A hard world, she thought, and but little entitled to obedience or respect from the wretches trampled down in its iron course. Edward should not, at all events, depart foodless on his morning's errand; neither should her boy lack breakfast. On this she was now determined, and with shaking hands and flushed cheek, she hastily set about preparing the bird for the morning meal—a weak and criminal act if you will; but a mother seldom reasons when a child lacks food: she only feels.

Edward Lovegrove very easily reconciled himself to the savoury breakfast which awaited him in the morning; and he and his son were doing ample justice to it—the wife, though faint with hunger, could not touch a morsel—when the latch of the door suddenly lifted, and in hurried Thompson the miller, and chief constable of the Hundred, followed by an assistant. A faint scream escaped from Mrs. Lovegrove, and a fierce oath broke from her husband's lips, as they recognized the new-comers, and too readily divined their errand.

"A charming breakfast, upon my word!" exclaimed the constable, laughing. "Roasted pheasant—no less! Our information was quite correct, it appears."

"What is the meaning of this, and what do you seek here?" exclaimed Edward Lovegrove.

"You and this game, of which we are informed you are unlawfully possessed. I hope," added the constable, a feeling, good sort of man—"I hope you will be able to prove both that this half-eaten pheasant and the hare I see hanging yonder were presented to you by some person having a right to make such gifts?"

A painful and embarrassing pause ensued. It would have been useless, as far as themselves were concerned, to have named Charity Symons, even had Lovegrove or his wife been disposed to subject him to the penalties of the law and the anger of his employer.

"After all," observed the constable, who saw how matters stood, "it is but a money penalty."

"A money penalty!" exclaimed Lovegrove. "It is imprisonment—ruin—starvation for my wife and child. Look at these bare walls—these threadbare garments—and say if it can mean anything else!"

"I am sorry for it," rejoined Thompson. "The penalty is a considerable one: five pounds for each head of game, with costs; and I am afraid, if Sir John Devereux' agent—lawyer Nichols—presses the

charge, in default of payment, six months' imprisonment! Sir John's preserves have suffered greatly
of late."

" It is that rascal, that robber Nichols' doing then !"
fiercely exclaimed Lovegrove. " I might have guessed
so ; but if I don't pay him off both for old and new
one of these days——"

" Tut, tut ! " interrupted the constable : " it's no
use calling names, nor uttering threats we don't mean
to perform. Perhaps matters may turn out better
than you think. In the mean time you must appear
before Squire Digby, and so must your hare and what
remains of your breakfast."

Arrived before the magistrate, the prisoner, taken
in " *flagrant délit*," had of course no valid defence to
offer. The justice remarked upon the enormity of
the offence committed, and regretted exceedingly that
he could not at once convict and punish the delin-
quent ; but as the statute required that two magistrates should concur in the conviction, the case would
be adjourned till that day week, when a petty sessions
would be held. In the mean time he should require
bail in ten pounds for the prisoner's appearance.
This would have been tantamount to a sentence of
immediate imprisonment, had not the constable, who
had been formerly intimate with the Lovegroves,
stepped forward and said, that if the prisoner would
give him his word that he would not abscond, he

would bail him. This was done, and the necessary formalities complete, the husband and wife took their sad way homewards.

What was now to be done? Their furniture, if sold at its highest value, would barely discharge the penalties incurred, and they would be homeless, penniless, utterly without resource! The wife wept bitterly, accusing herself as the cause of this utter ruin; her husband indulged in fierce and senseless abuse of Nichols, and in a paroxysm of fury seized a sheet of letter-paper, tore it hastily in halves, and scribbled a letter to the attorney full of threats of the direst vengeance. This crazy epistle he signed " A Ruined Man," and without pausing to reflect on what he was doing, despatched his little boy to the post-office with it. This mad proceeding appeared to have somewhat relieved him; he grew calmer, strove to console his wife, went out and obtained credit at the chandler's—the first time they had made such a request—for a few necessaries; and after a short interval, the unfortunate couple were once more discussing their sad prospects with calmness and partially-renewed hope. More than once Edward Lovegrove wished he had not sent the letter to Nichols; but he said nothing to his wife about it, and she, it afterwards appeared, had been so pre-occupied at the time, as not to heed or inquire to whom or of what he was writing.

On the third day after Edward Lovegrove's appearance before the magistrate, he set off about noon for Christchurch, in order to dispose of his flute—a sacrifice which could no longer be delayed. It was growing late, and his wife was sitting up in impatient expectation of his return, when an alarm of "Fire" was raised, and it was announced that a wheat-rick belonging to Nichols, who farmed in a small way, was in flames. Many of the villagers hastened to the spot; but the fire, by the time they arrived, had been effectually got under, and after hanging about the premises a short time, they turned homewards. Edward Lovegrove joined a party of them, and incidentally remarked that he had been to Christchurch, where he had met young Nichols, and had some rough words with him: on his return, the young man had passed him on horseback when about two miles distant from the elder Nichols' house, and just as he (Lovegrove) neared the attorney's premises, the rick burst into flames. This relation elicited very little remark at the time, and bidding his companions good-night, Lovegrove hastened home.

"The constables are looking for you," said a young woman, abruptly entering the chandler's shop, whither Edward Lovegrove had proceeded the following morning to discharge the trifling debt he had incurred.

"For me?" exclaimed the startled young man.

"Yes, for you; and," added the girl with a meaning look and whisper, "*if you were near the fire* last night,

I would advise you to make yourself scarce for a time."

Her words conveyed no definite meaning to Edward Lovegrove's mind. The fire! Constables after him! He left the shop, and took, with hasty steps, his way to the cottage, distant over the fields about a quarter of a mile.

" Lawyer Nichols' fire," he muttered as he hurried along. " Surely they do not mean to accuse me of that!"

The sudden recollection of the threatening letter he had sent glanced across and smote, as with the stroke of a dagger, upon his brain. " Good God! to what have I exposed myself?"

His agitation was excessive ; and at the instant the constables, who had been to his home in search of him, turned the corner of a path, a few paces ahead, and came full upon him. In his confusion and terror he turned to flee, but so weakly and irresolutely, that he was almost immediately overtaken and secured.

" I would not have believed this of you, Edward Lovegrove!" exclaimed the constable.

" Believed what?" ejaculated the bewildered man.

" That you would have tried to revenge yourself on Lawyer Nichols by such a base, dastardly trick. But it's not my business to reproach you, and the less you say the better. Come along."

As they passed on towards the magistrate's house,

an eager and curious crowd gradually collected and accompanied them ; and just as they reached Digby Hall, a distant convulsive scream, and his name frantically pronounced by a voice which the prisoner but too well recognized, told him that his wife had heard of his capture, and was hurrying to join him. He drew back, but his captors urged him impatiently on ; the hall-door was slammed in the faces of the crowd, and he found himself in the presence of the magistrate and the elder Nichols.

The attorney, who appeared to be strongly agitated, deposed in substance that the prisoner had been seen by his son near his premises a few minutes before the fire burst out ; that he had abused and assaulted young Mr. Nichols but a few hours previously in the market at Christchurch ; and that he had himself received a threatening letter, which he now produced, only two days before, and which he believed to be in the prisoner's handwriting——

The prisoner, bewildered by terror, eagerly denied that he wrote the letter.

This unfortunate denial was easily disposed of, by the production, by the constable, of a half-sheet of letter-paper found in the cottage, the ragged edge of which precisely fitted that of the letter. Edward Lovegrove would have been fully committed at once, but that the magistrate thought it desirable that the deposition of Arthur Nichols should be first formally taken. This course was reluctantly acquiesced in by the prosecutor, and the prisoner was remanded to the next day.

The dismay of Charity Symons, when he found that his well-intentioned present had only brought additional suffering upon the Lovegroves, was intense and bitter; but how to help them he knew not. He had half made up his mind to obtain—no matter by what means—a sight of certain papers which he had long dimly suspected would make strange revelations upon matters affecting Mary Lovegrove, when the arrest of her husband on a charge of incendiarism thoroughly determined him to risk the expedient he had long hesitatingly contemplated. The charge, he was quite satisfied in his own mind, was an atrocious fabrication, strongly as circumstances seemed to colour and confirm it.

The clerk, as he sat that afternoon in the office, silently pursuing his ill-paid drudgery, noticed that his employer was strangely ill at ease. He was restless, and savagely impatient of the slightest delay on the most necessary question. Evening fell early—it was now near the end of October, and Symons, with a respectful bow, left the office. A few minutes afterwards, the attorney having carefully locked his desk, iron-chest, &c., and placed the keys in his pocket, followed.

Two hours had elapsed, when Symons re-entered the house by the back way, walked through the kitchen, softly ascended the stairs, and groped his way to the inner, private office. There was no moon, and he dared not light a candle; but the faint starlight fortunately enabled him to move about without stumbling or noise. He mounted the office-steps, and inserted the edge of a sharp broad chisel between the lock and the lid of a heavy iron-bound box marked " C." The ease and suddenness with which the lid yielded to the powerful effort he applied to it overthrew his balance, and he with difficulty saved himself from falling on the floor. The box was not locked, and on putting his hand into it, he discovered that it was entirely empty! The tell-tale papers had been removed, probably destroyed! At the moment Symons made this exasperating discovery, the sound of approaching footsteps struck upon his startled senses, and shaking with fright, he had barely time to descend the steps, and coop himself up in a narrow cupboard under one of the desks, when the Nichols, father and son, entered the office—the former with a candle in his hand.

" We are private here," said the father in a low, guarded voice; " and I tell you you *must* listen to reason."

" I don't like it a bit," rejoined the young man. " It's a cowardly, treacherous business; and as for swearing I saw him near the fire when it so strangely burst out, I won't do it at any price."

" Listen to me, you foolish, headstrong boy," retorted the elder Nichols, "before you decide on beggary for yourself, and ruin—the gallows, perhaps, for me."

"Wh-e-e-e-w!   Why, what do you mean?"

"I will tell you.   You already know that Mary Woodhouse married Robert Clarke against his uncle's consent; you also know that Robert Clarke died about five years after the marriage, and that the seventy pounds a year which the uncle allowed his nephew to keep him from starvation was continued to be paid through me to his widow."

"Yes, I have heard all this before."

"But you do *not* know," continued the attorney in an increasingly-agitated voice, "that about six years after Robert Clarke's death, the uncle so far relented towards the widow and daughter—though he would never see either of them—as to increase the annuity to two hundred pounds, and that at his death, four years since, he bequeathed Mrs. Clarke five hundred pounds per annum, with succession to her daughter; all of which sums, I, partly on account of your riot and extravagance, have appropriated."

"Good Heaven—what a horrible affair!   What would you have me do?"

"I have told you.   The dread of discovery has destroyed my health, and poisoned my existence. Were he once out of the country, his wife would doubtless follow him; detection would be difficult; conviction, as I will manage it, impossible."

There was more said to the same effect; and the son, at the close of a long and troubled colloquy, departed, after promising to " consider of it."

He had been gone but a few minutes; the elder Nichols was silently meditating the perilous position in which he had placed himself, when a noiseless step approached him from behind, and a heavy hand was suddenly placed upon his shoulder. He started wildly to his feet, and confronted the stern and triumphant glance of the once humble and submissive Charity Symons. The suddenness of the shock overcame him, and he fainted.

Mary Lovegrove, whose child had sobbed itself to sleep, was sitting in solitude and darkness in the lower room of the cottage, her head bowed in mute and tearless agony upon the table, when, as on a previous evening, a tap at the back window challenged her attention. It was once more Charity Symons. " What do you here again ?" exclaimed the wretched wife with some asperity of tone: " you no doubt intended well; but you have nevertheless ruined, destroyed me."

" Not so," rejoined the deformed clerk, his pale, uncouth, but expressive features gleaming with wild exultation in the clear starlight. " God has at last enabled me to requite your kindness to a contemned outcast. Fear not for to-morrow. Your husband is safe, and you are rich." With these words he vanished.

On the next morning a letter was placed in the magistrate's hands from Mr. Nichols, stating that circumstances had come to the writer's knowledge which convinced him that Edward Lovegrove was entirely innocent of the offence imputed to him; that the letter, which he had destroyed, bore quite another meaning from that which he had first attributed to it; and that he consequently abandoned the prosecution. On further inquiry, it was found that the attorney had left his house late the preceding night, accompanied by his son, had walked to Christchurch, and from thence set off post for London. His property and the winding-up of his affairs had been legally confided to his late clerk. Under these circumstances the prisoner was of course immediately discharged; and after a private interview with Symons, returned in joy and gladness to his now temporary home. He was accompanied by the noisy felicitations of his neighbours, to whom his liberation and sudden accession to a considerable fortune had become at the same moment known. As he held his passionately weeping wife in his arms, and gazed with grateful emotion in her tearful but rejoicing eyes, he whispered, "That kind act of yours towards the despised hunchback has saved me, and enriched our child. ' Blessed are the merciful, for they shall obtain mercy!' "

THE WIFE'S STRATAGEM.

Captain Marmaduke Smith is, judging from his present mundane, matter-of-fact character—about the last man one would suspect of having been at any time of his life a victim to the " tender passion." A revelation he volunteered to two or three cronies at the club the other evening undeceived us. The captain on this occasion, as was generally the case on the morrow of a too great indulgence, was somewhat dull-spirited and lachrymose. The weather, too, was gloomy; a melancholy barrel-organ had been groaning dreadfully for some time beneath the windows; and, to crown all, Mr. Tape, who has a quick eye for the sentimental, had discovered, and read aloud, a common, but sad story of madness and suicide in the evening paper. It is not, therefore, so surprising that tender recollections should have revived with unusual force in the veteran's memory.

" You would hardly believe it, Tape," said Captain Smith, after a dull pause, and emitting a sound somewhat resembling a sigh, as he relighted the cigar

which had gone out during Mr. Tape's reading—
"you would hardly believe it perhaps; but I was
woman-witched once myself!"

"Never!" exclaimed the astonished gentleman
whom he addressed. "A man of your strength of
mind, captain? I can't believe it; it's impossible!"

"It's an extraordinary fact, I admit; and, to own
the truth, I have never been able to account exactly
for it myself. Fortunately, I took the disorder as I
did the measles—young; and neither of these com-
plaints is apt to be so fatal then, I'm told, as when
they pick a man up later in life. It was, however, a
very severe attack while it lasted. A very charming
hand at hooking a gudgeon was that delightful Coralie
Dufour, I *must* say."

"Any relation to the Monsieur and Madame Dufour we saw some years ago in Paris?" asked Tape.
"The husband, I remember, was remarkably fond of
expressing his gratitude to you for having once wonderfully carried him through his difficulties."

Captain Smith looked sharply at Mr. Tape, as if
he suspected some lurking irony beneath the bland
innocence of his words. Perceiving, as usual, nothing in the speaker's countenance, Mr. Smith—blowing at the same time a tremendous cloud to conceal
a faint blush which, to my extreme astonishment, I
observed stealing over his unaccustomed features—
said gravely, almost solemnly: "You, Mr. Tape, are
a married man, and the father of a family, and your

own experiences therefore in the female line must be ample for a lifetime ; but you, sir," continued the captain patronizingly, addressing another of his auditors, " are, I believe, as yet " unattached," in a legal sense, and may therefore derive profit as well as instruction from an example of the way in which ardent and inexperienced youth is sometimes entrapped and bamboozled by womankind. Mr. Tape, oblige me by touching the bell."

The instant the captain's order had been obeyed, he commenced the narrative of his love adventure, and for a time spoke with his accustomed calmness ; but towards the close he became so exceedingly discursive and excited, and it was with so much difficulty we drew from him many little particulars it was essential to hear, that I have been compelled, from regard to brevity as well as strict decorum, to soften down and render in my own words some of the chief incidents of his mishap.

Just previous to the winter campaign which witnessed the second siege of Badajoz, Mr. Smith, in the zealous exercise of his perilous vocation, entered that city in his usual disguise of a Spanish countryman, with strict orders to keep his eyes and ears wide open, and to report as quickly as possible upon various military details which it was desirable the British general should be made acquainted with. Mr. Smith, from the first moment the pleasant proposition was hinted to him, had manifested considerable reluctance to undertake the task ; more especially as General Phillipon, who commanded the French garrison, had not very long before been much too near catching him to render a possibly still more intimate acquaintance with so sharp a practitioner at all desirable. Nevertheless, as the service was urgent, and no one, it was agreed, so competent as himself to the duty—indeed, upon this point Mr. Smith remarked that the most flattering unanimity of opinion was exhibited by all the gentlemen likely, should he decline the honour, to be selected in his place—he finally consented, and in due time found himself fairly within the walls of the devoted city. "It was an uncomfortable business," the captain said, "very much so—and in more ways than one. It took a long time to accomplish ; and what was worse than all, rations were miserably short. The French garrison were living upon salted horse-flesh, and you may guess, therefore, at the condition of the civilians' victualling department. Wine was, however, to be had in sufficient plenty ; and I used frequently to pass a few hours at a place of entertainment kept by an Andalusian woman, whose bitter hatred of the French invaders, and favourable disposition towards the British, were well known to me, though successfully concealed from Napoleon's soldiers, many of whom—*sous-officiers* chiefly—were her customers. My chief amusement there was playing at dominoes for a few glasses. I played when I had

R

a choice with a smart, goodish-looking sous-lieutenant of voltigeurs—a glib-tongued chap, of the sort that tell all they know, and something over, with very little pressing. His comrades addressed him as Victor, the only name I then knew him by. He and I became very good friends, the more readily that I was content he should generally win. I soon reckoned Master Victor up; but there was an old, wiry *gredin* of a sergeant-major sometimes present, whose suspicious manner caused me frequent twinges. One day especially I caught him looking at me in a way that sent the blood galloping through my veins like wildfire. A look, Mr. Tape, which may be very likely followed in a few minutes afterwards by a halter, or by half-a-dozen bullets through one's body, is apt to excite an unpleasant sensation."

"I should think so. I wouldn't be in such a predicament for the creation!"

"It's a situation that would hardly suit you, Mr. Tape," replied the veteran with a grim smile. "Well, the gray-headed old fox followed up his look with a number of interesting queries concerning my birth, parentage, and present occupation, my answers to which so operated upon him, that I felt quite certain, when he shook hands with me, and expressed himself perfectly satisfied, and sauntered carelessly out of the place, that he was gone to report his surmises, and would be probably back again in two twos with a file of soldiers and an order for my arrest. He had put me so smartly through my facings, that although it was quite a cold day for Spain, I give you my honour that I perspired to the very tips of my fingers and toes. The chance of escape was, I felt, almost desperate. The previous evening a rumour had circulated that the British general had stormed Ciudad Rodrigo, and might therefore be already hastening in his seven-league boots towards Badajoz. The French were consequently more than ever on the alert, and keen eyes watched with sharpened eagerness for indications of sympathy or correspondence between the citizens and the advancing army. I jumped up as soon as the sergeant-major had disappeared, and was about to follow, when the mistress of the place approached, and said, hastily, ' I have heard all, and if not quick, you will be sacrificed by those French dogs; this way.' I followed to an inner apartment, where she drew from a well-concealed recess a French officer's uniform, complete. ' On with it!' she exclaimed as she left the room. ' I know the word and countersign.' I did not require twice telling, you may be sure; and in less than no time was togged off beautifully in a lieutenant's uniform, and walking at a smart pace towards one of the gates. I was within twenty yards of the *corps-de-garde*, when whom should I run against but Sous-Lieutenant Victor! He stared, but either did not for the moment recognize me, or else doubted the evidence of his own senses. I quickened my steps—the guard challenged —I gave the words, 'Napoleon, Austerlitz!'—passed on, and, as soon as a turn of the road hid me from view, increased my pace to a run. My horse, I should have stated, had been left in sure hands at about two miles' distance. Could I reach so far, there was, I felt, a chance. Unfortunately, I had not gone more than five or six hundred yards, when a hubbub of shouts, and musket-shots, in my rear announced that I was pursued. I glanced round; and I assure you, gentlemen, I have seen in my life many pleasanter prospects than met my view—Richmond Hill, for instance, on a fine summer day. Between twenty and thirty voltigeurs, headed by my friend Victor, who had armed himself, like the others, with a musket, were in full pursuit ; and once, I was quite satisfied, within gun-shot, my business would be very effectually and speedily settled.

"I ran on with eager desperation; and though gradually neared by my friends, gained the hut where I had left the horse in safety. The voltigeurs were thrown out for a few minutes. They knew, however, that I had not passed the thickish clumps of trees which partially concealed the cottage; and they extended themselves in a semicircle to enclose, and thus make sure of their prey. Juan Sanchez, luckily for himself, was not at home ; but my horse, as I have stated, was safe, and in prime condition for a race. I saddled, bridled, and brought him out, still concealed by the trees and hut from the French, whose exulting shouts, as they gradually closed upon the spot, grew momentarily louder and fiercer. The sole desperate chance left was to dash right through them ; and I don't mind telling you, gentlemen, that I was confoundedly frightened, and that, but for the certainty of being instantly sacrificed without benefit of clergy, I should have surrendered at once. There was, however, no time for shilly-shallying. I took another pull at the saddle-girths, mounted, drove the only spur I had time to strap on sharply into the animal's flank, and in an instant broke cover in full and near view of the expecting and impatient voltigeurs ; and a very brilliant reception they gave me— quite a stunner in fact! It's a very grand thing, no doubt, to be the exclusive object of attention to twenty or thirty gallant men, but so little selfish, gentlemen, have I been from my youth upwards in the article of ' glory,' that I assure you I should have been remarkably well pleased to have had a few companions—the more the merrier—to share the monopoly which I engrossed as I came suddenly in sight. The flashes, reports, bullets, *sacrés*, which in an instant gleamed in my eyes, and roared and sang about my ears, were deafening. How they all contrived to miss me I can't imagine, but miss me they did ; and I had passed them about sixty paces, when who should start up over a hedge, a few yards in advance, but my domino-player Sous-Lieutenant Victor ! In an instant his musket was raised within two or three, fect of my face. Flash!—bang! I felt a blow as if from a thrust of red-hot steel; and for a moment made sure that my head was off. With difficulty I kept my seat. The horse dashed on, and I was speedily beyond the chance of capture or pursuit. I drew bridle at the first village I reached, and found that Victor's bullet had gone clean through both cheeks. The marks, you see, are still plain enough."

This was quite true. On slightly separating the gray hairs of the captain's whiskers, the places where the ball had made its entrance and exit were distinctly visible.

" A narrow escape," I remarked.

" Yes, rather; but a miss is as good as a mile. The effusion of blood nearly choked me; and it was astonishing how much wine and spirits it required to wash the taste out of my mouth. I found," continued Mr. Smith, "on arriving at head-quarters, that Ciudad Rodrigo had fallen as reported, and that Lord Wellington was hurrying on to storm Badajoz before the echo of his guns should have reached Massena or Soult in the fool's paradise where they were both slumbering. I was of course for some time on the sick-list, and consequently only assisted at the assault of Badajoz as a distant spectator—a, part I always preferred when I had a choice. It was an awful, terrible business," added Mr. Smith with unusual solemnity. " I am not much of a philosopher that

I know of, nor, except in service hours, particularly given to religion, but I remember, when the roar and tumult of the fierce hurricane broke upon the calm and silence of the night, and a storm of hell-fire seemed to burst from and encircle the devoted city, wondering what the stars, which were shining brightly overhead, thought of the strife and din they looked so calmly down upon. It was gallantly done, however," the veteran added in a brisker tone, " and read well in the Gazette; and that perhaps is the chief thing."

" But what," I asked, " has all this to do with the charming Coralie and your love-adventure ?"

" Everything to do with it, as you will immediately find. I remained in Badajoz a considerable time after the departure of the army, and was a more frequent visitor than ever at the house of the excellent dame who had so opportunely aided my escape. She was a kind-hearted soul, with all her vindictiveness; and, now that the French were no longer riding rough-shod over the city, spoke of those who were lurking about in concealment—of whom there were believed to be not a few—with sorrow and compassion. At length the wound I had received at Lieutenant Victor's hands was thoroughly healed, and I was thinking of departure, when the Andalusian dame introduced me, in her taciturn expressive way, to a charming young Frenchwoman, whose husband, a Spaniard, had been slain during the assault or sack of the city. The intimacy thus begun soon kindled on my part into an intense admiration. Coralie was gentle, artless, confiding as she was beautiful, and moreover—as Jeannette, her sprightly, black-eyed maid informed me in confidence—extremely rich. Here, gentlemen, was a combination of charms to which only a heart of stone could remain insensible, and mine at the time was not only young, but particularly sensitive and tender, owing in some degree, I dare say, to the low diet to which I had been so long confined; for nothing, in my opinion, takes the sense and pluck out of a man so quickly as that. At all events I soon surrendered at discretion, and was coyly accepted by the blushing lady. 'There was only one obstacle,' she timidly observed, 'to our happiness.' The relatives of her late husband, by law her guardians, were prejudiced, mercenary wretches, anxious to marry her to an old hunks of a Spaniard, so that the property of her late husband, chiefly consisting of precious stones—he had been a lapidary—might not pass into the hands of foreigners. I can scarcely believe it now," added Mr. Smith with great heat; "but if I didn't swallow all this stuff like sack and sugar, I'm a Dutchman ! The thought of it, old as I am, sets my very blood on fire.

"At length," continued Mr. Marmaduke Smith, as soon as he had partially recovered his equanimity —"at length it was agreed, after all sorts of schemes had been canvassed and rejected, that the fair widow should be smuggled out of Badajoz as luggage in a large chest, which Jeannette and the Andalusian landlady—I forget that woman's name—undertook to have properly prepared. The marriage ceremony was to be performed by a priest at a village about twelve English miles off, with whom Coralie undertook to communicate. 'I trust,' said that lady, 'to the honour of a British officer'—I had not then received my commission, but no matter—'that he, that you, Captain Smith, will respect the sanctity o my concealment till we arrive in the presence of the reverend gentleman who,' she added with a smile like a sunset, 'will, I trust, unite our destinies for ever.' She placed, as she spoke, her charming little hand in mine, and I, you will hardly credit it, tumbled down on my knees, and vowed to religiously respect the dear angel's slightest wish! Mr. Tape, for mercy's sake, pass the wine, or the bare recollection will choke me!"

I must now, for the reasons previously stated, con. tinue the narrative in my own words.

Everything was speedily arranged for flight. Mr. Smith found no difficulty in procuring from the Spanish commandant an order which would enable him to pass his luggage through the barrier un- searched; Jeannette was punctual at the rendezvous, and pointed exultingly to a large chest, which she whispered contained the trembling Coralie. The chinks were sufficiently wide to admit of the requisite quantity of air; it locked inside, and when a kind of sailcloth was thrown loosely over it, there was nothing very unusual in its appearance. Tenderly, tremulously, did the rejoicing lover assist the precious load into the hired bullock-cart, and off they started, Mr. Smith and Jeannette walking by the side of the richly-freighted vehicle.

Mr. Smith trod on air, but the cart, which had to be dragged over some of the worst roads in the world, mocked his impatience by its marvellously slow progress, and when they halted at noon to give the oxen water, they were still three good miles from their destination.

"Do you think?" said Mr. Smith in a whisper to Jeannette, holding up a full pint-flask which he had just drawn from his pocket, and pointing towards the chest—"do you think?—Brandy and water—eh?"

Jeannette nodded, and the gallant Smith gently approached, tapped at the lid, and in a soft low whisper proffered the cordial. The lid was, with the slightest possible delay, just sufficiently raised to admit the flask, and instantly reclosed and locked. In about ten minutes the flask was returned as silently as it had been received. The enamoured soldier raised it to his lips, made a profound inclination towards his concealed *fiancée*, and said gently, "*A votre santé, charmante Coralie!*" The benignant and joyous expression of Mr. Smith's face, as he

vainly elevated the angle of the flask in expectation
of the anticipated draught, assumed an exceedingly
puzzled and bewildered expression. He peered into
the opaque tin vessel; pushed his little finger into
its neck to remove the loose cork or other substance
that impeded the genial flow; then shook it, and
listened curiously for a splash or gurgle. Not a
sound! Coralie had drained it to the last drop!
Mr. Smith looked with comical earnestness at Jeannette, who burst into a fit of uncontrollable laughter.

"Madame is thirsty," she said, as soon as she
could catch sufficient breath; "it must be so hot in
there."

"A full pint!" said the captain, still in blank astonishment, "and strong—very!"

The approach of the carter interrupted what he
further might have had to say, and in a few minutes
the journey was resumed. The captain fell into a
reverie which was not broken till the cart again
stopped. The chest was then glided gently to the
ground; the driver, who had been previously paid,
turned the heads of his team towards Badajoz, and
with a brief salutation departed homeward.

Jeannette was stooping over the chest, conversing
in a low tone with her mistress, and Captain Smith
surveyed the position in which he found himself with
some astonishment. No house, much less a church
or village, was visible, and not a human being was to
be seen.

"Captain Smith," said Jeannette, approaching the puzzled warrior with some hesitation, "a slight *contre-temps* has occurred. The friends who were to have met us here, and helped to convey our precious charge to a place of safety. are not, as you perceive, arrived; perhaps they do not think it prudent to venture quite so far."

"It is quite apparent they are not here," observed Mr. Smith; "but why not have proceeded in the cart?"

"What, captain! Betray your and madame's secret to yonder Spanish boor. How you talk!"

"Well, but my good girl, what *is* to be done? Will madame get out and walk?"

"Impossible—impossible!" ejaculated the amiable damsel. "We should be both recognized, dragged back to that hateful Badajoz, and madame would be shut up in a convent for life. It is but about a quarter of a mile," added Jeannette, in an insinuating, caressing tone, "and madame is not so *very* heavy."

"The devil!" exclaimed Mr. Smith, taken completely aback by this extraordinary proposal. "You can't mean that I should take that infer—— that chest upon my shoulders!"

"*Mon Dieu!* what else *can* be done?" replied Jeannette with pathetic earnestness; "unless you are determined to sacrifice my dear mistress—she whom you pretended to so love—you hard-hearted, faithless man!"

Partially moved by the damsel's tearful vehemence, Mr. Smith reluctantly approached, and gently lifted one end of the chest, as an experiment.

"There are a great many valuables there besides madame," said Jeannette, in reply to the captain's look, "and silver coin is, you know, very heavy."

"Ah!" exclaimed the perplexed lover. "It is deucedly unfortunate—still—— Don't you think," he added earnestly, after again essaying the weight of the precious burden, "that if madame were to wrap herself well up in this sail-cloth, we might reach your friend the priest's house without detection?"

"Oh, no—no—no!" rejoined the girl. "*Mon Dieu!* how can you think of exposing madame to such hazard?"

"How far did you say it is?" asked Captain Smith, after a rather sullen pause.

"Only just over the fields yonder—half a mile perhaps."

Mr. Smith still hesitated, but finally the tears and entreaties of the attendant, his regard for the lady and her fortune, the necessity of the position, in short, determined him to undertake the task. A belt was passed tightly round the chest, by means of which he could keep it on his back; and after several unsuccessful efforts, the charming load was fairly hoisted, and on the captain manfully staggered, Jeannette bringing up the rear.

Valiantly did Mr. Smith, though perspiring in every pore of his body, and dry as a cartouch-box—for madame had emptied the only flask he had—toil on under a burden which seemed to grind his shoulder-blades to powder. He declared he must have lost a stone of flesh at least before, after numerous restings, he arrived, at the end of about an hour, at the door of a small house, which Jeannette announced to be the private residence of the priest. The door was quickly opened by a smart lad, who seemed to have been expecting them; the chest was deposited on the floor, and Jeannette instantly vanished. The lad, with considerate intelligence, handed Mr. Smith a draught of wine. It was scarcely swallowed when the key turned in the lock, the eager lover, greatly revived by the wine, sprang forward with extended arms, and received in his enthusiastic embrace—whom do you think?

" Coralie, half stifled for want of air, and nearly dead with fright?" suggested Mr. Tape.

" That rascally Sous-Lieutenant Victor ! half-drunk with brandy-and-water," roared Captain Smith, who had by this time worked himself into a state of great excitement. " At the same moment in ran Jeannette, and, I could hardly believe my eyes, that Jezabel Coralie, followed by half-a-dozen French voltigeurs, screaming with laughter! I saw I was done," continued Mr. Smith, " but not for the moment precisely how, and but for his comrades, I should have settled old and new scores with Master Victor very quickly. As it was, they had some difficulty in getting him out of my clutches, for I was, as you may suppose, awfully savage. An hour or so afterwards, when philosophy, a pipe, and some capital wine — they were not bad fellows those voltigeurs—had exercised their soothing influence, I was informed of the exact motives and particulars of the trick which had been played me. Coralie was Victor Dufour's wife. He had been wounded at the assault of Badajoz, and successfully concealed in that Andalusian woman's house; and as the best, perhaps only mode of saving him from a Spanish prison, or worse, the scheme of which I had been the victim was concocted. Had not Dufour wounded me, they would, I was assured, have thrown themselves upon my honour and generosity—which honour and generosity, by the bye, would never have got Coralie's husband upon my back, I'll be sworn!

" 'You will forgive us, *mon cher capitaine?*' said that lady with one of her sweetest smiles, as she handed me a cup of wine. 'In love and war, you know, everything is fair.'

" A soldier, gentlemen, is not made of adamant. I was, I confess, softened; and by the time the party broke up, we were all the best friends in the world."

" And so that fat, jolly-looking Madame Dufour we saw in Paris, is the beautiful Coralie that bewitched

Captain Smith?" said Mr. Tape thoughtfully —
"Well!"

"She was younger forty years ago, Mr. Tape, than
when you saw her. Beautiful Coralies are rare, I
fancy, at her present age, and very fortunately, too,
in my opinion," continued Captain Smith; "for
what, I should like to know, would become of the
peace and comfort of society, if a woman of sixty
could bewitch a man as easily as she does at sixteen?"

HUNCHBACK OF STRASBOURG.

In the department of the Bas-Rhin, France, and not more than about two leagues north of Strasbourg, lived Antoine Delessert, who farmed, or intended farming, his own land—about a ten-acre slice of "national" property, which had fallen to him, nobody very well knew how, during the hurly-burly of the great Revolution. He was about five-and-thirty, a widower, and had one child, likewise named Antoine, but familiarly known as Le Bossu (hunchback)—a designation derived, like his father's acres, from the Revolution, somebody having, during one of the earlier and livelier episodes of that exciting drama, thrown the poor little fellow out of a window in Strasbourg, and broken his back. When this happened, Antoine, *père*, was a journeyman *ferblantier* (tinman) of that city. Subsequently he became an active, though subordinate member of the local Salut Public ; in virtue of which patriotic function he obtained Les Prés, the

s

name of his magnificent estate.   Working at his trade was now, of course, out of the question.   Farming, as everybody knows, is a gentlemanly occupation, skill in which comes by nature; and Citizen Delessert forthwith betook himself, with his son, to Les Prés, in the full belief that he had stepped at once into the dignified and delightful position of the ousted aristocrat to whom Les Prés had once belonged, and whose haughty head he had seen fall into the basket. But envious clouds will darken the brightest sky, and the new proprietor found, on taking possession of his quiet, unencumbered domain, that property has its plagues as well as pleasures.   True, there was the land, but not a plant, or a seed thereon or therein, nor an agricultural implement of any kind to work it with.   The walls of the old rambling house were standing, and the roof, except in about a dozen places, kept out the rain with some success; but the nimble, unrespecting fingers of preceding patriots had carried off, not only every vestige of furniture, usually so called, but coppers, cistern, pump, locks, hinges— nay, some of the very doors and window-frames! Delessert was profoundly discontented.   He remarked to Le Bossu, now a sharp lad of some twelve years of age, that he was at last convinced of the entire truth of his cousin Boisdet's frequent observation— that the Revolution, glorious as it might be, had been stained and dishonoured by many shameful excesses; an admission which the son, with keen remembrance

of his compulsory flight from the window, savagely
endorsed.

" Peste ! " exclaimed the new proprietor, after a
lengthened and painful examination of the dilapida-
tions and general nakedness of his estate ; " this is
embarrassing. Citizen Destouches was right. I must
raise money upon the property, to replace what those
brigands have carried off.   I shall require three thousand francs at the very least."

The calculation was dispiriting ; and, after a night's
lodging on the bare floor, damply enveloped in a few
old sacks, the financial horizon did not look one whit
less gloomy in the eyes of Citizen Delessert. Destouches, he sadly reflected, was an iron-fisted notary-
public, who lent money, at exorbitant interest, to dis-
tressed landowners, and was driving, people said, a
thriving trade in that way just now. His pulse
must, however, be felt, and money be obtained,
however hard the terms. This was unmistakably
evident ; and, with the conviction tugging at his heart,
Citizen Delessert took his pensive way towards Strasbourg.

" You guess my errand, Citizen Destouches ? " said
Delessert, addressing a flinty-faced man of about his
own age, in a small room of Numéro 9, Rue Béchard.

" Yes—money : how much ? "

" Three thousand francs is my calculation."

" Three thousand francs ! You are not afraid of
opening your mouth, I see. Three thousand francs

humph! Security, ten acres of middling land, uncul-
tivated, and a tumble-down house; title, *droit de
guillotine.* It is a risk, but I think I may venture.
Pierre Nadaud," he continued, addressing a black-
browed, sly, sinister-eyed clerk, " draw a bond, secured
upon Les Prés, and the appurtenances, for three
thousand francs, with interest at ten per cent.——"

" Morbleu! but that is famous interest!" interjected
Delessert, though timidly.

" Payable quarterly, if demanded," the notary continued, without heeding his client's observation;
" with power, of course, to the lender to sell, if
necessary, to reimburse his capital, as well as all
accruing *dommages-intérêts.*"

The borrower drew a long breath, but only muttered,
" Ah, well; no matter! We shall work hard, Antoine
and I."

The legal document was soon formally drawn.
Citizen Delessert signed and sealed, and he had only
now to pouch the cash, which the notary placed upon
the table.

" Ah ça!" he cried, eyeing the roll of paper proffered to his acceptance with extreme disgust. " It is
not in those *chiffons* of assignats, is it, that I am to
receive three thousand francs, at ten per cent.?"

" My friend," rejoined the notary, in a tone of great
severity, " take care what you say. The offence of
depreciating the credit or money of the Republic is a
grave one."

" Who should know that better than I ? " promptly replied Delessert. " The paper money of our glorious Republic is of inestimable value ; but the fact is, Citizen Destouches, I have a weakness, I confess it, for coined money—*argent métallique.* In case of fire, for instance, it——"

" It is very remarkable," interrupted the notary with increasing sternness—" it is very remarkable, Pierre," (Pierre was an influential member of the Salut Public,) " that the instant a man becomes a landed proprietor, he betrays symptoms of *incivisme*—is discovered to be, in fact, an *aristocq* at heart."

" I an *aristocq !* " exclaimed Delessert, turning very pale ; " you are jesting, surely. See, I take these admirable assignats—three thousand francs' worth at ten per cent.—with the greatest pleasure. Oh, never mind counting among friends."

" Pardon ! " replied Destouches, with rigid scrupulosity. " It is necessary to be extremely cautious in matters of business. Deducting thirty francs for the bond, you will, I think, find your money correct ; but count yourself."

Delessert pretended to do so, but the rage in his heart so caused his eyes to dance and dazzle, and his hands to shake, that he could scarcely see the figures on the assignats, or separate the one from the other. He bundled them up at last, crammed them into his pocket, and hurried off, with a sickly smile upon his face, and maledictions, which found fierce utterance as soon as he had reached a safe distance, trembling on his tongue.

"Scélérat! coquin!" he savagely muttered. "Ten per cent. for this moonshine money! I only wish—but never mind, what's sauce for the goose is sauce for the gander. I must try and buy in the same way that I have been so charmingly sold."

Earnestly meditating this equitable process, Citizen Delessert sought his friend Jean Souday, who lived close by the Fossé de Tanneurs (Tanners' Ditch). Jean had a somewhat ancient mare to dispose of, which our landed proprietor thought might answer his purpose. Cocotte was a slight waif, sheared off by the sharp axe of the Place de la Révolution, and Souday could therefore afford to sell her cheap. Fifty francs *argent métallique* would, Delessert knew, purchase her; but with assignats, it was quite another affair. But courage! He might surely play the notary's game with his friend Souday: that could not be so difficult.

"You have no use for Cocotte," suggested Delessert, modestly, after exchanging fraternal salutations with his friend.

"Such an animal is always useful," promptly answered Madame Souday, a sharp, notable little woman, with a vinegar aspect.

"To be sure—to be sure! And what price do you put upon this useful animal?"

" Cela dépend "—replied Jean, with an interrogative glance at his helpmate.

" Yes, as Jean says, that depends — entirely depends——" responded the wife.

" Upon what, citoyenne ? "

" Upon what is offered, parbleu ! We are in no hurry to part with Cocotte ; but money is tempting."

" Well, then, suppose we say, between friends, fifty francs ? "

" Fifty francs ! That is very little ; besides, I do not know that I shall part with Cocotte at all."

" Come, come ; be reasonable. Sixty francs ! Is it a bargain ? "

Jean still shook his head. " Tempt him with the actual sight of the money," confidentially suggested Madame Souday ; " that is the only way to strike a bargain with my husband."

Delessert preferred increasing his offer to this advice, and gradually advanced to 100 francs, without in the least softening Jean Souday's obduracy. The possessor of the assignats was fain at last to adopt Madame Souday's iterated counsel, and placed 120 paper francs before the owner of Cocotte. The husband and wife instantly, as silently, exchanged with each other, by the only electric telegraph then in use, the words, " I thought so."

" This is charming money, friend Delessert," said Jean Souday ; " far more precious to an enlightened mind than the barbarous coin stamped with effigies of kings and queens of the *ancien regime*. It is very tempting ; still, I do not think I can part with Cocotte at any price."

Poor Delessert ground his teeth with rage, but the expression of his anger would avail nothing ; and, yielding to hard necessity, he at length, after much wrangling, became the purchaser of the old mare for 250 francs—in assignats. We give this as a specimen of the bargains effected by the owner of Les Prés with his borrowed capital, and as affording a key to the bitter hatred he from that day cherished towards the notary, by whom he had, as he conceived, been so egregiously duped. Towards evening, he entered a wine-shop in the suburb of Robertsau, drank freely, and talked still more so, fatigue and vexation having rendered him both thirsty and bold. Destouches, he assured everybody that would listen to him, was a robber, a villain—a vampire blood-sucker, and he, Delessert, would be amply revenged on him some fine day. Had the loquacious orator been eulogizing some one's extraordinary virtues, it is very probable that all he said would have been forgotten by the morrow, but the memories of men are more tenacious of slander and evil-speaking ; and thus it happened that De-lessert's vituperative and menacing eloquence on this occasion was thereafter reproduced against him with fatal power.

Albeit, the now nominal proprietor of Les Prés, assisted by his son and Cocotte, set to work manfully at his new vocation, and, by diut of working twice as hard, and faring much worse than he did as a journey-man *ferblantier*, contrived to keep the wolf, if not far from the door, at least from entering in. His son, Le Bossu, was a cheerful, willing lad, with large, dark, inquisitive eyes, lit up with much clearer intelligence than frequently falls to the share of persons of his age and opportunities. The father and son were greatly attached to each other ; and it was chiefly the hope of bequeathing Les Prés, free from the usurious gripe of Destouches, to his boy, that encouraged the elder Delessert to persevere in his well-nigh hopeless husbandry. Two years thus passed, and matters were beginning to assume a less dreary aspect, thanks chiefly to the notary's not having made any demand in the interim for the interest of his mortgage.

"I have often wondered," said Le Bossu one day as he and his father were eating their dinner of *soupe aux choux* and black bread, " that Destouches has not called before. He may now as soon as he pleases, thanks to our having sold that lot of damaged wheat at such a capital price. Corn must be getting up tremendously in the market. However, you are ready for Destouches' demand of six hundred francs, which it is now."

" Parbleu! quite ready ; all ready counted in those charming assignats; and that is the joke of it. I wish the old villain may call or send soon——"

A gentle tap at the door interrupted the speaker.

The son opened it, and the notary, accompanied by his familiar, Pierre Nadaud, quietly glided in.

"Talk of the devil," growled Delessert audibly, "and you are sure to get a whisk of his tail. Well, messieurs," he added more loudly, "your business?"

"Money—interest now due on the mortgage for three thousand francs," replied M. Destouches, with much suavity.

"Interest for two years," continued the sourly-sardonic accents of Pierre Nadaud; "six hundred francs precisely."

"Very good: you shall have the money directly." Delessert left the room; the notary took out and unclasped a note-book; and Pierre Nadaud placed a slip of *papier timbré* on the dinner-table, preparatory to writing a receipt.

"Here," said Delessert, re-entering with a roll of soiled paper in his hand, "here are your six hundred francs, well counted."

The notary re-clasped his note-book, and returned it to his pocket; Pierre Nadaud resumed possession of the receipt paper.

"You are not aware, then, friend Delessert," said the notary, "that creditors are no longer compelled to receive assignats in payment?"

"How! What do you say?"

"Pierre," continued M. Destouches, "read the extract from *Le Bulletin des Lois*, published last week." Pierre did so with a ringing emphasis which would have rendered it intelligible to a child; and the unhappy debtor fully comprehended that his papermoney was comparatively worthless! It is needless to dwell upon the fury manifested by Delessert, the cool obduracy of the notary, or the cynical comments of the clerk. Enough to say, that M. Destouches departed without his money, after civilly intimating that legal proceedings would be taken forthwith. The son strove to soothe his father's passionate despair, but his words fell upon unheeding ears; and after several hours passed in alternate paroxysms of stormy rage and gloomy reverie, the elder Delessert hastily left the house, taking the direction of Strasbourg. Le Bossu watched his father's retreating figure from the door until it was lost in the clouds of blinding snow that was rapidly falling, and then sadly resumed some indoor employment. It was late when he retired to bed, and his father had not then returned. He would probably remain, the son thought, at Strasbourg for the night.

The chill, lead-coloured dawn was faintly struggling on the horizon with the black, gloomy night, when Le Bossu arose. Ten minutes afterwards, his father strode hastily into the house, and threw himself, without a word, upon a seat. His eyes, the son observed, were bloodshot, either with rage or drink— perhaps both; and his entire aspect wild, haggard, and fierce. Le Bossu silently presented him with a measure of *vin ordinaire*. It was eagerly swallowed, though Delessert's hand shook so that he could scarcely hold the pewter flagon to his lips.

"Something has happened," said Le Bossu presently.

"Morbleu!—yes. That is," added the father, checking himself, "something *might* have happened, if ——Who's there?"

"Only the wind shaking the door. What *might* have happened?" persisted the son.

"I will tell you, Antoine. I set off for Strasbourg yesterday, to see Destouches once again, and entreat him to accept the assignats in part payment at least. He was not at home. Marguérite, the old servant, said he was gone to the cathedral, not long since reopened. Well, I found the usurer just coming out of the great western entrance, heathen as he is, looking as pious as a pilgrim. I accosted him, told my errand, begged, prayed, stormed! It was all to no purpose, except to attract the notice and comments of the passers-by. Destouches went his way, and I, with fury in my heart, betook myself to a wine-shop—Le Brun's. He would not even change an assignat to take for what I drank, which was not a little; and I therefore owe him for it. When the gendarmes cleared the house at last, I was nearly crazed with rage and drink. I must have been so, or I should never have gone to the Rue Béchard, forced myself once more into the notary's presence, and— and——"

" And what ? " quivered the young man, as his father abruptly stopped, startled as before into silence by a sudden rattling of the crazy door. " And what ? "

" And abused him for a flinty-hearted scoundrel, as he is. He ordered me away, and threatened to call the guard. I was flinging out of the house, when Marguérite twitched me by the sleeve, and I stepped aside into the kitchen. 'You must not think,' she said, 'of going home on such a night as this.' It was snowing furiously, and blowing a hurricane at the time. 'There is a straw pallet,' Marguérite added, ' where you can sleep, and nobody the wiser.' I yielded. The good woman warmed some soup, and the storm not abating, I lay down to rest—to rest, do I say?" shouted Delessert, jumping madly to his feet, and pacing furiously to and fro—"the rest of devils! My blood was in a flame; and rage, hate, despair, blew the consuming fire by turns. I thought how I had been plundered by the mercenary ruffian sleeping securely, as he thought, within a dozen yards of the man he had ruined—sleeping securely just beyond the room containing the *secrétaire* in which the mortgage-deed of which I had been swindled was deposited——"

" Oh, father ! " gasped the son.

" Be silent, boy, and you shall know all. It may be that I dreamt all this, for I think the creaking of a door, and a stealthy step on the stair, awoke me ; but perhaps that, too, was part of the dream. However, I was at last wide awake, and I got up and looked out on the cold night. The storm had passed, and the moon had temporarily broken through the heavy clouds by which she was encompassed. Marguérite had said I might let myself out, and I resolved to depart at once. I was doing so, when, looking round, I perceived that the notary's office-door was ajar. Instantly a demon whispered, that although the law was restored, it was still blind and deaf as ever—could not see or hear in that dark silence—and that I might easily baffle the cheating usurer after all. Swiftly and softly I darted towards the half-opened door—entered. The notary's *secrétaire*, Antoine, was wide open! I hunted with shaking hands for the deed, but could not find it. There was money in the drawers, and I—I think I should have taken some —did perhaps, I hardly know how—when I heard, or thought I did, a rustling sound not far off. I gazed wildly round, and plainly saw in the notary's bed-room—the door of which, I had not before observed, was partly open—the shadow of a man's figure clearly traced by the faint moonlight on the floor. I ran out of the room and out of the house with the speed of a madman, and here—here I am!" This said, he threw himself into a seat, and covered his face with his hands.

"That is a chink of money," said Le Bossu, who had listened in dumb dismay to his father's concluding narrative. " You had none, you said, when at the wine-shop."

" Money ! Ah, it may be as I have said—Thunder of heaven ! " cried the wretched man, again fiercely springing to his feet, " I am lost ! "

" I fear so," replied a commissaire de police, who had suddenly entered, accompanied by several gendarmes, " if it be true, as we suspect, that you are the assassin of the notary Destouches."

The assassin of the notary Destouches ! Le Bossu heard but these words ; and when he recovered consciousness, he found himself alone save for the presence of a neighbour, who had been summoned to his assistance.

The *procès verbal* stated, in addition to much of what has been already related, that the notary had been found dead in his bed, at a very early hour of the morning, by his clerk Pierre Nadaud, who slept in the house. The unfortunate man had been stifled by a pillow, it was thought. His *secrétaire* had been plundered of a very large sum, among which were Dutch gold ducats, purchased by Destouches only the day before, of the value of more than 6000 francs. Delessert's mortgage-deed had also disappeared, although other papers of a similar character had been left. Six crowns had been found on Delessert's person, one of which was clipped in a peculiar manner, and was sworn to by an *épicier* as that offered him by the notary the day previous to the murder, and re fused by him. No other portion of the stolen property could be found, although the police exerted themselves to the utmost for that purpose.

There was, however, quite sufficient evidence to convict Delessert of the crime, notwithstanding his persistent asseverations of innocence. His known hatred of Destouches, the threats he had uttered concerning him, his conduct in front of the cathedral, Marguérite's evidence, and the finding the crown in his pocket, left no doubt of his guilt, and he was condemned to suffer death by the guillotine. He appealed, of course, but that, everybody felt, could only prolong his life for a short time, not save it.

There was one person, the convict's son, who did not for a moment believe that his father was the assassin of Destouches. He was satisfied in his own mind that the real criminal was he whose step Delessert had dreamed he heard upon the stair, who had opened the office-door, and whose shadow fell across the bedroom floor; and his eager, unresting thoughts were bent upon bringing this conviction home to others. After a while, light, though as yet dim and uncertain, broke in upon his filial task.

About ten days after the conviction of Delessert, Pierre Nadaud called upon M. Huguet, the procureur-general of Strasbourg. He had a serious complaint to make of Delessert, *fils*. The young man, chiefly, he supposed because he had given evidence against his father, appeared to be nourishing a monomaniacal hatred against him, Pierre Nadaud. "Wherever I go," said the irritated complainant, "at whatever hour, early in the morning and late at night, he dogs my steps. I can in no manner escape him, and I verily believe those fierce, malevolent eyes of his are never closed. I really fear he is meditating some violent act. He should, I respectfully submit, be restrained —placed in a *maison de santé*, for his intellects are certainly unsettled; or otherwise prevented from accomplishing the mischief I am sure he contemplates."

M. Huguet listened attentively to this statement, reflected for a few moments, said inquiry should be made in the matter, and civilly dismissed the complainant.

In the evening of the same day, Le Bossu was brought before M. Huguet. He replied to that gentleman's questioning by the avowal, that he believed Nadaud had murdered M. Destouches. "I believe also," added the young man, "that I have at last hit upon a clue that will lead to his conviction."

"Indeed! Perhaps you will impart it to me?"

"Willingly. The property in gold and precious gems carried off has not yet been traced. I have discovered its hiding-place."

"Say you so? That is extremely fortunate."

"You know, sir, that beyond the Rue des Vignes there are three houses standing alone, which were

gutted by fire some time since, and are now only
temporarily boarded up.   That street is entirely out of
Nadaud's way, and yet he passes and repasses there
five or six times a day. When he did not know that I
was watching him, he used to gaze curiously at those
houses, as if to notice if they were being disturbed for
any purpose.   Lately, if he suspects I am at hand, he
keeps his face determinedly *away* from them, but still
seems to have an unconquerable hankering after the
spot. This very morning, there was a cry raised close
to the ruins, that a child had been run over by a
cart. Nadaud was passing ; he knew I was close by,
and violently checking himself, as I could see,
kept his eyes fixedly *averted* from the place, which
I have no longer any doubt contains the stolen
treasure."

"You are a shrewd lad," said M. Huguet, after a
thoughtful pause. "An examination shall at all events
take place at nightfall. You, in the mean time, remain
here under surveillance."

Between eleven and twelve o'clock, Le Bossu was
again brought into M. Huguet's presence.   The commissary who arrested his father was also there. "You
have made a surprising guess, if it *be* a guess," said
the procureur.   "The missing property has been
found under a hearthstone of the centre house."   Le
Bossu raised his hands, and uttered a cry of delight.
"One moment," continued M. Huguet.   "How do we

know this is not a trick concocted by you and your father to mislead justice ? "

" I have thought of that," replied Le Bossu calmly. " Let it be given out that I am under restraint, in compliance with Nadaud's request; then have some scaffolding placed to-morrow against the houses, as if preparatory to their being pulled down, and you will see the result if a quiet watch is kept during the night." The procureur and commissary exchanged glances, and Le Bossu was removed from the room.

It was verging upon three o'clock in the morning when the watchers heard some one very quietly remove a portion of the back-boarding of the centre house.   Presently, a closely-muffled figure, with a dark lantern and a bag in his hand, crept through the opening, and made direct for the hearth-stone; lifted it, turned on his light slowly, gathered up the treasure, crammed it into his bag, and murmured with an exulting chuckle as he reclosed the lantern and stood upright, " Safe—safe at last."   At the instant, the light of half-a-dozen lanterns flashed upon the miserable wretch, revealing the stern faces of as many gendarmes. " Quite safe, M. Pierre Nadaud ! " echoed their leader. " Of that you may be assured." He was unheard : the detected culprit had fainted.

There is little to add. Nadaud perished by the guillotine, and Delessert was, after a time, liberated.

Whether or not he thought his ill-gotten property had brought a curse with it, I cannot say ; but, at all events, he abandoned it to the notary's heirs, and set off with Le Bossu for Paris, where, I believe, the sign of "Delessert et Fils, Ferblantiers," still flourishes over the front of a respectably-furnished shop.

THE PENINSULAR WAR.

ONE evening at our club we had the satisfaction of hearing Captain Marmaduke Smith relate an adventure in which he had been concerned in Spain, and which I shall try to give as nearly as possible in the language of the narrator. The reader is aware, for he has already made the captain's acquaintance, that he was somewhat of an oddity, and his story on this occasion was suggested by a hot discussion among us on the subject of patriotism.

"Don't tell me of patriotism," said the captain; " I have seen such queer exhibitions of the article in my day, that I am pretty well tired of hearing anything more about it. I could give you a story of Spanish patriotism that would astonish you; however, it's no use talking of the affair."

" The story—let us have the captain's story by all means," replied several voices. " Come, captain, begin."

"Well, well, if I must, I must, though I would rather have the matter forgotten. You of course all know that I am not exactly an Englishman?"

"Indeed! We always thought ——"

"Never mind; I shall explain. My father was a Scotsman, my mother was an Irishwoman, and I was born in Gibraltar; so that you see I am an Anglo-Scoto-Irish Spaniard—a nondescript animal— though I hope not the worse subject of her Majesty, God bless her! By my father, who was a mariner at Gibraltar, I was sent to England for my education; and in consequence of my great merit—ahem!—a commission was easily got for me in the army. Well, that is a good while ago now. I served in the Peninsula, and was promoted—mark you, *not* by brevet. The Peninsula, you will observe, was a sort of native country to me—I spoke Spanish as fast as English. During one of the lulls in the campaign of 1811 I got leave of absence in order to visit Gibraltar. My father and only parent was lying dangerously ill, and requested my presence. Before I had got to Gibraltar, he had died, leaving me his sole heir, which was a great consolation. When I came to look into his property, I found that it included a handsome schooner, the 'Blue-Eyed Maid,' which lay in the harbour, loaded with a capital cargo of printed cotton goods. The craft was waiting for a skipper, and none could be had. An idea struck me—'Why not turn skipper myself for the occasion?' The voyage

was designed to be only as far as Bilboa—a regular
smuggling transaction. I need hardly tell you, for
all the world knows it, that Gibraltar is useful to us
chiefly as a smuggling depôt. The Spaniards want
our goods ; their Government will not let them buy
them in a regular way; and we, kind creatures, let
them have them without giving any trouble to the
custom-house. Now, here was a fine opportunity for
me distinguishing myself as a contrabandista. My
leave of absence having yet some time to run, I
determined on taking the command myself; for
although I had every proper confidence in Bill
Jenkins the mate, yet knowing the weakness of human nature, and especially of smuggling human
nature, in such cases, I judged it might be as well
to be my own cashier. On Christmas eve everything
was ready for a start; the anchor was atrip, and a
fresh breeze was blowing from the south-west, which
promised, if it did but last, a swift and pleasant run.
I had just reached the bottom of the flight of rock-
steps leading to the signal station, where I had been
to take a last look at the weather, when I was accosted by an old, odd, withered-looking gentleman—
his hair and beard white as snow, and dressed in an
old-fashioned grandee suit of velvet, with a short
cloak over his shoulders, and a Spanish cocked-hat
and feather on his head. He had a letter from a
well-known merchant of Gibraltar, recommending
him as a safe, trustworthy gentleman. His object,

he explained, was to procure a passage in the 'Blue-Eyed Maid' to Bilboa, then in the occupation of the French. As our rendezvous was a little to the south of the mouth of the Ebro, I had no difficulty in acceding, for a 'consideration,' to his request. An hour afterwards we were on board, and I had an opportunity of more closely observing our new companion. He seemed a stunted, dried-up specimen of grandee pedigree and arrogance. He could not be less, judging from his palsied limbs, tremulous shrill voice, and shrunken features, than eighty years of age. His eyes, too, were filmy and dull, except when anything occurred to rouse him—an allusion to the French especially—and then a fire would glare out of the old decaying sockets—whether of heaven or the other place this story will best tell—enough to scorch one. He looked at such times for all the world like an Egyptian mummy animated by a fiend from the bottomless pit.

" We were soon under-weigh, and cracking along at a spanking rate. The old Don kept very quiet, giving little or no trouble, except that some one or other of us was continually tumbling over him; for the restless creature would totter about the deck all day and nearly all night, muttering to himself, and every now and then irreverently flapping down on his knees. This conduct at last greatly scandalized Bill Jenkins, who argued that a man who threw out such an enormous number of that sort of signals must have an uncommon queer cargo; and Bill darkly hinted that if extra bad weather should come on, or any out-of-the-way mishap occur, he should know who to thank for it. Nothing, however, happened contrariwise till we were within a hundred miles of our destination; when, just as day broke, the look-out band reported a strange sail on the weather-beam. All eyes and the only glass on board were immediately turned in the direction of the stranger, who finally proved to be a French war corvette. Bill Jenkins glanced at me, and then at the Spaniard, as much as to say, I told you what would come of having that precious rascal on board; and then made preparations to hoist every stitch of canvas the schooner could carry. But spite of all our exertions, the corvette gained rapidly upon us, and the prospect of a French prison became momentarily more and more distinct, and apparently inevitable. Our grandee seemed struck with utter madness: he stormed, raved, gesticulated, and execrated the advancing ship with a fury scarcely human! As something more to the purpose, we were preparing, with sorrowful hearts, to throw over the best and heaviest of the cargo, in order to lighten the schooner, when Jenkins, who had gone up with the glass to the foretop, sung out—'Avast heaving there; here comes a customer for the Frenchman— hurrah!' We all ran to the side, and gazed to where Bill's arm pointed; and there, sure enough, about four miles a-head—the wind was right on our beam—was a British ship of war, just rounding a headland, and coming on like a race-horse. Up went our ensign—we had hitherto modestly concealed it—in a brace of shakes; we crowed out three lusty cheers, and fired our two little brass popguns, as valiant as turkey-cocks, at the corvette. As soon as the Frenchman perceived his new friend, he luffed up into the wind, and seemed for a few minutes doubtful whether to show fight or a clean pair of heels. The British vessel was the 'Scorpion' sloop of war, and about a fair match for the gentleman who had so nearly snapped up my father's son and his inheritance of marketable sundries. But the Frenchman finally made up his mind for a tussle. In little more than ten minutes the 'Scorpion' swept close by us, and we were hailed from the quarter-deck with, 'What schooner's that?' 'The Blue-Eyed Maid of London,' was the prompt reply. 'Heave-to, and wait here till our return,' was the as quick rejoinder. 'Ay, ay, sir!' shouted Bill Jenkins, at the same time respectfully touching his hat, and adding in a lower voice, 'We'll see you smothered first!' In those days, gentlemen, merchant vessels were by no means desirous of too intimate an acquaintance with his Majesty's cruisers. They had a pestilent way of carrying off the best hands, and both skippers and sailors, like the sheep in a story-book, used to make ugly comparisons between the wolves and the shepherds: so we kept on under as much sail as the sticks would bear. The appearance of the British cruiser had changed the delirious rage of the Spaniard into the wildest joy; and when the fight, of which we had a capital view at a pleasant and rapidly-increasing distance—a circumstance, let me tell you, which adds wonderfully to the agreeableness of such glorious spectacles—indeed, to tell the honest truth, I doubt if they are ever thoroughly enjoyed in any other manner——"

"I always understood," interrupted a thin, squeaky voice, struggling through the smoke from a corner of the room; "I always understood that warriors delight in battle."

"Did you, Tape?" rejoined Captain Smith: "then your innocence has been shamefully imposed upon. A great pleasure *over* a battle *may* be; but ball-favours in actual course of distribution are anything but pleasant to the two-legged targets expectant. He who thinks otherwise, you may depend upon it never played at the game. But to return to my story. The Spaniard, I was saying, capered like a maniac—which in truth he was, and that's the best thing, you'll admit presently, can be said of him—at every mishap that befell the Frenchman's spars or rigging-gear; and when, after both ships had been some time hull down, Bill Jenkins announced from the mizzen-truck, with a roar like a small hurricane, that the tricolor was struck, he fairly yelled with delight, and was so overcome with joy that he fainted away, and had to be carried below. A man must have lived in Spain in those days to know to what a pitch national animosity can be carried; and this Senor Cortina, to add to his aversion for the French as the invaders of his country, had suffered, I afterwards learned, personal wrong and violence at their hands. His chateau, after a foolish resistance, had been sacked and burned, and his daughter ill-treated by the savage soldiery. After a few hours' repose he was again on deck, ejaculating as before; and by what I could piece out from detached sentences I now and then overheard, I believed him to be imploring strength and help for the accomplishment of some great and awful duty which he had made a vow to perform.

"Nothing further occurred till we made the entrance of the Ebro, where we stood on and off for a couple of days and nights. At last our signals were answered, and we made a successful run of the entire cargo. As soon as I had pocketed the cash, I paid the crew liberally, and despatched the schooner back to Gibraltar, intending to join my regiment overland. I lingered a few days at the *podesta*, where my late passenger had put up, and became, in consequence, an actor in the affair which followed.

"One day, after a late dinner, I told Senor Cortina who I was, and the occupation I usually followed. His dull old eyes flashed with joy, and having first pressed a considerable present on my acceptance, and hinted that he wished to confer privately with me in the morning, he retired to his chamber. The sight and feel of the money effected a decided change for the better in my opinion of the old gentleman's rabid patriotism, and I began to think somewhat highly of one who evinced such touching gratitude towards an ally. The next morning I was summoned immediately after breakfast to his apartment, where he sat as cold, stern, and rigid as an iron image. All his flightiness was gone, and he was as solemn as a judge. His first sentence was a stunner! 'I want you, Mr. Smith, to convey a message to an officer of the garrison of Bilboa.' 'Bilboa?' says I, almost lifted off my feet with surprise. 'Yes,' he replied, cool as a cucumber—'Bilboa. The service is, I am aware, dangerous; but the reward shall be ample.' This was to the point, and sensible. 'What is the officer's name, senor?' 'Colonel Delisle,' he replied, naming one of the most active and success-ful officers in King Joseph's service. He was, I had before heard, a Spaniard born, though he now bore a French name ; that, I believe, of his wife. You must know, gentlemen, that many Spaniards, through dislike of the old corrupt system of government, which, they said, had ruined the country, joined the intrusive monarch, as he was called, in hopes of establishing through him a more enlightened rule. They were called Afrancesados, and were more bit-

terly hated by the ' patriots ' than were the French
themselves. ' Colonel Delisle ! ' I exclaimed ; ' why,
what on earth can *you* have to say to him ?' ' He is
my son,' was the reply. I was dumbfounded. 'Yes,'
resumed the old man, his cold, hard eye glittering
like a serpent's, ' Colonel Delisle is my son ; and as
I feel that I have not many weeks, perhaps not many
days, to live, I wish to see him once more ere I die.
I wish you to convey this message to him. I cannot
enter Bilboa myself, for a price is set upon my capture. You are used to such enterprises ; and, as I
said, the reward shall be ample. This ring,' he
added, taking an old family affair from his finger,
will accredit your message.' Well, I at last consented to undertake the commission, and immediately
set about my preparations. They were completed in
about an hour ; and in the afternoon of the same
day I arrived safely at Bilboa, distant about eleven
miles from where we were stopping. I soon succeeded in procuring an interview with the colonel, a
fine soldierly-looking man, and at once imparted my
message. He was greatly agitated, and pressed me
with a hundred questions, which I answered or
evaded as well as I could. Finally, he agreed,
though with much hesitation, to meet his father,
for whom he seemed to entertain a strong affection,
a few miles without the town on the following day.
From his inquiries concerning his sister, I gathered

that he was ignorant of the burning and sacking of his paternal mansion, and I left him in happy ignorance on the subject.

" I got safely back to Senor Cortina; and when I informed him of the result, a flash as of demoniac joy lighted up his withered features, and fading in an instant, left them paler, stonier than before. I could not comprehend his strange expression of face; but the faintest suspicion of his motives never crossed my mind. It was arranged that I should meet the colonel, and conduct him to a small farm-house, about half a mile distant from the place of rendezvous, where the senor would be in waiting.

" Evening was rapidly closing in as I next day reached the appointed spot. I gave the concerted signal, and a tall figure immediately emerged from the concealment of a large clump of stunted fir-trees : it was the colonel ! He expressed surprise at not seeing his father; but, satisfied with my explanation, agreed at once to proceed to the farm-house. We set off at a smart pace, and were just entering a narrow sort of gorge leading through some intervening hills, when thirty or forty muskets were suddenly presented at us by a number of men who seemed literally to start out of the ground. The colonel glared fiercely for an instant in my face; and muttering, ' Accursed traitor ! ' sprang wildly up the declivity. The attempt was useless : he was instantly seized. Our arms were pinioned; and having first searched and stripped us of all the money and valuables we had about us, we were placed in the centre of the party, and marched off at a brisk pace. After about three hours' smart walking, we arrived at the head-quarters of the guerilla party into whose hands we had fallen. It was a wild-looking spot, encircled on all sides by bare and rugged hills. The night was cold, dark, and stormy, and the only objects we could discern were several stacks of piled muskets, baggage and horse-furniture scattered here and there, and a rude portable table, near which was placed a number of equally rude camp-stools. Not a word was spoken; and the only sounds we heard for a space, I should think, of more than twenty minutes, were what I took to be signal whistles, replied to at greater and lesser distances. At the end of that time men, wrapped in cloaks, stalked, silently as shadows, into the space in front of us, and seated themselves in grim silence near the table or trestled boards. I counted fifteen of them, when a whistle louder and shriller than any that had preceded it announced the arrival of the chief of the pleasant party. He took his seat in the centre of them. Pine torches were then lighted, at which the grim gentlemen kindled their cigars, and business commenced in very dangerous earnest.

"'Who, and what are you?' said the chief, addressing me in a voice as rough as a nutmeg-grater. I informed him. The explanation was satisfactory; for he immediately said, 'You are free.' I started

with joyful surprise, and was just about to claim
restitution of my stolen property, when I was si-
lenced by a peremptory, 'Who is your companion ?'
This was a poser; but as I had anticipated some
inquiry of the sort, I answered pretty readily that
he was a gentleman living in Bilboa, with whom I
had some pecuniary transactions; aud that we were
proceeding to a neighbouring farm-house to settle
matters when we were arrested. For the truth of
which statement, I added, one Senor Cortina, who
was still no doubt waiting there for us, would readily
vouch.

" A meaning smile, as I uttered the senor's name,
gleamed over the rugged features of the chief, and
was reflected on the countenauces of his companions. Puzzled and alarmed, I stopped abruptly,
and held my peace.

" ' Is this fellow's story true ?' said the president of
the court, addressing the colonel.

" The colonel was silent for a few seconds, and
then said, ' Yes; I am a peaceable and loyal inhabitant of Bilboa.'

" ' Does any one know him ? ' said the chief, looking around inquiringly. 'We must have no mistake
in this business.' There was a long and anxious
pause; but no one answered.

" ' I am sorry for it,' muttered the president, as if
speaking to himself; ' but it must be done.' He
then whispered one of his companions, who instantly

rose, and quickly disappeared in the surrounding gloom.

"A painful silence ensued. The colonel's countenance was dark and troubled, and I am pretty sure he partly guessed what was coming. At last two figures approached the circle. They were the guerilla officer returning to his seat, accompanied by Senor Cortina! I could scarcely believe my eyes, and trembled in every joint of my body. The old man looked harder, colder, stonier than ever; but as his eye fell upon his son, the same fierce gleam I had before so frequently noticed flashed from his eyes, and his features worked with convulsive passion. The fit lasted but a moment, and he was calm again. The chief had risen at his approach, and his manner, as he invited the senor to be seated, indicated both respect and compassion. The old man declined the proffered seat, and remained erect, motionless, and rigid.

"'Is the prisoner the man whom we seek?' asked the president in a nervous, agitated whisper.

"'Yes,' replied Senor Cortina, in a distinct, but somewhat hurried voice and manner, like a man repeating a lesson he has long conned over, and is anxious to be done with. 'He is Colonel Delisle, as he calls himself, in the usurper's service. His real name is Cortina: he is my son, and a Spaniard by blood and birth. He is one of the most active foes of his suffering countrymen. I was on my way to

England with my daughter, who, you may have heard ——' The old man paused, and again the expression of insane hate and fury flitted across his features. Recovering himself, he proceeded, but more hurriedly even than before. ' She died at Gibraltar, and I returned here with that worthy man (pointing to me), in order to atone by this sacrifice for the crime of having given birth to a traitor.'

" A deathlike silence followed. The stern countenances of the members of this rude court of military justice, as seen by the fitful glare of the torches, assumed a gloomier and more savagely-sinister aspect as the old man spoke ; but not a word or gesture of comment followed. Senor Cortina, upon a gesture from the president, was led away.

" ' You hear, Colonel Delisle ?' said the chief, as soon as he supposed the father was out of hearing.

" ' I do,' replied the victim, mastering, as well as he could, the frightful emotion which the old man's denunciation had excited. ' I do, and perceive that I am hopelessly entrapped into the power of remorseless ruffians by that mistaken, much-to-be-pitied old man, whom may God forgive, as I do ! I ask not for mercy from such as you ; indeed, I know it would be bootless to do so ; but I tell you to your teeth, that my love and devotion to Spain are as strong and pure as yours can be. I sought to liberate her—with foreign help, 'tis true ; for how else could it be done ? —from the vilest tyranny that ever debased and ruined a gallant nation; *you* fight to restore her, also by foreign aid, to thraldom of both soul and body. You are impatient: well, then, your sentence—and be brief!'

"It was soon passed—death without delay.

" 'Do you wish for a priest?' said the chief.

"An impatient gesture of refusal was the only answer. Half-a-dozen musketeers, at a signal from one of the officers, stepped forth from the ranks behind us: the colonel drew himself fiercely up, and looked them sternly and steadily in the face: the chief waved me away: the words, 'Make ready, present, fire!' were rapidly given: the death-shots rang sharply on the silence of the night; and the colonel fell stone-dead on the greensward. A soldier tapped me lightly on the shoulder, and bade me follow him. I mechanically obeyed, and soon found myself on the high road, where my guide, having first generously restored me three of the many gold pieces I had been robbed of, left me. I was so knocked up, so bewildered by what I had witnessed, that I sought shelter and repose in the first house I came to; and it was not till the fourth day after the colonel's execution that I arrived at my old lodgings. I was there informed that Senor Cortina had returned, bringing with him his son's body, which was interred in a neighbouring burying-ground, and that the old man had since passed most of his time there. I waited several hours for him, as I had not yet touched the reward, which, although I wished to Heaven I had never earned, still, as the mischief was done, I felt a natural desire to receive : but finding he did not arrive, and feeling anxious to be gone, I proceeded to the churchyard in search of him. As I approached, I saw him kneeling, with his back towards me, by the side of a new-made grave, at the head of which was a wooden crucifix. I called to him, at first gently, then louder ; receiving no answer, I went up, tapped him on the back, and found that he was dead ! The unnatural furor which had preyed on him had at length quenched the last spark of life. He was a victim to his own vengeful passions ! "

" What a horrible transaction altogether ! " said one or two of the party.

" Yes," said the captain in conclusion ; " it was an affair I shall never forget, although I do try to banish it from recollection. It was, however, after all, only one of thousands of cases of family desolation and murder that occurred during the Peninsular war. Gentlemen, good-night ! "

THE COUNTER-STROKE.

Just after breakfast one fine spring morning in 1837, an advertisement in the *Times* for a curate caught and fixed my attention. The salary was sufficiently remunerative for a bachelor, and the parish, as I personally knew, one of the most pleasantly situated in all Somersetshire. Having said that, the reader will readily understand that it could not have been a hundred miles from Taunton. I instantly wrote, enclosing testimonials, with which the Rev. Mr. Townley, the rector, was so entirely satisfied, that the return-post brought me a positive engagement, unclogged with the slightest objection to one or two subsidiary items I had stipulated for, and accompanied by an invitation to make the rectory my home till I could conveniently suit myself elsewhere. This was both kind and handsome; and the next day but one I took coach, with a light heart, for my new destination. It thus happened that I became acquainted, and in some degree mixed up, with the train of events it is my present purpose to relate.

The rector I found to be a stout, portly gentleman, whose years already reached to between sixty and seventy. So many winters, although they had plentifully besprinkled his hair with gray, shone out with ruddy brightness in his still handsome face, and keen, kindly bright-hazel eyes; and his voice, hearty and ringing, had not as yet one quaver of age in it. I met him at breakfast on the morning after my arrival, and his reception of me was most friendly. We had spoken together but for a few minutes, when one of the French windows, that led from the breakfast-room into a shrubbery and flower-garden, gently opened and admitted a lady, just then, as I afterwards learned, in her nineteenth spring. I use this term almost unconsciously, for I cannot even now, in the glowing summer of her life, dissociate her image from that season of youth and joyousness. She was introduced to me, with old-fashioned simplicity, as "My grand-daughter, Agnes Townley." It is difficult to look at beauty through other men's eyes, and, in the present instance, I feel that I should fail miserably in the endeavour to stamp upon this blank, dead paper, any adequate idea of the fresh loveliness, the rose-bud beauty of that young girl. I will merely say, that her perfectly Grecian head, wreathed with wavy *bandeaux* of bright hair, undulating with golden light, vividly brought to my mind Raphael's halo-tinted portraitures of the Virgin—with this difference, that in place of the holy calm and resignation of the painting, there was in Agnes Townley a sparkling youth and life, that even amidst the heat and glare of a crowded ball-room or of a theatre, irresistibly suggested and recalled the freshness and perfume of the morning—of a cloudless, rosy morning of May. And, far higher charm than feature-beauty, however exquisite, a sweetness of disposition, a kind gentleness of mind and temper, was evidenced in every line of her face, in every accent of the low-pitched, silver voice, that breathed through lips made only to smile.

Let me own, that I was greatly struck by so remarkable a combination of rare endowments; and this, I think, the sharp-eyed rector must have perceived, or he might not perhaps have been so immediately communicative with respect to the near prospects of his idolised grandchild, as he was the moment the young lady, after presiding at the breakfast-table, had withdrawn.

"We shall have gay doings, Mr. Tyrrell, at the rectory shortly," he said. "Next Monday three weeks will, with the blessing of God, be Agnes Townley's wedding-day."

" Wedding-day ! "

" Yes," rejoined the rector, turning towards and examining some flowers which Miss Townley had brought in and placed on the table. " Yes, it has been for some time settled that Agnes shall on that day be united in holy wedlock to Mr. Arbuthnot."

" Mr. Arbuthnot, of Elm Park ? "

"A great match, is it not, in a worldly point of view?" replied Mr. Townley, with a pleasant smile at the tone of my exclamation. "And much better than that : Robert Arbuthnot is a young man of a high and noble nature, as well as devotedly attached to Agnes. He will, I doubt not, prove in every respect a husband deserving and worthy of her ; and that from the lips of a doting old grandpapa must be esteemed high praise. You will see him presently."

I did see him often, and quite agreed in the rec-tor's estimate of his future grandson-in-law. I have not frequently seen a finer-looking young man—his age was twenty-six ; and certainly one of a more honourable and kindly spirit, of a more genial temper than he, has never come within my observation. He had drawn a great prize in the matrimonial lottery, and, I felt, deserved his high fortune.

They were married at the time agreed upon, and the day was kept not only at Elm Park, and in its neighbourhood, but throughout "our" parish, as a general holiday. And, strangely enough—at least I have never met with another instance of the kind— it was held by our entire female community, high as well as low, that the match was a perfectly equal one, notwithstanding that wealth and high worldly position were entirely on the bridegroom's side. In fact, that nobody less in the social scale than the repre-sentative of an old territorial family ought, in the nature of things, to have aspired to the hand of

Agnes Townley, appeared to have been a foregone conclusion with everybody. This will give the reader a truer and more vivid impression of the bride, than any words or colours I might use.

The days, weeks, months of wedded life flew over Mr. and Mrs. Arbuthnot without a cloud, save a few dark but transitory ones which I saw now and then flit over the husband's countenance at the time when he should become a father drew near, and came to be more and more spoken of. "I should not survive her," said Mr. Arbuthnot, one day in reply to a chance observation of the rector's, "nor indeed desire to do so." The gray-headed man seized and warmly pressed the husband's hand, and tears of sympathy filled his eyes; yet did he, nevertheless, as in duty bound, utter grave words on the sinfulness of despair under any circumstances, and the duty, in all trials, however heavy, of patient submission to the will of God. But the venerable gentleman spoke in a hoarse and broken voice, and it was easy to see he *felt* with Mr. Arbuthnot that the reality of an event, the bare possibility of which shook them so terribly, were a cross too heavy for human strength to bear and live.

It was of course decided that the expected heir or heiress should be entrusted to a wet-nurse, and a Mrs. Danby, the wife of a miller living not very far from the rectory, was engaged for that purpose. I had frequently seen the woman; and her name, as the rector and I were one evening gossiping over our tea, on some subject or other that I forget, came up.

"A likely person," I remarked; "healthy, very good-looking, and one might make oath, a true-hearted creature. But there is withal a timidity, a frightenedness in her manner at times which, if I may hazard a perhaps uncharitable conjecture, speaks ill for that smart husband of hers."

"You have hit the mark precisely, my dear sir. Danby is a sorry fellow, and a domestic tyrant to boot. His wife, who is really a good, but meek-hearted person, lived with us once. How old do you suppose her to be?"

"Five-and-twenty, perhaps."

"Six years more than that. She has a son of the name of Harper by a former marriage, who is in his tenth year. Anne wasn't a widow long. Danby was caught by her good looks, and she by the bait of a well-provided home. Unless, however, her husband gives up his corn speculations, she will not, I think, have that much longer."

"Corn speculations! Surely Danby has no means adequate to indulgence in such a game as that?"

"Not he. But about two years ago he bought, on credit, I believe, a considerable quantity of wheat, and prices happening to fly suddenly up just then, he made a large profit. This has quite turned his head, which, by the bye, was never, as Cockneys say, quite rightly screwed on." The announcement of a visitor interrupted anything further the rector might have to say, and I soon afterwards went home.

A sad accident occurred about a month subsequent to the foregoing conversation. The rector was out riding upon a usually quiet horse, which all at once took it into his head to shy at a scarecrow it must have seen a score of times, and thereby threw its rider. Help was fortunately at hand, and the reverend gentleman was instantly conveyed home, when it was found that his left thigh was broken. Thanks, however, to his temperate habits, it was before long authoritatively pronounced that, although it would be a considerable time before he was released from confinement, it was not probable that the lusty winter of his life would be shortened by what had happened. Unfortunately, the accident threatened to have evil consequences in another quarter. Immediately after it occurred, one Matthews, a busy, thick-headed lout of a butcher, rode furiously off to Elm Park with the news. Mrs. Arbuthnot, who daily looked to be confined, was walking with her husband upon the lawn in front of the house, when the great burley blockhead rode up, and blurted out that the rector had been thrown from his horse, and, it was feared, killed !

The shock of such an announcement was of course overwhelming. A few hours afterwards, Mrs. Arbuthnot gave birth to a healthy male-child ; but the young mother's life, assailed by fever, was for many days utterly despaired of—for weeks held to tremble so evenly in the balance, that the slightest adverse circumstance might in a moment turn the scale deathward. At length, the black horizon that seemed to encompass us so hopelessly, lightened, and afforded the lover-husband a glimpse and hope of his vanished and well-nigh despaired-of Eden. The promise was fulfilled. I was in the library with Mr. Arbuthnot awaiting the physician's morning report, very anxiously expected at the rectory, when Dr. Lindley entered the apartment in evidently cheerful mood.

" You have been causelessly alarmed," he said. " There is no fear whatever of a relapse. Weakness only remains, and that we shall slowly, perhaps, but certainly, remove."

A gleam of lightning seemed to flash over Mr. Arbuthnot's expressive countenance. " Blessed be God !" he exclaimed. " And how," he added, " shall we manage respecting the child ? She asks for it incessantly."

Mr. Arbuthnot's infant son, I should state, had been consigned immediately after its birth to the care of Mrs. Danby, who had herself been confined, also with a boy, about a fortnight previously. Scarlatina being prevalent in the neighbourhood, Mrs. Danby was hurried away with the two children to a place near Bath, almost before she was able to bear the journey. Mr. Arbuthnot had not left his wife for an hour, and consequently had only seen his child for a few minutes just after it was born.

"With respect to the child," replied Dr. Lindley, "I am of opinion that Mrs. Arbuthnot may see it in a day or two. Say the third day from this, if all goes well. I think we may venture so far; but I will be present, for any untoward agitation might be perhaps instantly fatal." This point provisionally settled, we all three went our several ways:—I to cheer the still suffering rector with the good news.

The next day but one, Mr. Arbuthnot was in exuberant spirits. "Dr. Lindley's report is even more favourable than we had anticipated," he said; "and I start to-morrow morning, to bring Mrs. Danby and the child "—— The postman's subdued but unmistakable knock interrupted him. "The nurse," he added, "is very attentive and punctual. She writes almost every day." A servant entered with a salver heaped with letters. Mr. Arbuthnot tossed them over eagerly, and seizing one, after glancing at the post-mark, tore it eagerly open, muttering as he did so, "It is not the usual handwriting; but from her, no doubt "—— "Merciful God!" I impulsively exclaimed, as I suddenly lifted my eyes to his, "what is the matter?" A mortal pallor had spread over Mr. Arbuthnot's before-animated features, and he was glaring at the letter in his hand as if a basilisk had suddenly confronted him. Another moment, and the muscles of his frame appeared to give way suddenly, and he dropped heavily into the easy-chair from which he had risen to take the letters. I was terribly alarmed, and first loosening his neckerchief, for he seemed choking, I said: "Let me call some one;" and I turned to reach the bell, when he instantly seized my arms, and held me with a grip of iron. "No—no—no!" he hoarsely gasped; "water—water!" There was fortunately some on a side-table. I handed it to him, and he drank eagerly. It appeared to revive him a little. He thrust the crumpled letter into his pocket, and said in a low, quick whisper: "There is some one coming! Not a word, remember—not a word!" At the same time, he wheeled his chair half-round, so that his back should be towards the servant we heard approaching

"I am sent, sir," said Mrs. Arbuthnot's maid, "to ask if the post has arrived."

"Yes," replied Mr. Arbuthnot, with wonderful mastery of his voice. "Tell your mistress I shall be with her almost immediately, and that her—her son is quite well."

"Mr. Tyrrel," he continued, as soon as the servant was out of hearing, "there is, I think, a liqueur-stand on the sideboard in the large dining-room. Would you have the kindness to bring it me, unobserved—mind that—unobserved by any one?"

I did as he requested; and the instant I placed the liqueur-frame before him, he seized the brandy

carafe, and drank with fierce eagerness. " For goodness' sake," I exclaimed, " consider what you are
about, Mr. Arbuthnot: you will make yourself ill."

" No, no," he answered, after finishing his draught.
" It seems scarcely stronger than water. But I—I
am better now. It was a sudden spasm of the heart,
that's all. The letter," he added, after a long and
painful pause, during which he eyed me, I thought
with a kind of suspicion—" the letter you saw me
open just now comes from a relative, an aunt, who
is ill, very ill, and wishes to see me instantly. You
understand?"

I *did* understand, or at least I feared that I did,
too well. I, however, bowed acquiescence ; and he
presently rose from his chair, and strode about the
apartment in great agitation, until his wife's bedroom bell rang. He then stopped suddenly short,
shook himself, and looked anxiously at the reflection
of his flushed and varying countenance in the magnificent chimney-glass.

" I do not look, I think—or, at least shall not, in
a darkened room—odder, more out of the way—that
is, more agitated—than one might, than one *must* appear, after hearing of the dangerous illness of—of—
an aunt ? "

" You look better, sir, than you did awhile since."

" Yes, yes, much better, much better. I am glad
to hear you say so. That was my wife's bell. She is
anxious, no doubt, to see me."

He left the apartment; was gone perhaps ten minutes; and when he returned, was a thought less nervous than before. I rose to go. "Give my respects," he said, "to the good rector; and as an especial favour," he added, with strong emphasis, "let me ask of you not to mention to a living soul that you saw me so unmanned as I was just now; that I swallowed brandy. It would appear so strange, so weak, so ridiculous."

I promised not to do so, and almost immediately left the house, very painfully affected. His son was, I concluded, either dead or dying, and he was thus bewilderedly casting about for means of keeping the terrible, perhaps fatal tidings from his wife. I afterwards heard that he left Elm Park in a postchaise, about two hours after I came away, unattended by a single servant!

He was gone three clear days only, at the end of which he returned with Mrs. Danby and—his son— in florid health, too, and one of the finest babies of its age—about nine weeks only—I had ever seen. Thus vanished the air-drawn Doubting Castle and Giant Despair which I had so hastily conjured up! The cause assigned by Mr. Arbuthnot for the agitation I had witnessed, was doubtless the true one; and yet—and the thought haunted me for months, years afterwards—he opened only *one* letter that morning, and had sent a message to his wife that the child was well!

Mrs. Danby remained at the Park till the little Robert was weaned, and was then dismissed very munificently rewarded. Year after year rolled away without bringing Mr. and Mrs. Arbuthnot any additional little ones, and no one, therefore, could feel surprised at the enthusiastic love of the delighted mother for her handsome, nobly-promising boy. But that which did astonish me, though no one else, for it seemed that I alone noticed it, was a strange defect of character which began to develope itself in Mr. Arbuthnot. He was positively jealous of his wife's affection for their own child! Many and many a time have I remarked, when he thought himself unobserved, an expression of intense pain flash from his fine expressive eyes, at any more than usually fervent manifestation of the young mother's gushing love for her first and only born! It was altogether a mystery to me, and I as much as possible forbore to dwell upon the subject.

Nine years passed away without bringing any material change to the parties involved in this narrative, except those which time brings ordinarily in his train. Young Robert Arbuthnot was a healthy, tall, fine-looking lad of his age; and his great-grandpapa, the rector, though not suffering under any actual physical or mental infirmity, had reached a time of life when the announcement that the golden bowl is broken, or the silver cord is loosed, may indeed be quick and sudden, but scarcely unexpected. Things had gone well, too, with the nurse, Mrs. Danby, and her husband; well, at least, after a fashion. The speculative miller must have made good use of the gift to his wife for her care of little Arbuthnot, for he had built a genteel house near the mill, always rode a valuable horse, kept, it was said, a capital table; and all this, as it seemed, by his clever speculations in corn and flour, for the ordinary business of the mill was almost entirely neglected. He had no children of his own, but he had apparently taken, with much cordiality, to his step-son, a fine lad, now about eighteen years of age. This greatly grieved the boy's mother, who dreaded above all things that her son should contract the evil, dissolute habits of his father-in-law. Latterly, she had become extremely solicitous to procure the lad a permanent situation abroad, and this Mr. Arbuthnot had promised should be effected at the earliest opportunity.

Thus stood affairs on the 16th of October, 1846. Mr. Arbuthnot was temporarily absent in Ireland, where he possessed large property, and was making personal inquiries as to the extent of the potato-rot, not long before announced. The morning's post had brought a letter to his wife, with the intelligence that he should reach home that very evening; and as the rectory was on the direct road to Elm Park, and her husband would be sure to pull up there, Mrs. Arbuthnot came with her son to pass the afternoon there, and in some slight degree anticipate her husband's arrival.

About three o'clock, a chief-clerk of one of the Taunton banks rode up in a gig to the rectory, and asked to see the Rev. Mr. Townley, on pressing and important business. He was ushered into the library, where the rector and I were at the moment rather busily engaged. The clerk said he had been to Elm Park, but not finding either Mr. Arbuthnot or his lady there, he had thought that perhaps the Rev. Mr. Townley might be able to pronounce upon the genuineness of a cheque for £300, purporting to be drawn on the Taunton Bank by Mr. Arbuthnot, and which Danby the miller had obtained cash for at Bath. He further added, that the bank had refused payment, and detained the cheque, believing it to be a forgery.

"A forgery!" exclaimed the rector, after merely glancing at the document. "No question that it is, and a very clumsily executed one, too. Besides, Mr. Arbuthnot is not yet returned from Ireland."

This was sufficient; and the messenger, with many apologies for his intrusion, withdrew, and hastened back to Taunton. We were still talking over this sad affair, although some hours had elapsed since the clerk's departure—in fact, candles had been brought in, and we were every moment expecting Mr. Arbuth-not—when the sound of a horse at a hasty gallop was heard approaching, and presently the pale and haggard face of Danby shot by the window at which the rector and myself were standing. The gate-bell was rung almost immediately afterwards, and but a brief interval passed before " Mr. Danby " was announced to be in waiting. The servant had hardly gained the passage with leave to show him in, when the impatient visitor rushed rudely into the room in a state of great, and it seemed angry excitement.

" What, sir, is the meaning of this ill-mannered intrusion ? " demanded the rector sternly.

" You have pronounced the cheque I paid away at Bath to be a forgery ; and the officers are, I am told, already at my heels. Mr. Arbuthnot, unfortunately, is not at home, and I am come, therefore, to seek shelter with you."

" Shelter with me, sir ! " exclaimed the indignant rector, moving, as he spoke, towards the bell. " Out of my house you shall go this instant."

The fellow placed his hand upon the reverend gentleman's arm, and looked with his bloodshot eyes keenly in his face.

" Don't ! " said Danby ; " don't, for the sake of yourself and yours ! Don't ! I warn you : or, if you like the phrase better, don't, for the sake of me and *mine*."

" Yours, fellow ! Your wife, whom you have so long held in cruel bondage through her fears for her son, has at last shaken off that chain. James Harper sailed two days ago from Portsmouth for Bombay. I sent her the news two hours since."

"Ah! Is that indeed so?" cried Danby, with an irrepressible start of alarm. "Why, then—— But no matter: here, luckily, comes Mrs. Arbuthnot *and her son*. All's right! She will, I know, stand bail for me, and, if need be, acknowledge the genuineness of her husband's cheque."

The fellow's insolence was becoming unbearable, and I was about to seize and thrust him forcibly from the apartment, when the sound of wheels was heard outside. "Hold! one moment," he cried with fierce vehemence. "That is probably the officers: I must be brief, then, and to the purpose. Pray, madam, do not leave the room for your own sake: as for you, young sir, I *command* you to remain!"

"What! what does he mean?" exclaimed Mrs. Arbuthnot bewilderedly, and at the same time clasping her son—who gazed on Danby with kindled eyes, and angry boyish defiance—tightly to her side. Did the man's strange words give form and significance to some dark, shadowy, indistinct doubt that had previously haunted her at times? I judged so. The rector appeared similarly confused and shaken, and had sunk nerveless and terrified upon a sofa.

"You guess dimly, I see, at what I have to say," resumed Danby with a malignant sneer. "Well, hear it, then, once for all, and then, if you will, give me up to the officers. Some years ago," he continued, coldly and steadily—" some years ago, a woman, a nurse, was placed in charge of two infant children, both boys; one of these was her own; the other was the son of rich, proud parents. The woman's husband was a gay, jolly fellow, who much preferred spending money to earning it, and just then it happened that he was more than usually hard up. One afternoon, on visiting his wife, who had removed to a distance, he found that the rich man's child had sickened of the small-pox, and that there was no chance of its recovery. A letter containing the sad news was on a table, which he, the husband, took the liberty to open and read. After some reflection, suggested by what he had heard of the lady-mother's state of mind, he recopied the letter, for the sake of embodying in it a certain suggestion. That letter was duly posted, and the next day brought the rich man almost in a state of distraction; but his chief and mastering terror was lest the mother of the already dead infant should hear, in her then precarious state, of what had happened. The tidings, he was sure, would kill her. Seeing this, the cunning husband of the nurse suggested that, for the present, his—the cunning one's—child might be taken to the lady as her own, and that the truth could be revealed when she was strong enough to bear it. The rich man fell into the artful trap, and that which the hus-

band of the nurse had speculated upon, came to
pass even beyond his hopes. The lady grew to idolize
her fancied child—she has, fortunately, had no other
—and now, I think, it will really kill her to part with
him. The rich man could not find it in his heart
to undeceive his wife—every year it became more
difficult, more impossible to do so; and very generously, I must say, has he paid in purse for the forbearance of the nurse's husband. Well now, then,
to sum up: the nurse was Mrs. Danby; the rich,
weak husband, Mr. Arbuthnot; the substituted child,
that handsome boy—*my son!*"

A wild scream from Mrs. Arbuthnot broke the
dread silence which had accompanied this frightful
revelation, echoed by an agonized cry, half tenderness, half rage, from her husband, who had entered
the room unobserved, and now clasped her passionately in his arms. The carriage-wheels we had heard
were his. It was long before I could recall with
calmness the tumult, terror, and confusion of that
scene. Mr. Arbuthnot strove to bear his wife from
the apartment, but she would not be forced away,
and kept imploring with frenzied vehemence that
Robert—that her boy should not be taken from her.

"I have no wish to do so—far from it," said
Danby with gleeful exultation. "Only folk must
be reasonable, and not threaten their friends with
the hulks——"

"Give him anything, anything!" broke in the

unhappy lady. "O Robert! Robert!" she added with a renewed burst of hysterical grief, "how could you deceive me so?"

"I have been punished, Agnes," he answered in a husky, broken voice, "for my well-intended but criminal weakness; cruelly punished by the ever-present consciousness that this discovery must one day or other be surely made. What do you want?" he after a while addded with recovering firmness, addressing Danby.

"The acknowledgment of the little bit of paper in dispute, of course: and say a genuine one to the same amount."

"Yes, yes," exclaimed Mrs. Arbuthnot, still wildly sobbing, and holding the terrified boy strained in her embrace, as if she feared he might be wrenched from her by force. "Anything — pay him anything!"

At this moment, chancing to look towards the door of the apartment, I saw that it was partially opened, and that Danby's wife was listening there. What might that mean? But what of helpful meaning in such a case could it have?

"Be it so, love," said Mr. Arbuthnot, soothingly. "Danby, call to-morrow at the Park. And now, begone at once."

"I was thinking," resumed the rascal with swelling audacity, "that we might as well at the same time come to some permanent arrangement upon black and white.   But never mind: I can always put the screw on; unless, indeed, you get tired of the young gentleman, and in that case, I doubt not, he will prove a dutiful and affectionate son—— Ah! devil!   What do you here?   Begone, or I'll murder you!   Begone, do you hear?"

His wife had entered, and silently confronted him. " Your threats, evil man," replied the woman quietly, " have no terrors for me now.   My son is beyond your reach.   Oh, Mrs. Arbuthnot," she added, turning towards and addressing that lady, " believe not——"

Her husband sprang at her with the bound of a panther.   " Silence!   Go home, or I'll strangle"—— His own utterance was arrested by the fierce grasp of Mr. Arbuthnot, who seized him by the throat, and hurled him to the further end of the room.   " Speak on, woman; and quick! quick!   What have you to say?"

" That your son, dearest lady," she answered, throwing herself at Mrs. Arbuthnot's feet, " is as truly your own child as ever son born of woman."

That shout of half-fearful triumph seems even now as I write to ring in my ears!   I *felt* that the woman's words were words of truth, but I could not see distinctly: the room whirled round, and the lights danced before my eyes, but I could hear

through all the choking ecstacy of the mother, and
the fury of the baffled felon.

"The letter," continued Mrs. Danby, "which my
husband found and opened, would have informed you,
sir, of the swiftly-approaching death of *my* child, and
that yours had been carefully kept beyond the reach
of contagion. The letter you received was written
without my knowledge or consent. True it is that,
terrified by my husband's threats, and in some measure reconciled to the wicked imposition by knowing
that, after all, the right child would be in his right
place, I afterwards lent myself to Danby's evil purposes. But I chiefly feared for my son, whom I fully
believed he would not have scrupled to make away
with in revenge for my exposing his profitable fraud.
I have sinned; I can hardly hope to be forgiven, but
I have now told the sacred truth."

All this was uttered by the repentant woman, but
at the time it was almost wholly unheard by those
most interested in the statement. They only comprehended that they were saved—that the child was
theirs in very truth. Great, abundant, but for the
moment, bewildering joy! Mr. Arbuthnot—his beautiful young wife—her own true boy (how could she
for a moment have doubted that he was her own true
boy!—you might read that thought through all her
tears, thickly as they fell)—the aged and half-stunned
rector, whilst yet Mrs. Danby was speaking, were exclaiming, sobbing in each other's arms, ay, and prais-

ing God too, with broken voices and incoherent words it may be, but certainly with fervent, pious, grateful hearts.

When we had time to look about us, it was found that the felon had disappeared—escaped. It was well, perhaps, that he had; better, that he has not been heard of since.

SELF-SACRIFICE.

The "days of chivalry," in the steel-armour and horse-prancing sense of the phrase, have doubtless passed away into the limbo reserved for all social extravagances; but the spirit which, in the eyes of thoughtful men, redeemed its else vain shows and tinsel accessories from unmitigated contempt, interfused with the prosaic drama of conventional modern life, survives in more than all its ancient vigour, and from time to time gleams forth and illumines the sober hues of our neutral-tinted civilization with the brilliant prismatic colours of the dawn. In other words, there are deeds constantly enacted in this matter-of-fact world of ours which, for real heroism, have no parallel in the glittering annals of plumed and painted chivalry. A romantic episode in the life of a gallant and well-known sea officer—for the ex-.ct verity of which I, and indeed many others still living, can vouch—affords, I think, a vivid illustration of this brief text.

Francis Travers, as I shall call him, was the only

son of a worthy and somewhat eccentric gentleman
of Devonshire, who had passed the greater part of
an active and successful life in the naval service of
the East India Company. He retired from active
pursuits at the—for this bustling go-a-head country
—early age of fifty-five; and having securely invested
the savings of his life—amounting to about twenty
thousand pounds—in the funds, retired to an old-
fashioned rustic residence called Marlands, to enjoy
in leisured solitary dignity—he had been long a
widower—the remainder of his allotted days. His
house, in common with those of most retired seamen, was speedily decorated with a wind-vane and
a flag-staff, on which was frequently exhibited bunt-
ing of every hue and device known and recognized
beneath the sun; but even with the help of these
interesting time-killers, the hours passed slowly and
heavily with the old mariner, and it was soon abundantly evident that to be thus everlastingly anchored,
stranded in one spot, was ruinous to his health as
well as temper. He grew daily more and more restless, fidgety, and irritable, and drank a great deal
more than he had been accustomed to. Finally, on
the very morning after the news arrived that his son
had creditably passed for a lieutenant in the Royal
Navy, Mr. Travers was found dead and cold in his
bed. The coroner's inquest recorded that he died by
" the visitation of God."

Lieutenant Travers, the sole heir of his father's

wealth, was at this time a fine specimen of a well-educated, intelligent naval officer; and rich, well-looking, and of robust health, might be fairly looked upon as an extremely fortunate person, whom in all probability a brilliant, cloudless future awaited. In the young officer's own opinion, however, all these aids and appliances were nothing if they failed to obtain for him the one sole object, after professional fame, of his ambition—the hand of the beautiful girl by whom, since his first visit to his father at Marlands, his whole being—heart, soul, sense—had been engrossed. His admiration of Mary Wharton was perhaps all the more enthusiastic and intense from having remained as yet strictly confined to his own breast. His heart alone knew and brooded over its own secret, and was likely, it seemed, to do so for an indefinite time to come, inasmuch as the daring sailor, who had already been twice wounded in desperate boat expeditions upon which he had volunteered, doubted much whether he should ever muster sufficient audacity to disclose his passion even to the fair lady herself.

It is the faith or imagination of the worshipper which invests the idol or the shrine with its transcendant attributes; and often as Francis Travers had counted up his own advantages—*videlicet*, a person which even *his* modesty could not but admit was not one to frighten the gentler sex; a professional reputation for skill and daring; and now, since the

death of his father, a handsome fortune—he pro·
nounced them all mere dross and rags when weighed
against the divine perfections of the lady. It is very
doubtful whether any other human being would have
arrived at the same conclusion. Mary Wharton was
indeed an amiable, graceful girl; and her beauty, if
not of the brilliant kind which at first view dazzles
the beholder, was scarcely less ultimately dangerous
in its pensive thoughtfulness, and in the beseeching
gentleness which, gleaming from out the transparent
depths of her sweet blue eyes, tinted the pale, finely-
turned cheek with varying charm. But excepting
this beauty of expression more than of form, and an
unquestionably amiable temper and disposition, she
had really nothing to boast. Of worldly fortune
she would not possess one shilling, and was neither
fashionably nor wealthily connected. Her father, Sir
Richard Wharton—a spendthrift, gambling baronet,
of old creation, it is true, but bankrupt alike in health
and fortune, known, in fact, to be overwhelmed with
debt—was scarcely very desirable as a father-in-law;
and yet Francis Travers, as he took leave of Lady
Wharton and her daughter, after attending his father's
funeral, could not help wondering, as he gazed upon
the fair, gentle girl, and felt her calm reservedness
of tone and manner sweep coldly across his beating
heart, at his presumptuous folly in having loved

> "—— A bright, particular star,
> And thought to wed it."

So strange are the tricks which the blind god some-times plays with the eyes and understandings of his more enthusiastic votaries.

The frigate to which Lieutenant Travers was first appointed, after knocking about the Channel through the winter, picking up a few trifling prizes, was ordered to Portsmouth, to be overhauled, and have defects made good; but being found thoroughly in-fected with dry-rot, was put out of commission, and ultimately broken up. The brush off Trafalgar had crippled Napoleon's marine; and as the breeze with Brother Jonathan had not yet sprung up, lieutenants were in somewhat less request than usual, and Travers took up his abode at Marlands, undisturbed for a con-siderable time by intimation or command from the Admiralty. Mary Wharton, more beautiful, more interesting than ever, received him, he imagined, with a much more cordial frankness than formerly; Lady Wharton seemed pleased with his return; whilst Sir Richard, who, he instinctively felt, had long since penetrated his secret, and with whom, by the way, he had always been a great favourite, expressed unqualified pleasure at seeing him. What wonder, then, that the illusions dispelled by former coldness should reappear beneath the genial warmth of such a reception? There was no rival in the case: of that he felt assured. Indeed, with the exception of the Rev. Edmund Harford, curate of the parish church, and Mary's cousin, Lady Wharton and her daughter lived at Archer's Lodge in almost entire seclusion. Sir Richard for three-fourths of the year resided in London, and when visiting Devonshire, surrounded himself with associates whose manners and pursuits were anything but congenial with those of his wife and daughter. As to the curate, accomplished scholar and eloquent divine as he was, and much as Miss Wharton seemed to take pleasure in his varied and brilliant conversation—not more, however, than did her mother and Travers himself—any notion of marriage with him was, the lieutenant felt, quite out of the question. Edmund Harford's salary as curate was only about ninety pounds a year—he had no influential connections to push him on in the church—and Travers thought he had ill read the human character if Lady Wharton, did any chance exist of Mary allying herself with poverty and wretchedness, would permit an intercourse likely to have so fatal a result. Thus reasoning, believing, hoping, Travers surrendered himself unresistingly to the influence by which he was enthralled. He walked, fished, played at billiards with the baronet, participated freely in all the various modes he adopted for killing time, except gaming, and awaited with torturing anxiety a favourable moment for terminating the feverish doubts which, reason as he might, still haunted him incessantly. A circumstance, sudden, unexpected, and terrible, cut short his hesitation, and pushed him to a decision he might have else delayed for months—perhaps years.

A dispute arose late one night between Sir Richard Wharton and one of his companions respecting alleged unfair play at cards. Injurious epithets were freely interchanged; and after a fruitless attempt by the persons present to adjust the quarrel amicably, an appeal to the arbitrement of the pistol was arranged for an early hour the next morning. The meeting took place, and both combatants were wounded at the first fire—Sir Richard, as it proved, mortally.

The baronet was hastily conveyed to the nearest public-house, and such medical aid as the locality afforded was instantly procured. On examining the wound, which was in the chest, and bled internally, the surgeon at once informed the sufferer that nothing could be done to prolong, much less to *save*, his life.

" I thought so—felt so!" murmured the unfortunate gentleman with white lips. " Accursed chance !" A few moments afterwards he added, " How long, think you, my life—this agony, may last ? "

" Not long: an hour perhaps—not more."

" So soon! I must be quick then. Let the room be cleared at once of all except my servant. James," he added, as soon as his orders were obeyed, " hasten to Marlands to Mr. Travers : tell him I must see him instantly. Be swift, for more than life depends upon your speed ! "

For the next half-hour the groans wrenched from the dying man, in his fast-closing struggle with the terrible foe that held him in his iron grasp, were alone heard in the apartment ; and then hurrying feet sounded along the passage, and Lieutenant Travers, greatly excited, rushed in.

" Can this terrible intelligence be true ? " he breathlessly exclaimed, " that you are——"

" Dying ? Yes ; a few more pulsations, my young friend, and that which men call life will be past, and I shall be nothing ! "

" May not something be still attempted ? Where is the surgeon ? "

" Gone, by my orders ! You, Francis Travers, can alone aid me in this extremity."

" I ! What can you mean ? "

" Not, indeed, to save my life—that is past hoping for ; but to rescue an ancient name, which I have already tarnished, from indelible disgrace and infamy. You love Mary Wharton ? "

" As my own soul ! " replied Travers, flushing scarlet.

" I have long known it. You are aware that the estates go to my nephew, and that she is portionless ? "

" Perfectly ; but that is a circumstance——"

" How much per annum of clear, available income do you possess ? " interrupted Sir Richard quickly.

So strange a question at such a moment startled Travers ; but after a moment's pause, he replied, " Including my professional income, about a thousand a-year."

" Enough ! Hand me a glass of water. Now, come nearer, Travers, for my eyes grow dim, and my speech, beneath the choking grasp of this fell death, is faint and difficult. You know that Lady Wharton and myself, though occasionally residing under one roof, have been for many years thoroughly estranged from each other. For this I know the world blames *me*, and, I admit, quite justly. Well, the world, wise and prying as it is, as yet neither knows nor guesses a thousandth part of the wrong I have done my wife and child."

" Sir Richard ! "

" When I married Ellen Harford, her fortune, secured to her by settlement, was invested in the funds in her maiden name : the annual interest amounted to about eight hundred pounds——"

" Indeed ! I never heard——"

" Perhaps not. This revenue Lady Wharton has constantly drawn, half-yearly, through Childs' banking-house. It was devoted by her to the maintenance of our establishment. A few months since, I—bend lower, that I may hiss the accursed confession in your ear!—I, pressed by enormous gaming debts, and infatuated by a belief that I might, had I the means of playing for large stakes, retrieve my losses, forged—do you hear?—*forged* my wife's name to a warrant of attorney, drew out the entire capital, played with, and lost all! And now—now," cried the miserable man with spasmodic violence, "you know all—know that by my act my wife, my child, are paupers—beggars—homeless—friendless; and, but for you, without resource or hope!"

"Merciful powers; *can* this be true?"

"As death!" rejoined the baronet, his husky accents again sinking to a feeble whisper. "And you, on whom I counted, hesitate, I see, to save my name from infamy, even though the reward be Mary Wharton——"

"Say not so!" passionately exclaimed Travers. "But how—by what means can I conceal—can I——"

"Easily. Continue to pay the dividend as usual through Childs' till you are—where are you?—till you are married. Lady Wharton will live with you and Mary, till—till—— You understand?"

"I think I do," stammered Travers. "But——"

"That's well!" A silence of several minutes succeeded, followed by incoherent murmurs, indicating that the senses of the dying man were wandering. "Cold, cold—and dark! Looed! and upon three trumps! Light the candles; we cannot see the cards! Ah! what shapes are these? Ellen, Mary! so stern too, now that Travers has promised—has promised——" The death-rattle choked his utterance, and in a few minutes Sir Richard Wharton had ceased to live.

About three weeks after the funeral of the deceased baronet, Lieutenant Travers received a letter, on service, from the Admiralty, announcing his appointment to a crack frigate fitting for sea at Portsmouth, and directing him to report himself on board immediately. This summons rendered further delay or hesitation impossible. He could not leave Marlands without coming to a frank explanation with Lady and Miss Wharton, and he resolved it should take place that very morning. Not a syllable had yet passed his lips relative to the extraordinary disclosure made by Sir Richard Wharton in his last moments, or to the wishes he had expressed regarding his daughter. In the event, Travers mentally argued, of the acceptance of his suit by Miss Wharton and her mother, there could be no reason for any concealment from them; *they* would not betray the late baronet's disgraceful secret. At all events, he would not, by first revealing to Mary Wharton that she was penniless, and afterwards proffering his hand and fortune, seem to wish to *purchase* her consent to a union with him. Full of these cogitations and resolves, he arrived at Archer's Lodge, where, to his extreme astonishment, he found the servants packing up the furniture, as for immediate removal. He hurried to the breakfast-room, where he found Lady Wharton and her daughter both busily engaged arranging books, music, and papers.

"What is the meaning of this?" he demanded with intense agitation. "Surely you are not leaving Archer's Lodge?"

"Indeed we are, Mr. Travers," replied Lady Wharton. "We received a letter yesterday, accepting an offer we had made for the lease of a house in Wales, close to Edmund's new curacy, which he says will suit us admirably."

"Us—Edmund!" gasped Travers.

"Mary, love, place these papers," said Lady Wharton, "in the writing-desk in my dressing-room. Mr. Travers," she added, as the door closed, "you are ill. The walk has perhaps fatigued you. Let me give you a glass of wine."

"No—no—no! What is it you say? Mary—Edmund! Speak, and quickly; my brain turns!"

"I feared this," said Lady Wharton soothingly, as she approached, and gently took his hand; "and perhaps I have been to blame in delaying the explanation which must now be made."

"What explanation—relative to whom?"

"To Mary and her cousin, Edmund Harford."

"Ha!"

"They are betrothed lovers, and have been so,

with my consent, for many months. Listen to me
calmly, Mr. Travers," continued Lady Wharton, terrified by the wild expression of the young man's
eyes. " Mary some time since wished me to give
you my confidence. I hesitated; for, alas! bitter
experience has taught me to place but little reliance
on the faith of men. I was wrong, I see; but pray
strive to calm yourself."

" Go on—go on. Let me at least now know all—
the worst, the worst!"

" I will be frank with you. The failing health of
Sir Richard Wharton has for some time warned me
that but a brief space remained to him on earth.
The frightful catastrophe of the other day but hastened his end, in all probability, by only a few months.
Mary's sole dependence was, in that event, I k new,
the marriage-portion secured to me, the interest of
which amounts to something over eight hundred
pounds per annum."

" I know—I have heard---- "

" Indeed!"

" Yes; but no matter. Proceed, I beg of you."

" The possession of an income in my own right,
amply sufficient for the needs of an unambitious
household, warranted me, I conceived, in consent-
ing to Mary's engagement with her cousin, whom
she has known from girlhood, and of whose worth no
one can speak too highly. My silence and reserve
have, I perceive, Mr. Travers, misled you; but for-

give me I did not know—I could not con-
ceive——"

"Let me pass, madam," exclaimed Travers, disen-
gaging his hand, and staggering towards the door.
"I will return presently."

A whirlwind of emotion was sweeping through his
brain as he hurried from the house into the adjoining
shrubbery. Wounded affection, despair, compassion,
tugged at his heart, and ruled it by turns. The open
air helped to cool and revive him; and after about an
hour's bitter conflict with himself, he returned to the
apartment where he had left Lady Wharton. She was
still there.

"May I have your ladyship's permission to see
Miss Wharton alone for a few minutes?" he asked.

Lady Wharton appeared surprised at the request,
but at once acceded to it. "I will send her to you
immediately," she replied, and left the room.

A considerable interval elapsed before Miss Wharton, trembling, blushing, painfully agitated, almost,
indeed, in tears, entered the apartment.

"Pardon my freedom—my importunity, Miss
Wharton," said Travers in as calm a tone as he
could command, as he led her to a seat, and placed
himself beside her. "I have a question to ask you,
of the last importance to you as to myself, and I
intreat you to answer it frankly as to a brother."

The lady bowed, and the lieutenant proceeded with
somewhat more firmness.

"You are, I am informed, dependent as to fortune upon Lady Wharton. Is it, then, I would ask, of your own free choice and will that you are contracted to your cousin—to the Reverend Mr. Harford? Nay, lady, be not offended at my boldness. It is in virtual compliance with the injunctions of Sir Richard Wharton, expressed in his last moments, that I ask this question."

The momentary glance of indignant surprise passed from Mary Wharton's face at the mention of her father's name. Her suffused eyes were again bent on the ground, whilst the rich colour came and went on her cheek, as she replied in a low, agitated voice—"Edmund and I have known, have been attached, almost betrothed to each other from his boyhood——"

"Enough, Miss Wharton," said Travers, hastily rising; "I will not trespass further on your indulgence. May all good angels guard and bless you!" he added, seizing her hand, and passionately kissing it; "and for your sake, him—— Farewell!" He hurried from the house, and the same evening took coach for London; made the necessary arrangements for continuing the payment of Lady Wharton's dividend through Childs', as before; then proceeded to Portsmouth, and joined his ship, which a few days afterwards sailed for the South American station.

Lady Wharton and her daughter removed, as they had intimated, to Wales, where Edmund Harford had obtained a curacy, scarcely of so much money-value as that which he had left in Devonshire. After the lapse of a twelvemonth he was married to Mary Wharton; still, however, retaining his curacy as a means of usefulness. The union was a happy one. In the enjoyment of an amply-sufficient income, and soon begirt with joyous infancy, their days fled past in tranquil happiness; and each succeeding year, as it rolled over them in their beautiful retreat, augmenting with some new blessing their sum of worldly felicity. If a thought of the noble-hearted man to whom they were unconsciously so deeply indebted crossed their minds, it was chiefly when a present for one of the children of some rich or curious produce of distant climes arrived; or a gazette of that stirring period announced one of the bold deeds which rapidly advanced Lieutenant Travers to post-captain's rank. Peace, for which the harassed, trampled world had so long sighed, was at last proclaimed, and Edmund Harford, who corresponded with Captain Travers, thought it possible he might now pay them a visit—perhaps take up his abode in the neighbourhood, for Marlands, they knew, had long since been disposed of. He, however, came not; and the next letter received announced that he had joined the expedition against Algiers under Lord Exmouth. Tidings of the triumph of the British fleet over that celebrated nest of pirates reached them in due season, accompanied by victory's ever-present crimson shadow—

the list of killed and wounded. Harford glanced anxiously at the sad column, and an exclamation of dismay and sorrow broke from him — Captain Travers was returned " mortally wounded!" Greatly pained and shocked as they all were by this intelligence, they were some days before they knew how deep cause they had for grief. About a fortnight, it might have been, afterwards, Mr. Harford, by Lady Wharton's directions, wrote to Messrs. Child to inquire the reason the last half-year's dividend had not been forwarded as usual. The answer—revealing as it did the crime of Sir Richard Wharton, the heroic sacrifice of Travers, and their own utter worldly ruin —stunned, overwhelmed them! " The reported death of Captain Travers," the bankers wrote, after fully explaining the source from which, since the death of Sir Richard Wharton, the remittances had been derived, " and a consequent claim to his property by a distant relative, as heir-at-law, necessarily precluded them from continuing the half-yearly payments."

All emotions of admiration, wonder, gratitude, excited by this discovery were soon absorbed by a consternation at the terrible prospect before them— suddenly deprived as they were, as by the stroke of an enchanter's wand, of their imaginary wealth. " Our children!" exclaimed Mrs. Harford with tearful vehemence, " what will become of them, nursed as they have been in ease and luxury ? "

" God will provide both for them and us, Mary,"

replied her husband. "If we exercise but faith and patience, I have no fear; but my heart swells to think that that noble-minded man should have passed away unassured, unconscious, of our deep gratitude and esteem."

"Do not deem me selfish, Edmund," rejoined Mrs. Harford. "I feel his generous kindness as deeply as yourself. It is for our children I am anxious—not for myself, not even for you."

"Be assured," said Lady Wharton, recovering from her panic, "that Captain Travers has not neglected to provide for such a probable contingency in his profession as sudden death. His unselfish devotedness to you, Mary, will shield you and yours from beyond the grave: of that be satisfied."

Lady Wharton was not mistaken in her judgment of the character of Captain Travers. By the very next post a letter arrived under cover of Messrs. Child, from a solicitor, informing them that, by a will executed by Captain Travers on the same day that he had directed the bankers to remit the usual amount to Lady Wharton, the whole of the property of which he might die possessed was bequeathed to Mary Wharton, now—he, the solicitor, was informed —Mary Harford, for her sole use and benefit, and not passing by marriage to the husband. "The instant official news of the death of Captain Travers arrived," it was added, "probate would be at once obtained on the will, and the proper steps taken to put Mrs. Harford in possession of the legacy."

All doubts were speedily set at rest. A carriage drove slowly up the avenue one evening, just as it was growing dusk, and Mr. Harford was informed that a gentleman wished to speak with him. He hastened out, and a pale, mutilated figure extended its hand to him, exclaiming in a feeble voice, "Edmund! Do you not know me?"

"Captain Travers!" almost shouted Harford. "Can it indeed be you?"

"A piece of me, Edmund," replied the wounded officer with an effort at a smile. "I am come to ask permission," he added in a graver tone, "to die here. I shall not, I think, be refused?"

He survived for several months, administered to with tenderest solicitude by Mrs. Harford and her husband. The last tones that sounded in his ear were those of Edmund Harford, reading with choking voice the prayers of the church for the dying; the last object his darkening eyes distinguished was the tearful countenance of the beloved of his youth and manhood; the last word his lips uttered was her name—Mary!